Bloodheir

Bloodheir

BOOK 6 IN THE BLOODBORN SERIES

SYDNEY WINWARD

Bloodheir

The Bloodborn Series, Book Six

Cover Design by Sydney Winward

Published by Silver Forge Books

Paperback ISBN 978-1-960461-05-6

Digital ISBN 978-1-960461-04-9

www.sydneywinward.com

To my mom, whose creativity constantly inspires me!

BOOKS BY SYDNEY WINWARD

The Bloodborn Series

Bloodborn

Bloodbond

Bloodscourge

Bloodbane

Bloodcurse

Bloodheir

Sunlight and Shadows Series

A Breath of Sunlight

A Taste of Shadows

A Glimpse of Music

A Kiss of Embers

A Balm of Healing

Letters to Love Series

Yours, Sterling

Forever, Mirabelle

Always, Ivette

Lord Death Series

A Waltz with Lord Death

Novellas

Through Wylder Meadows

Root Brew Float

On Silver Wings

Bloodmoon

Selkie

CHAPTER 1

VAMPIRES HELD THE upper hand in combat. Especially in war.

Sweat trickled down Jesper Degore's face, sticky against his helmet. It threatened to blind his eyes through the narrow steel slits as he attacked his enemy with feral grace, a sword in his hand.

He didn't dare blink away the tendril of blood dripping from one of his eyelashes—whether his own blood or his enemy's, he wasn't entirely sure. The scent of blood strewn across the battlefield west of Ichor Knell made his green eyes flash a dangerous shade of red as a lust for blood—human blood—nearly overwhelmed his senses. After hours on the killing field, he desperately wanted to feed, to savor the thick red liquid against his tongue.

But he kept fighting.

Because the enemy kept coming.

The gray clouds overhead blanketed the field littered with bodies. Hundreds of vampire soldiers wearing red uniforms with wyverns emblazoned on their weapons and shields pushed back human soldiers wearing yellow until most of them were trapped with the forest at their backs. A group of humans managed to break through the lines, shouting war cries, and three of them now circled Jesper like vultures waiting to feed on his carcass.

Pitted against the three massive opponents, their faces concealed by armor that barely contained bulking muscle, Jesper drew from the years of training he'd received by both his father, Adam Degore, and his grandfather, Dracula, and made quick work of the first two.

The remaining soldier pulled a dagger out of his boot, and Jesper hissed as the weapon grazed his arm. In the momentary distraction, the human kicked him onto his hands and knees.

He ducked beneath another swing and rolled onto his feet. His throat burned with desire when the blood from a fallen human soldier sang a siren call. He struggled to fight the urge to feed and lifted his weapon to face his opponent once more. Judging by the fact that the wound started to knit itself within moments, the man's weapon wasn't made of iron like his sword, but of steel.

With one quick swing of his weapon, he sliced through the man's neck, and the human immediately dropped, bleeding onto the ground.

The scent of blood filled his nostrils. He flexed his fingers as he pushed back the overwhelming desire to sink his fangs into the man's severed neck and feast on the blood spilling out of him. His throat burned as the delicious aroma of a promised feast slammed into him from all directions. He couldn't give in. Not yet.

He breathed heavily, surveying the battleground while he had a moment to catch his bearings. Both vampires and humans had fallen by the sword, though far more humans lay scattered throughout the field. Many opponents fled as if realizing the attack on the vampire city of Ichor Knell was futile, but a handful remained.

One such opponent, their captain, faced his grandfather in battle. The fierce dance of blades echoed off the dark clouds looming overhead. Dracula's expression was blank, not a single flicker of emotion giving away his next attack. He was the fiercest warrior Jesper had ever known. Fierce. Brutal. Unforgiving. A thousand years ago, he'd saved an entire race of vampires and became the shah as a result, second to none.

Jesper arced his sword through the air and started toward his next target currently locked in battle with another vampire. He raised his weapon and—

He froze when Dracula's opponent disarmed him. His heart stopped, the world coming to a halt when the captain stabbed his sword straight through Dracula's chest. An iron sword. One of the few things that could kill a vampire.

His pulse sounded loud in his ears when his heart started, then stopped, then started again. White, hot fury flowed through his veins. His legs seemed to move on their own accord as he rushed at the captain, so quick that his opponent didn't have time to swing his weapon. He grabbed the captain by a tuft of hair and slammed his weapon through his gut. The man gurgled as blood dripped from his mouth. He slumped forward, hitting the ground with a *thud*, his eyes wide in death.

After the fall of their captain, the remaining humans fled, and then the battlefield became as still as the black, beady eyes of a raven—a bad omen hanging over their heads.

Grandfather...

Dracula's breaths came short and quick. Thick, red blood soaked through his clothing and stained his armor. His hand clutched the open wound in his chest. Pain seared his eyes, deep like a chasm full of jutting rocks. And the first time in months, years even, he appeared fully grounded in the moment.

"No, no, no!" Jesper cried. He dropped to his knees at the same time Lucian Dragomir did, and together they attempted to lift his enormous mass. "Grandfather, just hold on. We'll get you to the infirmary."

"N-n-no," he stuttered, followed by a feeble attempt to push their hands away. "Th-th-the wound is too g-g-great. Willow. W-W-Willow!"

At the call of her name, Jesper's mother, Willow, materialized before them. The haze of red flakes from her power solidified until her horrified expression took shape. She took one look at Dracula and tears of panic welled in her eyes.

"Papa!" she wailed. "We'll get you help. Lucian, help me—"

"No." Dracula's trembling fingers grasped her hand and held it to his heart. "I-I-I'm ready. I have been for a l-l-long time now. I-I-I miss your mother so m-m-much."

Jesper watched the exchange with cold fear racing through him as if he'd suddenly found himself trudging through an icy mountain river. No, no, no. This could not happen. This absolutely could not happen.

Yet, his feet remained firm as if nailed to the ground.

"Papa, no." Red-tinted tears escaped her eyes and trailed down her chin, dripping onto Dracula's shoulder. "I beg you. Don't leave."

"I love y-y-you, cel mic." Instead of answering, she released a pained whimper. "Y-y-you are… Y-y-you are…" His grip on her hand slackened, and his head rolled to the side while his last breath exited his lungs. His chest didn't rise again.

She screeched loud enough to pierce the dark clouds and the heavens beyond.

Jesper pulled off his metal helmet and threw it aside, his dark red hair slicked to his forehead. He stared wide-eyed at his grandfather lying still on the ground. The greatest warrior to ever live. The fiercest vampire.

Dead.

After over a thousand years of his reign, Dracula had fallen.

And Jesper was his heir.

CHAPTER 2

"THEY'RE STILL OUT there," Jesper murmured under his breath as he stared out the palace window to the courtyard below.

Hundreds of candles flickered in the darkness of night, honoring the shah who had reigned over them for many, many centuries. Two weeks had passed since Dracula's death, and a black, festering hole of heartache still lingered within him. He'd been crowned Shah the day after his grandfather's death. It hadn't been a happy occasion, but rather one of much sorrow.

He glanced to his left to find his younger sister, Kiara, staring out another window. She wore a long black mourning dress, her face and light brown hair hidden beneath a black lace veil. Their mother hadn't left her room since the coronation, and their father had been scarce as well. It was typical of Sam, their brother, to have made a brief appearance at the funeral, and an even briefer one at the coronation.

"It's been two weeks," Kiara said in a melancholy tone. No one had loved Grandfather more than her. "I don't think any of them have moved a muscle."

Most vampires only needed to feed once every few weeks to a couple months, so it was entirely possible.

The two of them remained silent for several more minutes as they watched the gathered crowd below. A lump lodged in his throat, and he swallowed it before turning his head a fraction to look at her.

"Being Dracula's heir was supposed to be a joke." He turned the shah's ring around on his pinky finger—a thick black metal band inlaid with a single red ruby. A permanent reminder of his new position. "He was never supposed to die. Ever. I was never supposed to be crowned."

"Yet, here we are."

He nodded, the bleak pit consuming him once more. "Here we are."

The memory of his grandfather being impaled by the iron sword haunted him throughout each day and night, but it wasn't just the pain, the death that grieved him. No, it was what he had seen when Dracula had been disarmed. The brief flicker of hesitation. The flash of despair and hopelessness. He knew his grandfather well enough to know he could have saved himself. He could have escaped death. But...

"Do you ever think Grandfather wanted to die?" he asked, not daring to speak any louder than a whisper lest someone overhear them. When vampires had impeccable hearing, he couldn't risk it.

"Don't say such things, Brother."

He probably should have heeded her, but he couldn't let it go. "A month ago… I caught Dracula weeping beside Elisabeta's grave." He had been without his mate for six hundred long years. "When I couldn't find him the next morning, I went searching for him, only to find him sleeping by her headstone. He hadn't been the same since. Quiet. Withdrawn. Staring blankly at the walls during meetings. I think his soul gave up."

Kiara turned to him, the lace fabric of her veil shifting with the movement. "I don't want to hear it, Jesper. I cannot stomach the idea of him being so heartbroken that he'd allow someone to kill him."

Not wanting to upset her any further, he bit his tongue. Their grandfather was dead. Whether or not he'd allowed it didn't change anything.

Once again, he turned the ring around on his finger as he watched each small candle flame flicker in the darkness. All his life, he'd been preparing for the weight of the crown despite never believing he'd inherit the throne. He didn't have the luxury to continue mourning. It was time to get to work.

"Where are you going?" she asked when he started for the door.

"To build my court."

The castle was far too quiet for comfort. When people spoke, they spoke in whispers. When he walked past, they bowed and curtsied, and they kept their eyes on him until he rounded the next bend in the large black castle the size of a city in itself. They were watching. Waiting to see what he'd do with the kingdom. And he desperately hoped he wouldn't destroy everything his grandfather had built.

Following two familiar scents through the palace grounds, he found them kneeling at the front of the cathedral, candles covering every inch of the dais. The stained-glass windows lining each wall glittered under the candlelight, their sheen dampened as if they, too, were mourning. Lucian Dragomir and Nicolae Covaci stood when he approached, each bowing their heads. They'd never bowed to him before, and it unnerved him more than he cared to admit.

"Your Highness," Nicolae said by way of greeting.

Those two words sounded foreign to his ears, and he wondered for a moment if he would ever get used to hearing them.

Never one to make small talk and skirt around the topic, he said, "I need advisors. Both of you were a boon to my grandfather."

Lucian and Nicolae exchanged looks, and a pit formed in his stomach before Nicolae opened his mouth. "It is in your best interest to start anew. We are entering a new era of reign. Dracula served as the shah for a very long time, and we as his advisors. If Dracula is gone... Your Highness, you must adapt to the changing world, and so now we advise you to find younger vampires like yourself to stand beside you. Lucian and I..."

Nicolae glanced toward his friend, and Lucian continued for him. "We're old. We may not look it, but we're far older than anyone in this city. We've had our turn, now it's time for another generation to take over."

Like his grandfather, they were over a thousand years old, though they looked to be in their early thirties. And Jesper... He was only eighty-five, which was still considered young for a vampire.

A rare moment of uncertainty, he voiced his concerns. "But what if I fail? Without you... Without Dracula... I can't do this."

"You can," Lucian assured. "You are Dracula's *kin*. If he could start from scratch, so can you."

"And you will have to do it quickly," Nicolae added. "When word reaches outer kingdoms that Dracula has fallen, I fear for Ichor Knell. You must be ready."

Jesper feared for Ichor Knell as well, though he refused to show it on his face. Enemies soon would likely show up on their doorstep, trying to get their foot in the door by any means necessary.

No more bloodshed. He'd made the vow to himself as they'd lowered Dracula into his grave, buried next to his mate. He would not build this kingdom on bloodshed and brutality, but on honesty and justice. He only feared he might break his own vow someday.

"A word of advice?" Nicolae said with an encouraging smile despite the grief evident in his piercing blue eyes. "Start small. Dracula did. Perhaps begin by making sure the army is ready to meet resistance. Eventually, you will be able to handle mountains of responsibility."

Nicolae hadn't needed to say it. Ever since Jesper's grandfather had withdrawn from the public eye, Jesper had taken up the large mantle of responsibilities in his stead. However, he still felt lost. He'd always had his grandfather to fall back on, but now he had no one but himself. His safety net was gone.

And that terrified him.

With a dip of his head, he turned away and exited the cathedral. A rush of night air greeted him, and he took a moment to breathe in deeply to calm his racing mind. There was no room for error, no room for uncertainty, and certainly no room for fear.

He placed a hand on the hilt of the dagger at his belt for reassurance. Designs of gold and black stretched across either side of the hilt, the blade wicked sharp within the confines of the sheath. His father had given it to him for his fiftieth birthday, and it had stayed tucked close to his side ever since.

Forcing his expression into a neutral mask, he continued down the path leading back to the castle, but this time he cut through the courtyard. He nodded his head to those who made eye contact with him and acknowledged those who bowed.

When he spotted a head of large blond curls, he touched the male's shoulder and nodded his head toward a side entrance.

Leif Covaci followed him without question, and together, they located Cybil training in the barracks. Her face was slick with sweat, brown hair matted to her skin. She wore a men's tunic and trousers, and despite her small frame, she was faster than many of the male soldiers he knew and had incredible accuracy with the bow.

"You two look like you could use a round of drinks," Cybil said, panting hard as she returned the training sword to the rack. Many of the other soldiers in the barracks either paused or slowed their skirmishes as if in hopes to overhear their conversation. Jesper's privacy had never felt more invaded in his life since inheriting the throne.

"Drinks can wait," Jesper replied in an icy tone meant for the other soldiers listening in. "First, let's move away from prying eyes and ears."

Leif and Cybil exchanged a confused look, obviously unaware of what he wanted. Only when they ascended a flight of stairs and entered one of the private council chambers did he sink into a chair, his shoulders sagging. Cybil leaned against the table and inspected one of her many knives, perfectly polished and perfectly sharp. Leif watched him warily with his arms crossed.

"What's this about, Jesper?" Leif asked. "The three of us haven't been in the same room for at least a year."

He remembered Leif's and Cybil's fallout. Cybil, the deadly warrior with a temper the size of a mountain, had *stabbed* Leif for breaking off a courtship with her sister and breaking her heart. He was lucky the knife had been made of silver and not iron. He was also lucky he'd only been stabbed once.

Kicking his feet up onto the table, he leveled a stare at Leif first, then Cybil. "Things have changed."

Cybil snorted. "Obviously."

He glared at her and continued, "I need people by my side whom I trust. I am asking the two of you to become my advisors."

Metal clattered to the table as Cybil dropped her knife, her eyes wide. "You are jesting, right?"

"I never jest."

She watched him like a predator waiting to pounce on its next kill as if deliberating whether she could trust his words. Finally, she said, "Do you realize how long it took to convince Dracula to allow a *female* into his army? My whole damn life, that's how long. And even then, he only allowed me in as a guard and not a soldier. But an advisor?"

"Dracula is dead." The gaping hole he'd tried so hard to close over the past couple of weeks flared open again, and he desperately attempted to stuff the hole with neutral emotions. "I'm the shah now. If you want to be a soldier, I will allow it. However, I would rather you become my advisor."

After a moment of silence, she raised an eyebrow.

He raised his higher in a challenge. The staring match began. His coolheadedness snuffed out her hotheadedness until the water between them became a sizzling battlefield. At last, she picked up her knife and used it to twist her hair up into a bun. How she did it without cutting any of it, he had absolutely no idea.

"Fair enough, Your Highness." She gave him a mocking smile he hoped she wouldn't give him in public. "I'll be your advisor. But I get to be your number one. This fool," she jerked her head toward Leif, "gets to be your number two."

Leif pointedly ignored her jab, taking after his peaceful Covaci kin. "You know I'm with you," he said, not a flicker of hesitancy in his eyes.

Relief filled him, but he didn't let it show. To show vulnerability was weak. Begging was weak. Giving into emotion was weak. And he would not be weak.

Rapid pounding sounded on the door, and each of their heads snapped in the direction. "Your Highness," a male shouted on the other end, his words shallow as he gasped them out as if he'd run a good distance to get there. "Permission to enter."

Vampires couldn't enter a room without permission—one of the many drawbacks of their species.

"Come."

A guard burst into the room with blood on his hands and uniform. Jesper stood quickly and inhaled a deep breath through his nose. His nostrils flared as he scented the male. The blood belonged to a vampire.

"What happened?"

The guard wheezed, "I found them during the rotation shift. Both dead. We have an intruder within these walls. We must get you to safety."

Jesper's expression hardened, and he ignored the male's attempt to preserve his life by hiding him away. He was no coward. "How warm was the blood?"

"Fresh. Their deaths must have happened in the last thirty minutes."

"And the weapon used to kill them?"

"A halberd, I reckon. Iron. The wounds were not pretty."

He followed the guard from the room, his senses on high alert as he watched, listened, and smelled for a foreign threat looming inside the castle. Cybil trailed behind him as if she were his own personal guard, a knife in each of her hands. He made a mental note to remind her that being an advisor didn't mean personal guard duty around the clock—he was fully capable of taking care of himself.

There.

The scent he picked up was so subtle that he might have missed it if he weren't actively searching for it. Human male. But with a layer of vampire folded in. And it was close.

"Send your men on a search and comb the castle. Try not to cause alarm. We're looking for a human male who covered himself in the vampires' blood. Only one intruder."

Slowly, the guard's mouth dropped in disbelief, his eyes asking how he knew, but he waved him away. The guard obediently did as he asked, and when he turned to Cybil, he found her grinning.

"Why did you send him on a fool's errand?"

"To get him out of my way. Don't kill him, Cybil. I'm warning you now."

"Where's the fun in that?"

Giving her one last warning glare, he stalked down the seemingly empty hallway and stretched his hearing. He noticed curtains rustling in a breeze that entered from the open windows. He heeded the small red drop of blood on the long stretch of rug running from one end of the hallway to the other. He caught a sniff of the stinging metallic weapon and stifled breathing as if the intruder held a handkerchief to his mouth to muffle the sound.

Jesper didn't bother concealing himself as he continued forward, and when he passed the windows...

A muscular man shouted a war cry and jumped out at him with his halberd raised over his head. Before the man managed to strike, Jesper slashed out with an arm and smacked the halberd, the weapon flying. At the same time, he slammed his foot into the man's ribs, sending him sprawling backward on the carpet.

He hissed, his arm throbbing where it had made contact with the halberd. The iron had burned his skin, a searing red mark creating a rod-like line on his forearm. It had been a mistake to roll up his sleeves today. Next time—if there was a next time—he'd make sure to wear arm bracers to prevent himself from getting burned.

The man jumped to his feet, but then Cybil bounded forward and pressed a dagger to his back and hissed in his ear, "Take one more step and I'll gut you and spread your remains throughout the hallway."

Wisely, the man didn't move a muscle.

Vampire blood speckled the man's face, smeared across his cheeks and dried on his palms. By the looks of the cuts along his arms and torso, Ichor Knell's guards had at least put up a decent fight.

Jesper prowled forward as he studied the enemy. He was someone he'd never seen before, but the scent was familiar. Had he participated in the skirmish that had killed Dracula?

"Assassin?" Jesper murmured. "Or absurdly stupid? Where do you hail from?"

With a stoic expression, the man remained silent.

"You want to play this game?" Jesper hissed. "Then we'll play. Cybil, take him to the dungeons. We'll find out just how long it takes to get him to talk."

CHAPTER 3

FOUR.

That was the number of assassination attempts within the next two weeks. Two of them hadn't made it past Ichor Knell's border. One had jumped out of an emerald jewel tree and nearly landed on top of him, and the fourth assassin had tried to poison his goblet of blood. Idiot assassins. Didn't they understand just how keen his senses were? He'd sniffed out the poison long before the goblet entered his hand.

Jesper sighed and rubbed a hand down his face as he sat at a table in the private drawing room on his family's side of the castle—the Covaci and Dragomir covens occupied the other parts of the castle.

His parents and sister sat a little farther away occupied with their own tasks as he poured over documents regarding funds for the army. With Dracula dead, a couple of the cities they traded with had stopped trading. Their funds were taking a hit. The last thing he wanted to do was raise taxes, so he needed a solution and fast.

"Jesper…" a soft voice said, and he glanced up to find his mother sitting by the window beside Kiara, watching him with worry in green eyes similar to his. Though, her shade of red hair was lighter than his. At least she had gotten out of bed today. He'd feared she would stay locked in her room, forever in mourning.

"I'm fine, Mother." He schooled his expression to hide the stress building inside his head.

"I'm terribly worried for you. I cannot bear it if you were killed."

He shook his head and stared more intensely at the parchment full of words he didn't want to read. "You weren't supposed to find out about the assassination attempts. Who told you?"

"Your father."

The scraping of a sharpening blade ceased, and Jesper snapped his head in the direction of his father and glared. His father winced and resumed sharpening, not even bothering to apologize.

"Remind me again when you two are going back to your cottage? I have things handled here."

She pulled her wrap tighter around her shoulders as if a sudden chill took up residence in the room. "As soon as I know you're safe."

A snort escaped him without his permission, but he stared intensely at the documents to avoid looking at her. As long as he was Shah, there would always be a target on his back. Dracula had dealt with them for a good while into his reign, and Jesper suspected he would as well until proper treaties and alliances were in place.

"And I also want to see you eased into your new role," she added.

This time, he shoved his work away and leveled a stare at her, at least until she gave him a warning glower and he backed down. His mother didn't deserve it. He knew better. The stress must have been getting to him.

Treading more gently, he said, "I've overseen many of Grandfather's tasks for a while now. I've been *eased into the role* long enough. I'd be more comfortable knowing *you* were safe."

"Good luck getting her to leave," his father muttered, which received him a glare from his mother.

His father had been born a human, and despite being just over a hundred years old, he still was one. Dracula had saved his life by allowing him to conjoin his soul with Elisabeta, his deceased mate, and ever since, he healed quickly and never aged. But he was still mortal. Of course, his father could take care of himself, especially with his past of being a blood hunter—fierce warriors with a vow to kill dark creatures like vampires and werewolves. But mortality still hung over his head like a guillotine waiting to strike.

Then again, there were guillotines over everyone's heads if Dracula of all people could meet his end.

A pang echoed in his heart at the thought, but he quickly snuffed it out like a candlestick's flame.

Before he could try once more to convince her to leave the city, the door opened and two vampires stumbled inside, their lips locked in a kiss tighter than manacles on a prisoner's wrists. Walking backward, his younger brother, Sam, tripped over a chair leg and just barely managed to keep them from falling. Natalia giggled and pulled him down again to continue the kiss.

"Here we go again," Jesper muttered, followed by a sigh of exasperation from their father.

Rolling his eyes, he turned to his brother. "Do you mind doing that elsewhere? Some of us are trying to work."

"Oh, don't be such a prick," Sam said when he finally bothered to untangle himself from his mate. He poured himself a drink from the stash in the corner and plopped down in one of the armchairs. Natalia immediately slid onto his lap and stroked his arm, a purr in the back of her throat. "I wouldn't expect someone like you to understand. Have you ever courted a single female? I doubt you have the slightest idea of how to woo."

Jesper turned a page in his stack of documents, unaffected by his jab. It was one he received all too often. "I'm not interested in courting. It's a frivolous waste of time and energy. I have better things to do."

Sam laughed, and when he took a swig of his drink, his smile lingered. "Oh, you wouldn't be saying that if you knew, Brother. Nothing is better than having a mate."

"I doubt it."

Vampires mated for life, and even after having his mate for as long as he had, for approximately fifty years, Sam still went about with her as if they were newly mated. Irritating wasn't a strong enough word for it.

"What about Cybil?" Sam asked as if trying to add firewood to the flame. "She's pretty."

His expression neutral, he ignored his brother's comment and scribbled a note on one of the documents with a quill. Since Cybil had become an advisor, all she'd wanted to do was oversee the guards and soldiers, and getting her to attend any meetings was near impossible. A stark contrast to Leif, who attended each and every one diligently and took notes on each subject, including every comment or jest made throughout the meeting. He couldn't decide yet if he'd made a good choice with his advisors.

At least he trusted them.

"I caught her making eyes at you," Sam continued to goad. "She's smitten to the core."

Again, he wanted to snort, but he didn't want to give his brother the satisfaction of getting a reaction out of him. Smitten? With him? Jesper was no fool. He wasn't exactly the type of male to have females drooling all over him. That was more of Sam's talent. And besides, he wasn't interested. Not at all.

"How many handkerchiefs have you received from admirers?" Sam asked.

Would he never stop?

Finally, he slammed down his quill and stood abruptly, frowning at Sam's blatant grin. "As many as would fit up your rear end and push your guts into your own mouth."

Sam laughed, and Jesper's eye twitched with annoyance. "Twenty, then? I think my *rear end* could handle that many handkerchiefs. Has Cybil given you a handkerchief?"

He gathered up his documents and stormed toward the door, making sure to give Sam's leg a good kick on his way. "My personal life is none of your business. Stay out of it."

"Jesper," Kiara pleaded as she looked up from her sketchbook. "Please stay. I can't handle Sam's nonsense otherwise."

Her plea made him pause, but one look at Sam trailing his lips across Natalia's arm only reaffirmed his decision to leave. There was a reason Dracula had named Jesper his heir rather than Sam. His brother had the laziest work ethic he'd ever witnessed. Until it came to wooing his mate.

"Care to stretch your legs a bit?" he asked, jerking his head toward the door. "I hoped you could help me with something. *Away* from unhelpful and ghastly opinions." He glowered at Sam, who only chuckled at his comment before whispering something in Natalia's ear. Even with the impeccable hearing of a vampire, Jesper couldn't make out the words, nor did he care to.

Kiara picked up her sketchpad, holding it close to her chest as she joined him in the hallway. Not once did he relax, especially when he knew assassins could be lurking in these hallways right under his nose. If Kiara ever got hurt, he would never forgive himself, especially because she was his responsibility. She had chosen to live with him at court rather than with their parents in the country.

They turned the corner and—

He grunted in surprise when they ran into Cybil, who stood with her back against the wall, her arms folded and her foot propped against the stone. She looked guilty, and he knew right then that she'd overheard the entire conversation with his family. Her cheeks turned red, but she didn't look away from fluster as other females might.

Cybil wasn't one to eavesdrop, but she always managed to poke her nose where it didn't belong. He knew exactly what she was doing here.

"I don't need a bodyguard, Cybil," he growled. "I'm capable of looking after myself."

"So grumpy today," she tsked. "Could it have anything to do with your brother's arrival?"

It had everything to do with it. Absolutely everything.

"You are my advisor," he reminded her, "not my bodyguard."

"The tasks are one of the same to me."

He sighed and ran a hand down his face. How infuriating. Well, if she insisted on following him, he might as well enjoy her company. "Give me a bit of space, will you? Meet me for drinks later."

She stared at him, and stared, until finally she pushed away from the wall. "Fine. But if you find yourself with a knife in your back, don't come crying to me. And don't get too incapacitated. You'll need a semi-clear head."

The moment she disappeared, Kiara turned to him. "I'm starting to think Sam was right."

"He wasn't. He never is. We've gone out for drinks since the beginning of time."

When he made a grab for her notebook, she held it just out of reach. "Don't you dare go flipping through my sacred space. But I'll show you what I came up with."

Kiara opened to a page depicting a masterful drawing of a crown with sharp black spires to imitate the spires of the castle, a sheen to the onyx metal. Inlaid in the design were deep red rubies the color of his eyes when blood touched his lips.

"Oh, that's good." He nodded his head in approval. "This will strike fear in the hearts of my enemies, that's for sure."

She flipped the page to show him a more delicate version to match the original, with more rubies and a swirling black pattern for the headpiece. Despite the beautiful drawing, he frowned.

"If you're expecting a future mate to wear it, then you've wasted your time."

"It will happen someday, Jesper."

"No, it won't." Quickly, he redirected the topic before he had a chance to dwell on his few failed romantic attempts in his past. "I think what you've designed for me is perfect. Grandfather never wore a crown, but he didn't need to."

At well over six feet, Dracula had made a distinct impression, and no one could possibly mistake his identity. Jesper needed to remind his subjects, as well as other kingdoms, who and what he was. And that reminder started with a stunningly lethal crown.

His sister smiled brightly. "I thought you would like it. It will look even better on your head."

CHAPTER 4

RAIN POURED HEAVILY from the clouds, soaking the entire landscape in glittering darkness like pools of fresh blood coating the kingdom in the stain of one's enemies. Clattering droplets provided the perfect cover to mask one's movements, to drown out one's footsteps, and to especially hide one's scent from the bloodsucking creatures roaming the land.

Alavara Elroris rubbed her hands together, and a brief spark of blue lit up her palms, glowing under muted moonlight. She touched a hand to the side of a brick building, and it stuck fast with the magic flowing through her veins. One hand placement after the other, she climbed the side of the building before swinging her legs up and over a wooden beam, allowing herself to dangle upside down.

Slowly, to avoid making any noise, she pulled out an iron-tipped arrow from her quiver and angled her bow to face toward the open window of the tavern. He was there. She'd been following him for some time now, waiting for the perfect opportunity to make her move.

A wicked grin spread across her face as she sprinkled a smidge more of the powder from the pouch in her belt. She suspected the vampire king already knew he was being followed, but he hadn't yet made a move to stop her. Perhaps she could draw him out with a well-aimed arrow.

Even beneath the awning, rain droplets spattered her face as if wet blood already flecked her skin. A man with dark red hair sat within view of the window, a tankard on the table in front of him. In all honesty, she had not expected the new king of vampires to be so handsome. He had a seriousness to him she felt sure could wilt a flower just by looking at it, but handsome all the same. The deep red hair, the prominent jaw, a straight nose, and green eyes. She couldn't decide if he was handsome or beautiful. Both, perhaps.

And he left himself open to take an arrow to the throat.

She nocked her arrow and pulled back on the bowstring, and then held her breath as she first took aim at the man's pretty neck. Just because she could. It would be easy to kill him with an iron arrow to the skull. But she wanted him alive, not dead.

She blinked several times as fog clouded her mind, and she shook away the sudden confusion. No matter how hard she tried to recall why she wanted him alive, the haze of her father's magic swirled heavily inside her head.

Ignoring the sensation, she aimed a smidge to the left for his shoulder.

A much smaller female body stepped in front of the vampire king and hid him from view, her back to the window as if guarding him from a potential threat lingering outside.

Alavara snarled and let her bow slacken. More than once tonight, that same woman had thwarted her plans. She wanted to put an arrow through *her* neck if only to get her out of the way. But as soon as she killed the woman, the king would be on alert, and she would have lost her chance.

No. Better to wait until he was alone.

She smiled as she remembered the tankard sitting in front of him. Alone *and* intoxicated. What a perfect match for an attack.

CHAPTER 5

EVEN AFTER SEVERAL rounds of drinks, Jesper's burdens hadn't lightened but only grew heavier with each step he took through the castle hallways. A messenger had found him at the tavern and informed him quietly that enemy soldiers had been spotted within their borders. He'd dispatched a group of scouts to check it out, and since, he couldn't stop thinking about it. An assassin or two, he could manage. But a whole army?

No more bloodshed.

The vow echoed in his mind for the hundredth time, his grandfather's still body a reminder of the cost of war.

He shuddered as an image of Kiara entered his thoughts, still and lifeless as she lay in a casket. He would do anything, give up anything, to keep something so horrendous from happening.

For a moment, he wondered if he should send her somewhere far away in case something should happen to Ichor Knell. At least until the many impending threats disappeared.

Scuff.

Finally.

It had taken long enough for the assassin to make a move. He'd been anticipating it all night. He never should have told Cybil about their little shadow. She could have gotten hurt trying to protect him from the threat outside the tavern window. It was all he could do just to shake off his friend to keep her from accompanying him through the castle.

It took all his self-control not to tense at the nearly imperceptible sounds, to keep walking forward while also stumbling a bit to make himself appear drunk. He hummed a jaunty tune and stumbled again. Listening. Waiting.

Whoosh.

The kiss of a breath brushed his neck, and then something sharp pressed against his throat. He stopped walking and ceased his humming as he stared at the iron dagger glinting in the torchlight of the empty hallway. The weapon at his throat surprised him, far too quick for him to have avoided. But it wasn't anything he couldn't handle.

Now, who in this entire kingdom could be as near silent as shadows?

He was impressed against his better judgement.

"So, this is the new vampire king?" a female voice murmured in his ear like a lover's caress. "How pathetic."

So quickly that she didn't have time to react, he spun, wrenched her knife free of her grip, and slammed her against the wall with the bracer on his forearm digging into her neck. Her hood shrouded most of her face, but he saw the surprise showing in the shape of her mouth. He twisted the dagger now in his own hand and leaned close enough for *her* to feel *his* breath on her skin.

"I wasn't raised by a blood hunter to be a pathetic fool."

The female's jaw visibly clenched, and when her fingers moved as if to brave an escape from his hold, he held her tighter against the wall. He raised the knife—careful to only touch the hilt to avoid getting burned by the iron blade—and used the tip to latch onto her hood and pull it away from her face. Her dark *dark* brown eyes glared at him, her skin flawless and smooth, her pink lips puckered into a menacing frown, and her long, straight hair was nearly as dark as her eyes. The assassin was tall for a female. Tall and slender with the grace of a prowling feline.

But what stood out most were her ears. Long, pointed ears.

"I have never seen a dark elf before," he said with wicked amusement dancing in his eyes. Though, he'd anticipated their inevitable arrival, as relations with the dark elves had always been strained during Dracula's reign. "I can't help but wonder what your blood might taste like."

"Quite awful, or so I'm told."

Her voice was filled with midnight shadows, and he knew just one word, just one movement, could hurt him should she use magic.

"I've been anticipating your kind's arrival, dark elf." In a flicker of a movement, he deposited the knife into his coat pocket and clamped a metal band around her wrist—another precaution. Both ends of the metal sealed together, blocking out any attempt to break free of its enchantment. She gasped, her body slumping against his hold as the band suppressed the magic within her.

"Like it?" he purred. "A gift from Luca Frey, dwarven chieftain."

The elf groaned as if in pain, barely able to keep herself on her feet.

"Jesper!" someone cried as they rounded the corner, and Cybil appeared moments later, followed by singing metal as she drew her sword. He might have rolled his eyes in annoyance at running into her again if it hadn't been for the assassin slumped against him. Though, he watched her carefully in case she decided to spring a hidden weapon on him.

Honestly, he could take care of himself.

"Let's escort our newest arrival to the dungeon, shall we?"

Together, they hauled the elven assassin to the dungeon and threw her into one of the empty cells. The dungeon reeked of rotten blood, waste, and mildew, and it was all he could do not to cover his sensitive nose at the stench. His keen eyes easily adjusted to the darkness, and he wondered for a moment how well she could see in the dark herself. Elves were immortal, like vampires, and they were capable of magic.

His prisoner held herself upright against the far wall as if refusing to allow her knees to buckle in his presence. "You're not going to kill me, vampire?" she scoffed. "I didn't realize the new sovereign was a lump of soft dough."

"Continue to mock me, elf," he dared, his eyes flashing a deep red as he prowled closer to her like the predator he was. "Believe me, if I wanted you dead, you would be already. You can either tell me who you are, where you came from, and why you're here. Or..." He nodded his head toward the burly vampire sitting in the corner, sharpening a blade to a lethal point. "He can do the honor for me. I've heard elves don't heal quickly without magic."

She gave him a menacing glare, terrifying enough to curdle milk, and for a moment, he wondered if she might snap her teeth at him. "I know where you sleep, vampire," she laughed, her voice as smooth as the silk of a rose petal.

He almost smiled. Almost. "And I know where *you* sleep." To the dungeon guards, he ordered, "Strip her of her clothes, give her a spare set, and take the remaining weapons on her person—two pins in her hair, a dagger strapped to her thigh, some kind of powder in the pouch on her belt, and a smaller dagger between her breasts. I don't know where she stashed her bow and quiver, but we'll find them soon enough."

The elf's mouth fell open as if she could hardly believe he scented all the hidden weapons on her. "I will not undress in front of men. Send me a woman instead. I know what happens in dungeons when kings turn a blind eye."

A rare laugh escaped him before he clamped down on his jaw and scowled at her. "You are in vampire territory now, where we only take one mate for the rest of our lives. No one would want to waste their innocence on someone like you." Still, he gave the order. "Send for a maid. I don't think I need to remind you to keep your hands to yourself."

Not sparing the elf another glance, he left the dungeon where Cybil decided to stay and headed in the direction of his rooms while keeping his senses on high alert. Another assassination attempt. But something didn't seem right about this one. She'd had a chance to try to slash his throat with her iron dagger, and she didn't take it. Why?

"Your Majesty," one of the guards from the dungeon huffed while lumbering toward him, red-faced as he held out a necklace on a golden chain. "We found this on the prisoner."

The metal *clinked* as it fell into his palm, and he found himself staring at the royal emblem of the head of a gryphon screeching into the skies, its wings unfurled.

He swore under his breath as he ran a thumb over the crest. "It seems we are entertaining royalty. If she had come in through the front door rather than the back, perhaps we would have received her better."

"Should we release her?"

"No. If they're stupid enough to send a daughter of Varesia to do their dirty work, then we're brazen enough to keep her in our dungeons. Tell no one she's here, and don't torture this prisoner. We'll get answers from her another way."

After the guard bowed and disappeared, he located Leif in the library despite the late hour. The other vampire glanced up, shadows flickering across his face as he read by candlelight. "Leif, find records on the Varesia royal family if you will. We need to do a little research on our new enemy."

Leif's face blanched. "They're our enemy? But they've never dared to set foot in Ichor Knell."

"True, but Dracula has never been dead before. We have the princess locked in the dungeon, and I have a new knife."

His eyes sparkled with humor as he turned the knife over in his fingers. Such a well-crafted, balanced weapon. He only regretted it was made of iron and not something less lethal to a vampire like steel or silver.

How it was possible for Leif's face to pale even more, he didn't know. "Princess Alavara?"

"Is that her name?" he mused. "It means *elf warrior*. Seems fitting, as she is quieter than the full moon and must be lethal enough to warrant sending her here on her own. It's her mistake for thinking the new shah would be a docile puppet on a throne."

Lethal...

He couldn't help but wonder why they sent her. The assassination attempt was feeble at best, unless she was only supposed to be a distraction.

Yet, he'd heard of no other instances of attacks within the castle. It didn't stop him from checking on Kiara and then his mother. Both were fine and sleeping soundly in their beds.

Still, he slept fitfully that night.

CHAPTER 6

ALAVARA AWOKE TO a commotion coming from the upper castle. She sat up, fully alert as she continued to listen to frantic shouts and calm, collected orders. Jesper Degore proved to be calm where it counted, but his constant schooled expressions made it difficult for her to determine what was going on in that mind of his. Right now, she hoped it was shock, surprise, panic, dread.

Oh, and fury.

She heard the dungeon door open and slam shut with a deafening *crash*. The chill of the stones beneath her entered her bones as she pushed herself to her feet, standing tall and proud with her chin held high. The dress they'd given her was far too short for her figure, reaching her lower calves rather than her ankles. There was no time to blush at the impropriety of it. She refused to give the king the satisfaction of witnessing her rosy cheeks.

To her dismay, the furious door slammer wasn't Jesper but the ill-tempered female named Cybil. For an exhilarating moment, she thought she'd managed to push the vampire king over the edge of his calm exterior.

"What did you do?" Cybil growled through the bars.

Leaning against the wall, she flexed her fingers as she inspected the small bruises on her knuckles from punching one of the guards from getting too close the other night. The band clamped around her wrist suppressed her magic, which churned her stomach with nausea and stole the strength right from her legs. But she'd heal herself soon enough when she got the blasted thing off her wrist.

"Are you going to take me to your king or not?" she asked.

"Shah," Cybil corrected with a snarl. "He is my shah."

"And a bit more than that, it seems." At last, she lifted her head, satisfied when the little vampire's face contorted with rage.

Cybil said nothing more as she unlocked the cell, and an escort of five male soldiers joined as they led her up a flight of stairs, down a long hallway, around several corners, and finally dragged her into what appeared to be the throne room.

Two thrones rested at the top of the dais. Marble floors stretched from each of the four corners. Windows, sconces, and red-velvet furniture lined the walls. Jesper stood near the front of the room with his arms behind his back, his expression giving away nothing as she neared. He stared at her, and she stared right back.

"Princess Alavara Elroris," he drawled while slowly swinging her necklace by the chain. "What a surprise you have left on our doorstep. I can't help but wonder how you did it."

She grinned from ear to ear and gave the king a mocking bow. "My father sends his regards."

"Plenty of regards, if you are referring to his ten thousand soldiers camped not even a few miles away. Oh, but not even that. There are *four other armies* lying in wait as well."

Four?

Surprise jolted through her, but she tried her best to blink it back before the king noticed. Her father had been busy in her absence, it seemed. Who were their other allies? Or were they allies at all?

Jesper forced her out of her thoughts as he threw something in her direction. The pouch of powder they'd taken from her the other night plopped onto the floor, spilling half of the precious substance.

"What is this?"

No use lying now. "A glamor. Coupled with my magic, you will see and hear what I want you to see and hear. I spread it around your entire city right under your nose." Of course, the glamor had been near impossible to come by, and it only worked with strong magic.

"Ah." He approached slowly, still swinging her necklace at his side. "Very clever, I must admit. While I was preoccupied with the threat I thought I caught, I didn't bother setting my sights outside the city." He snapped the necklace into his palm and gave her a cold stare. "Have you ever witnessed a vampire fight, Princess?" When she didn't answer, he continued, "One of my soldiers can take down at least twenty of your men. It will only take five hundred of mine to take down ten thousand of yours. If this is a battle you want to wage, you better think long and hard about what this will cost you."

"And what it will cost *you*."

"Have you no concern about the lives of those who fight for you?"

Clamping her mouth shut, she continued to stare at him, all while taking in her surroundings. Two soldiers blocked every exit, plus the five soldiers who flanked her. Oh, and Cybil. Alavara didn't want to get in a fight with the small flamehead.

Each soldier carried either a sword or a dagger, and only two door soldiers held spears. She'd go for that exit, as they'd be easier to get past than the men who commanded swords. As for the bracelet suppressing her magic... She doubted she could get it off herself. She'd have to return to her people to be free of it.

The moment the king turned his attention to the necklace, she struck, lashing out with her knee to the groin of the nearest soldier. When he went down, she turned to the next and jabbed the pressure points in his arms before he even managed to reach for his weapon. His arms went limp.

The surprise of the attack had passed, and she quickly found herself swerving, ducking, leaping, and slipping like water in the obstacle course of jutting rocks. She plunged her fingers into pressure points in legs, arms, and necks, and one by one, they went down.

She clenched her jaw at the unnerving way Jesper simply stood and watched with cold, calculating eyes. Almost as if he were watching the way she fought and was memorizing every move she made.

She ducked beneath a sword and growled, elbowing the male in the side before taking the weapon from him. Why wasn't the king doing anything?

The final spar came between her and Cybil.

The clamor of dozens of boots on stone reached her ears, letting her know she only had moments to make an escape. Expecting Cybil to think she played by the rules, she threw her sword onto the ground, allowing it to clatter at the vampire's feet. The moment she looked down in confusion, Alavara lunged forward and jabbed her fingertips into her neck's pressure point, and she released a gurgle of surprise. The distraction was enough to dart toward the two guards holding spears. Fear shone in their eyes as she neared. As she'd guessed, they weren't able to hold their line within close quarters, and in seconds, they were on the ground as if their limbs suddenly didn't work.

A chuckle rose within her throat as she slipped out the doors.

The captain of the guard, Cornell, drew his sword, but Jesper placed a hand on his arm to stop him as he watched the elf slip out the doors like a graceful feline.

"Let her go."

"Sire?"

No more bloodshed.

"I said let her go. Not even an elf can easily outrun a vampire."

He brought the elven necklace to his nose and breathed in deeply, honing in on her berry-like scent. His eyes flashed red as the hunt officially began.

Alavara gasped for air as she finally allowed herself to cease sprinting. How much time had passed? Minutes? Hours? Days? Her father's army was only miles out, so it couldn't have been more than an hour, but it still felt like a lifetime.

Her knees wobbled when she drew on her magic, only for the bracelet to block her efforts. Nausea claimed her stomach as a result, and she leaned heavily against the trunk of a tree, focusing on breathing in and out slowly.

Midnight. It was midnight judging by the darker-than-usual skies and the crickets chirping around her. How much time had she spent in the dungeon? They'd given her six meals, but they'd never come on a schedule as if they'd wanted to confuse her sense of time.

"I'm not easily impressed," a deep voice said behind her.

She spun around, reaching for the weapon on her belt that was no longer there. The vampire king leaned casually against a tree with his arms folded, watching her with a predator's gaze. Her heart quickened, and she cursed herself to allow her body that much rein. Jesper's mouth twitched as if he could hear each beat inside her ribcage. Being a vampire, he probably could.

"What do you call your style of fighting?" he asked when her mouth refused to work. How had he found her? And so quickly? Were there others? Or did he come alone? He continued, "You took down eight of my men in a matter of minutes. *Without* a weapon. If you wanted to escape the dungeons, you could have."

Alavara remained very still, as if any sudden movement might encourage him to attack. She remembered the night he caught her. His agility had surprised her, and she didn't want to see the full extent of what he was capable of.

In less time than it took to blink, his fangs sprouted from his gums, and she jumped, backing farther away to put as much distance between them as possible.

"If I remember correctly," he said, pushing away from the tree and advancing, "I was curious to find out what a dark elf's blood tasted like."

"Vampires only drink human blood."

He shrugged. "I never said I wanted to drain you. I only want a little taste."

The vampire was toying with her, as if she were a mouse and he the cat.

Using the only weapons on her person, she raised her hands and readied herself for a fight. He lifted his arm—

—and tossed a piece of gold-glinting jewelry in the air. She caught it with deft fingers, only to find the Varesia royal emblem staring back at her.

"I don't wish to see any of my soldiers die. Elves are immortal like vampires, except one thing you don't understand is that when my people lose their mates, they lose them forever, and they can never take another mate again. It's beyond even my comprehension, the agony, the heartache. I don't wish that on my people, nor would I like to see your people butchered over a pointless war."

She gazed at him cautiously. "What are you asking?"

Jesper retracted his fangs and stopped advancing. "I would like the king of each army to come to my palace, and together, we can devise a treaty fair on all accounts. No lives need to be lost. No bloodshed."

"I don't think you are in a position to make bargains, vampire."

He moved so quickly that she couldn't follow where he'd gone. One moment he disappeared, and she hardly had a chance to stumble backward before he reappeared behind her, pinning her against him with her back to his chest. Two sharp points pressed against her neck, and she didn't need to see them to know what they were. She struggled against him, but the movement only managed to dig the tips of his fangs into her skin, drawing blood.

"Oh, I think I am, Princess," he whispered. "What a lovely neck you have. I wonder what it would look like pulsing with my venom."

Her entire body froze with fear, and she didn't dare move a muscle. The threat lingered in the air—if she refused to do as he asked, he would turn her into the very creature he was.

"Fine," she gulped, her heart beating wildly. "I will suggest a treaty, and I will get my father and the other kings to join you. When?"

He pushed away from her, but only slightly. "Two days. Mid-morning. We will provide food and shelter for whoever they decide to bring along with them. And if I detect betrayal, I will find you."

When his grip slackened on her, she leaped away from him and pressed her fingers to the two puncture wounds on her neck. They were shallow, but enough to make her wince when she touched them.

The vampire king's eyes glinted in amusement as he wiped her blood from his chin and sucked it off his finger. "Hmm..." he mused. "Now I know."

Though, whether her blood tasted like a sweet treat or a sewer, he didn't let on.

Her eyes widened when she noticed the magic-suppressor bracelet in his other hand, and her gaze darted to her bare wrist where the bracelet had been only moments before. How had she not noticed him take it off?

But when she glanced back up, he was gone.

CHAPTER 7

JESPER STOOD AT the window and watched as kings and soldiers rode into the city on horseback, flying their kingdoms' flags. He named each as they approached closer.

At the front was Varesia, and behind them was Tatteson, a kingdom in the dry regions of the continent belonging to humans. Bredor, riding behind them, also belonged to humans, as well as Misty Loch. Those humans lived on an island in the middle of an enormous lake. And riding in last were the pale elves from Serpentine. Each one of them were his enemies, and even if they drew up a treaty today, he would always keep one eye open.

"Do you suppose they are all allies?" his mother asked beside him.

"It's too much of a coincidence for them not to be," his father replied. He wore a sword strapped to his back, and while wearing his leather armor, he looked formidable like the blood hunter he used to be.

Although Jesper had opted to greet the kings without armor, he kept his fangs bared to remind everyone what he was. The red ruby shah ring on his finger sparkled brilliantly even in the little light seeping through the clouds overhead, but it served to remind them *who* he was.

His gaze remained on the riders below, his fangs snapping down in annoyance when he noticed Alavara among them. Instead of the elven two-piece garb they'd caught her in, she wore a long, flowing white dress with golden trim, with half of her hair pulled up while the other half lay against her shoulders. Her hairstyle blatantly showed off her pointed ears, and just below was her neck hidden by her hair. He wondered if the puncture wounds had been healed with magic or if they still marred her skin.

The chain of the Varesia necklace lay against her neck, dipping low until it disappeared into her bodice. Part of him wished he'd kept the piece of jewelry, if only to hoard it as a prize.

"That's her?" Kiara whispered, barely peeking over the side of the window to gaze out. "She doesn't look like a trained killer."

"Believe me," he replied icily, "she is."

"But she's too beautiful."

Until now, he hadn't paid attention to her fair appearance, but he supposed his sister was correct. It changed nothing except made her all the deadlier.

Kiara left her place by the window, and his gaze followed her toward the table in the middle of the room, an ornate, dark bronze box sitting on top. She unlatched the box, and his throat constricted when she pulled out a magnificently terrifying black crown with red rubies.

"Go raise hell." She smiled and placed the black crown on top of his head. It fit perfectly, as if it were always meant to sit above his brow.

Not able to say anything lest his emotions get the best of him, he kissed his sister on top of her head, his mother on the cheek, and then he clapped his father's shoulder on his way toward the door. Who knew where Sam and Natalia had ended up? Probably in someone else's bed because they were unable to make it to their own.

Taking a deep breath, he entered the largest council chambers with his family at his heels where the others were waiting. Upon their entrance, dozens of people fell silent, all eyes on him. He kept his gaze steely, not an inch of warmth as he stared at each king, all wearing crowns of their own. Even Alavara wore her own crown, though hers draped across her forehead in an intricate weave, a blue jewel directly in the middle.

Near each king stood their guards and council members, and on one side of the room were his own guards and council members, Leif and Cybil included. Up on the balcony that overlooked the room were many more vampires there to watch the proceedings.

"Is the audience really necessary?" King Ruvyn, Alavara's father, asked as he nodded to the balcony.

Jesper immediately hated the man, if only for the first words to escape his mouth. "We encourage Ichor Knell's citizens to participate in court proceedings, if only to watch and listen. Anything I deem private is held somewhere else, and this is far from private. Your army has made that clear enough."

When no one else made any comments, he gestured to the long square table in the middle of the room. "Take a seat."

The kings and council members did as he asked, a rumble of movement before all was still with the exception of shifting papers and squirming backsides. His own family continued to stand, including Cybil who looked ready to take a dagger for him at a moment's notice. He resisted the urge to roll his eyes. He loved his friend, but by Ylios, she was intense.

He felt Alavara's gaze on him, but he refused to look at her. Refused. This predicament was her fault. And he had fallen for it. Which meant he was the foolish one. Only one month on the throne and he already managed to get himself five armies on his doorstep. For a moment, he wondered if Dracula would be ashamed to call him his kin. But he vowed to do everything in his power to protect the ones he loved. Anything and everything.

"The fact that you are here," Jesper said, looking each king in the eye, "means you are as interested in limiting bloodshed as I am."

The meeting commenced, and while each king took a turn speaking, they each turned to King Ruvyn as if to receive a confirmation of their words. The looks were subtle, the nods subtler, but Jesper caught them. It didn't sit well with him.

King Ruvyn cleared his throat, and all eyes turned in his direction. The elf's eyes were as dark as his daughter's, though his hair was a couple shades lighter.

"There is only one thing I require," Ruvyn said with a wicked glint in his eye. "Unless you want my army to march on yours, you will comply."

Jesper's gaze hardened. "And what is your demand?"

The elf king's mouth turned up into a sinister grin. "You will wed my daughter, Princess Alavara, and form a union between our two kingdoms."

Every vampire in the room burst into an outrage, shouting and snarling and demanding injustice until the din was so loud he couldn't hear himself think. He held up a hand, and the entire room quieted.

He slowly turned his head in Alavara's direction, looking at her for the first time since the meeting began. Not a trace of emotion crossed her features. She'd been planning on this outlandish proposition. Had she known about her father's demands the other night in the woods?

Casually resting his chin on his hand, he said, "That's not how vampires find their mates."

"Maybe not. But elves and humans alike establish peace in this matter. You will take my daughter as your mate, or there will be no peace between our kingdoms."

His casual demeanor turned into icy steel as he watched the four other kings nod their heads in agreement. He stared at Alavara, and she stared back. Oh, they had no idea what they were asking, and he would make sure they knew it wasn't even an option.

"I will not have an elf on a vampire throne." His eyes gleamed wickedly. "She would have to be turned."

Horror flitted across her features, her long, slender hands curling into fists atop the table. She obviously hadn't expected him to say that. She seemed afraid of the idea of becoming a vampire. But as far as he was concerned, she never would become one because she would never become his mate.

But then his heart stopped when Ruvyn waved away the idea with his hand. "It does not matter to me what race she is. If you want to turn her, then turn her. But she *will* become your mate."

Now it was Jesper's turn to ball his hands into fists. His nose twitched as he held back a snarl. How *dare* they try to force him to take a mate. *How dare they!*

Judging by the vampire hisses echoing across the room, his people were outraged as well.

Ruvyn turned to each of the kings. "I think we can all agree with this match. Shah Jesper Degore of Ichor Knell and Princess Alavara Elroris of Varesia. If any of you object, speak now."

None of the kings objected. If they supported the proposition, then none would sign a treaty unless it happened. Their armies would march on Ichor Knell, and many, *many* vampires would die. They'd lost a decent number of soldiers in the last war when Dracula had fallen. They weren't prepared for another battle, especially not one of this magnitude.

Kiara could die.

No more bloodshed.

His balled fists shook at his sides as he tried his utmost hardest to rein in his anger. He'd never wanted to rip out so many throats in his life.

"Of course, there is another matter," Ruvyn stated. "I understand vampires mate for life. The consummation *must* happen. Therefore, as is our custom for elven royalty, there will be witnesses on the union night."

Vampires roared and hissed, shaking the entire room and rattling the windows with their objections. Jesper's gaze turned deadly as he stared back at the elven king, his entire frame shaking with barely controlled anger. Knowing he was either about to rip out some throats or destroy the table between them, he stood abruptly and managed to control himself just long enough to spit out, "Any other demands?"

"No."

"Then my council will meet and discuss your demands, and then we will all reconvene tomorrow morning."

Before anyone else said another word, he spun on his heel and strode out of the room.

"How *dare* they!" Jesper roared as he punched the striking bag with all his might, nearly knocking his father back as he attempted to hold it in place. "It's cruel. It's unjust!" He punched it again, this time forcing his father's feet off the ground.

As if knowing he needed to release his anger, his father said nothing. Though, his fuming expression nearly matched his own.

Jesper punched the bag again and again. "He pitted me into a trap, and he knows it."

He was glad he'd dismissed everyone in the training room so no one could watch him explode. "Witnesses?" he snarled. One punch. Two punches. "A forced union with *her*? I'm going to kill him just for suggesting it."

"Normally, I would be expected to disagree," his father huffed, his face red. "But if you don't end him, I will."

Another punch, this one causing the ceiling to creak. "Finding a mate is a sacred opportunity!" Something in his hand cracked at the impact against the striking bag, but he didn't feel the pain, and it didn't deter him for a single moment. "This isn't just for a few decades before I die. This is for the rest of my miserable, immortal life!" The ceiling groaned again when he hit the bag.

The next punch broke the bag from the ceiling, and when it crashed to the ground, Jesper screeched and jumped on top, tearing into it with his fingernails as sharp as daggers. Stuffing flew in all directions, but his eyes were red with bloodlust. They couldn't possibly force him to do this. They *couldn't*.

Jesper's screech was something wild and animalistic. Finally, Alavara had seen him explode with fury, and she wasn't amused in the slightest. His fingernails tore into the striking bag as if it were made of cotton and not leather. Instinct caused her hand to reach toward her dagger as she imagined what those fingernails could do to *her* if he felt so inclined.

She darted behind the corner, her back against the wall as she focused on breathing. In and out. In and out. She'd come to try to speak to him in private, but during a screeching fit of fury was one of the worst possible times.

His screeches burned her ears long after she pushed away from the wall. She clutched her mother's necklace in her hands as she found her way to her rooms at the farthest end of the castle. It was as if Jesper had wanted to be as far from her as possible, even long before he knew about her father's plan. The vampire king did not care for her in the slightest, and after what she'd just witnessed, she doubted he ever would.

A tall figure stood in front of her door, and her heart quickened when she looked into the dark eyes of her father.

Do not let him see your fear.

Her mother had spoken the words to her countless times, and she held tightly onto them now as she followed her father into her room. Only when the door closed did he turn to her with a triumphant grin.

"The vampire king cannot say no. We've caught him in our trap."

Your trap.

But she supposed it was hers as well, seeing that she was simply a pawn in his game.

The disgust in Jesper's eyes at the mere mention of taking her as his mate haunted her. Though, whether it was disgust at the idea of not being able to choose for himself or disgust at *her*, she didn't know. Part of her didn't want to know.

To bide her time as she formed words on her tongue, she glanced around the room. A four-poster bed with a red velvet canopy. A simple writing desk tucked in the corner. A couple of armchairs on either side of a small round table. She threw back the curtains, only to be met with a grand view of a black stone wall. The insult wasn't lost on her. He'd put her in this room for a reason, if only to remind her exactly what he thought of her.

His future mate.

"Father," she finally said as she slowly turned around. "Perhaps there is another way—"

Her words died in her mouth as her father pulled out the necklace hanging from his neck, elegant swirls stretched like a cage around a glowing blue orb. The orb pulsed softly like a half-hearted plea.

"How many more memories of your mother will you force me to steal?" her father growled.

"Please." She swallowed, eyeing the necklace swirling with memories she remembered losing but not what lay within. Her father had killed her mother years ago after she'd gotten in the way of his quest for power one too many times, and then he'd made her death look like an accident. "*Please*. I beg you. Don't do it."

He closed his fist around the orb, and she sank to her knees, pressing her forehead to the ground in submission. She would give her very life, her very soul, to keep him from taking more memories, to keep him from destroying her mind with his power. She would do anything he asked of her.

"Now you realize how serious I am. Make yourself useful. If their council is to gather, I want to know exactly what is said at the meeting and who says it. Go. Now."

Alavara nodded. "Yes, Milord."

CHAPTER 8

FIVE HOURS.

It took *five hours* for Jesper to calm himself enough to summon his council. Even then, he trudged into his private council chambers, the door slamming against the wall. The six vampires in the room leaped to their feet, each bowing hastily. He stared at the door for a moment and took several deep breaths as he reached deep inside himself to find his inner calm.

And then he softly shut the door behind him.

"Your Highness," Arad said, bowing again as he stepped forward and handed him a piece of parchment. "The other kings have demands as well, but we think they are reasonable."

He scanned the short list. Open trade between Bredor and Ichor Knell. A parcel of land to station an embassy for Serpentine. Safe passage through vampire lands for those from Tatteson. King Stian of Misty Loch requested lumber and was willing to trade copper ore for it.

"I agree. These are reasonable demands. Write them into the treaty." He signaled for the scribe in the corner to begin the creation.

Arad shuffled his feet, a look of uncertainty in his expression. "And then there is the matter of the union."

A hush filled the room.

This was the last thing he wanted to talk about, but the only thing they truly needed to discuss. He paced back and forth across the room and finally stopped at the head of the table, planting his palms on the cool wood. He addressed all six council members.

"What did you notice about the meeting with the other kings?"

Leif muttered under his breath, "That we have a lot of enemies."

"False. We have exactly *one* enemy. The elf king." Muttering broke out around the table, at least until he stilled it with the raise of his hand. "The others look to him to make the decisions. He has complete control. To appease him means to appease them."

"You want to go through with the union?" another council member named Ivan asked.

"Hell no. I'm open to any ideas on how to get around it."

Cybil spoke up, a murderous look on her face. "I suppose we need to understand *why* the elf king wants the union. It's not to put an elf on the throne, as you already mentioned you would turn her, and he wasn't deterred."

"Money?" Leif volunteered.

"Power?" Theo guessed.

Jesper shook his head in exasperation. "What could they get from us with the union that they couldn't have by plowing their armies through our kingdom? We each know Ichor Knell would be destroyed if they march on us. I tried to feign a surplus of soldiers and supplies with the princess, and I think she bought it. But we don't have the resources for war."

He ran his fingers through his hair. The situation became more and more hopeless by the minute.

"There is something to be said about legitimacy," Leif said, and all eyes turned to him. "If King Ruvyn marched on us, he would be considered a tyrant. If there was peace through a union, his power comes from a more legitimate source."

"And you think putting his daughter on our throne would give him power? He would have *nothing*. I would make sure of it."

"Unless there is something more to his plan."

For what seemed like hours, the council discussed what Ruvyn's motives might be, but they couldn't even begin to guess aside from putting Alavara on the throne. They talked at length about alternatives to the union, but each suggestion fell flat.

The longer the council discussed, the more Jesper saw red. Red from the blood covering Dracula's corpse. Red from the bodies that would pile in the fields if war came upon them. And the worst—red from the blood that could soak into Kiara's clothing and matt her hair. He felt like an animal trapped in a corner, and no matter which way he turned, an iron sword lay at the base of his throat.

His eyes burned as he tried to push the images away, but they refused to leave.

After hours of futile discussion, he finally stood. The room fell silent, everyone watching him closely. He turned his head to the scribe, and with one painful swallow, he gave the order. "Write it into the treaty that in two days' time, there will be a union between Jesper Degore and Alavara Elroris."

"Jesper, no," Cybil begged.

He couldn't bear to look her in the eye.

"I don't believe we have any other choice. I lost my grandfather. I will not lose anybody else. If I have to sacrifice myself to maintain peace, then so be it."

No more bloodshed.

Without another word, he walked out of the meeting. The hallway was empty save for the occasional servant scrambling with the needs of their new guests. He strode past them and into the vacant courtyard for a desperate breath of fresh air.

The cool evening breeze did nothing to vanquish the despair churning inside him. If anything, the anguish only amplified.

Cybil followed Jesper outside into the courtyard, and as if he heard her approach, he turned slowly. The despair in his eyes nearly killed her. She would do anything to take it away. So, she would offer the only thing she had to offer.

She walked toward him with nervousness beating as a loud drum in her veins. Each step closer to him increased the tempo. One stride. Two strides. He inhaled a sharp breath of surprise as she reached for him and clutched onto the front of his shirt, meeting his gaze unflinchingly.

"King Ruvyn only made such a demand because you do not have a mate," she whispered, not daring to allow her voice to climb any higher. "Take..." She swallowed and clutched even tighter onto his shirt. "Take me as your mate. Then they cannot claim you."

Pleading was below her, but even so, her eyes were begging him to accept her offer. She could not bear to see him in such low spirits, and even though she wouldn't dare say it out loud, she loved him. For a long time now, her heart had belonged to him, and it always would.

He stared at her, and while anyone else might mistake his expression as cold and unfeeling, she understood him well enough to know he was considering it.

Her blood boiled with need, her body lying in wait for his answer. They only needed to slip into the trees, or an empty broom closet, or she would even throw caution to the wind and allow him to take her right there if it meant saving him from a fate that might destroy him.

"You say you do not have a choice," she said, holding his steady gaze. "But I am giving you one now. I would do anything for you, Jesper. Anything."

He blinked once, twice, before he lifted his hands and placed them beneath her elbows. "What you are offering me… It's dangerous, Cybil. What if Ruvyn marches his army on us if we don't give him what he wants?"

"And what if he doesn't? Only you get to decide what is best for your kingdom. We can find other cards to place on the table to satisfy the elven king."

Though whatever those cards were, she had no clue.

His throat bobbed up and down as he swallowed. "It's a risk I'm not willing to take, not unless there was any chance I could love you." He swallowed again. "Will you allow me to kiss you?"

Against her will, her heart thrummed in her chest. Never in her life had she dared to hope he'd say those words to her. She knew he'd never seriously courted anyone before. She also knew he had no desire to do it. The fact that he was asking her this meant more to her than the world.

Not trusting her voice, she nodded. When he lowered his head, her grip tightened. Their lips touched, gentle but firm.

Every fiber of her wanted to yield to him, to savor his touch, to touch him. Heat flared in her veins, but she forced herself to hold still as the kiss lingered, not daring to move.

Please, she silently begged. *Please.*

But he pulled away instead of taking the kiss deeper. The frown on his face broke her heart into pieces.

"I don't feel anything," he said. "There's nothing there."

Hot tears escaped her eyes and blurred her vision. They trailed down her cheeks, dripped off her jaw. Her hands fell slack at her sides. "Nothing?" Her chin trembled.

"I'm sorry, Cybil."

She wiped her cheeks with the palms of her hands, and though she had been brave enough to look him in the eye before, she couldn't do so now. "I'm glad you considered all of your options. I truly hope you can find happiness with her, Jesper. Because I cannot bear to see you sad."

Each step she took away from him pained her. But now at least she knew. He would never have been able to love her as she loved him. Why did it have to hurt so much?

CHAPTER 9

THE NEXT MORNING, the entire castle filled with hushed whispers. Vampires stared as Jesper walked past, their feet shuffling nervously. The fate of the entire kingdom rested on his shoulders, and he didn't doubt they wondered whether they should be readying themselves for a siege or for a new kumari, a vampire queen.

Voices chattered within the large council room, and he paused for a moment as he checked himself. He didn't feel a desire to rip out any throats, nor break a table clean in half. He was in no danger of hurting anyone. Rather, his emotions felt subdued, exhausted.

He took a deep breath and entered the room. He knew all eyes were on him, but he only gazed back at Alavara. His future mate. The union would be held tomorrow. Too soon. But he hoped it would appease the elven king to pull back his armies. He would rest much easier without the noose around their necks.

Finally, he broke her gaze and turned his attention to the other kings. "My scribes have devised a treaty I'm sure will sit well with all of you. I am not willing to bend any farther than this, and if you so much as try, then my signature won't go anywhere near it."

They'd made six copies of the treaty, each worded exactly the same, and each would receive six signatures. Everyone would have a copy of their own.

Four of the kings nodded their heads in approval, but as Jesper suspected they would, they each turned their attention to King Ruvyn as if waiting for confirmation.

The elven king took his time reading the document, but his grin widened more and more by the second. "Tomorrow, Your Highness? I do like your way of doing things. Alavara, it looks like you will become a vampire queen sooner than expected."

Even from across the table, he heard her breathe in sharply, her gaze darting to his. He wasn't sure what to make of her surprise. Did she not think he would agree to the union? Or did the surprise stem from the fear of transitioning into a vampire?

Either way, he was too drained to care. The union would be held tomorrow morning. They would become mates. She would transition into a vampire soon after, and then they'd make their union complete tomorrow night to ensure she felt the vampire bloodbond as he would. Hopefully, Ichor Knell would know peace again.

"I would like all of your armies out of my kingdom immediately," he said, looking each king in the eye. "This treaty is to ensure peace. Keeping your armies on the premises is anything but."

Ruvyn replied for them, "They will move their armies. I will keep a portion of mine here, just to make sure everything goes smoothly."

"It will not be your business to run any part of my kingdom, and that includes where your daughter is concerned. *I* will ensure her introduction as Kumari goes smoothly, and me alone."

The elven king held his arms out in acceptance, dipping his head slightly. "As you wish. But it has been a long journey to get here. You would not offer your future father-in-law hospitality for a time?"

What he really wanted to do was punch his future father-in-law in the jaw. Or gut him. Or both.

It seemed his stores of anger weren't quite depleted, but he didn't allow it to show.

"Of course," he said carefully. "Hospitality is yours whenever you need it. But don't make me remind you that this is *my* kingdom."

Ruvyn nodded and pulled back his sleeves before being the first to sign all six documents. The treaties were passed around the table until they lay in front of him. He took a deep breath and then another, and then he dipped the quill in ink.

Someone whimpered behind him. Cybil.

He turned just enough to give her a sorrowful look. "You are dismissed, Cybil."

When she didn't move, Kiara placed a hand on her back to soothe her as she guided her out of the room. With her gone, he touched the quill to the parchment, and just like that, he signed away the rest of his life with a single stroke.

Alavara ran her fingers up and down the golden chain of her mother's necklace, her footsteps silent as she slipped down the hallway. She was well aware of the distrustful stares she received, but no one approached her, and she didn't care to speak to any of them, anyway. Every fiber of her being screamed at her, telling her this was wrong. But she had little choice in the matter.

The mere thought of challenging her father released another torrent of black fog in her mind. She fought against his magic, but the more she fought, the more it consumed her mind. What was fighting against? What did her father want her to do and why?

Frustration screamed in her head as she tried to remember, but the information evaded her, hovering just out of reach.

In hardly enough time, she found herself standing in front of a large oak door, an elegant but simple design etched into the wood. She took a deep breath, raised her hand, and knocked.

No answer.

For a moment, she wondered if she stood in front of the wrong door. The castle was so large, it was all too easy to mistake one door for another.

One more time, she knocked, and this time announced her presence. "Your Highness, it's Alavara. I thought we should talk."

A pause. Then his muffled voice on the other side said, "The door is open."

She turned the handle, slipped inside, and quickly closed the door behind her. Not for a second did she dare turn her back to the vampire king. For as fast as he moved, she felt certain he could put a knife in her back before she even had a chance to draw a single breath.

Jesper Degore sat behind a desk, his elbows resting on the top with his fingers steepled together. Darkness clouded his expression as if a storm loomed overhead. Shadows flickered across his face, cast by the candle lighting up the stack of parchments in front of him. He was fierce. He was unforgiving. He was darkness.

A vampire...

He was the very creature she would turn into tomorrow.

"What did you want to talk about?" he asked quietly, his deep voice sending shivers down her spine.

She lifted a shoulder. "Anything? Will we not be tied together by a bond far deeper than marriage?" Or at least she'd heard as much about the mysterious vampire bloodbond. She could only feel it if she were a vampire rather than an elf. "I thought we should get to know each other."

"I know everything I need to know."

His expression didn't lighten.

Her mouth turned downward. Guilt darted toward her, but she swiped it away with an expert wave of her hand. "Tell me, vampire. Will I screech as loudly as you do when I turn?"

Immediately, his dark expression turned into surprise, his steepled fingers falling flat on the table. "You witnessed that? How much, exactly, did you see?"

"Enough to know that becoming my mate is the last thing you want."

The chair he sat on scraped against the floor when he stood. With his hands flat on the table, he growled at her, "Becoming your mate is not the problem. The issue is being cornered, feeling like nothing more than a helpless animal. I wanted to tear out a lot of throats. I would have torn yours out as well."

She touched the base of her throat as she stared back into his serious eyes, remembering how easily he'd ripped apart the striking bag. "Will you kill me then? After my father leaves?

There is nothing in the treaty that says you can't do away with me."

"No," he murmured. The fact that he turned his back to her to store several papers away in the filing cabinets behind the desk told mountains of his confidence in himself with her in the room. "I will not. Mates are unable to kill each other, let alone hurt each other too badly. Our bond will prevent it. You will be safe from me, and I will be safe from you."

Mates...

A shudder of fear raced down her spine, straight to her toes. "Have you ever seen it done? Have you ever witnessed a transition?"

He paused, and then looked at her over his shoulder. "Once. If you insist on learning something about me, then here it is. I was born a vampire. My brother, Sam, was not. My father is a human, so there was a chance we would either be a vampire or a human. Sam was born a human." He leaned against the desk, and she dared to take a single step closer. "I was six when Sam was born, and I still remember my mother weeping when she learned of his mortality. She refused to turn him because she could not bear to put him through so much pain. He grew up as a human, and he was always envious of me. I was stronger. Faster. More lethal. And he considered himself ordinary. When he was sixteen, he decided he didn't want to live like a mortal anymore." He paused. "He begged my mother to turn him, and she did."

Without her consent, her heartbeat quickened when he pushed away from the table and approached, now close enough to cast a shadow over her. "Believe me, elf," he whispered, touching a strand of her hair with fingernails that could likely cut glass. "You will only wish for death. I will rest easy knowing you will not get your wish."

"What happened after?" she managed to get out. Between her fear of him gutting her and her nervousness at being near him, her mouth somehow worked. "How did he fare after the transition?"

"Well enough, I suppose. Sam always had a big heart where women were concerned. Lots of women. All the time. Some younger than him. Some older. When he was nineteen, my mother learned he had taken a mate a year prior, and they'd managed to keep it a secret all that time. She was furious and sent Sam to live with Dracula here in Ichor Knell, forcing him to take responsibility for Natalia."

He was volunteering much more information than she'd asked for, but she didn't want to remind him.

"Eighteen is very young to take a mate," she said, "even for an elf to marry."

The vampire king lifted her hair to his nose, a look of concentration on his face. "And how old are you? I can't tell by scenting you alone."

"Sixty-seven."

"I am eighty-five."

"Ah. I somehow expected you to be a lot older."

"So do a lot of people."

"Dracula was over a thousand years old."

As if her words reminded him of who she was and why she was there in the first place, he dropped his hand to his side and scowled. "Get out."

She returned his scowl. So quickly, their near-pleasant encounter had turned into frigid ice. "Then I will see you tomorrow."

With the intention of saying goodbye, she reached for his hand, but the moment their fingers touched, it felt as if the entire world flipped upside down. A burst of heat shot up her arm, the sudden connection sizzling like a thunderbolt bursting through the sky. He gasped as if he felt it, too, snatching his hand away like she had shocked him. She watched as his expression turned from surprise, to confusion, to anger.

He pointed to the door. "Out."

The moment she stepped foot into the hallway, he slammed the door shut behind her. She stood still for a moment and cradled her hand to her chest. Her skin still felt warm where it had made contact with him.

She recognized the feeling for what it was. Connection. Potential. Excitement. The start of something too beautiful to destroy.

No. She could have wept right there in the hallway, not caring if anyone saw. *No, this wasn't supposed to happen.*

CHAPTER 10

MOST PEOPLE DESCRIBED their union day as the happiest day of their lives. Jesper couldn't possibly begin to relate.

Nausea clawed at him as if he were a lioness's half-eaten meal, ripping into him from the very moment he woke from a fitful slumber. The ache of loss gripped him hard knowing he would not form a union with a female he loved. This was it. He would not get another chance for the rest of his very long life.

Kiara fussed over him throughout the morning, making sure he consumed a decent meal of warm blood, picking out what he would wear to the ceremony, and she even took the liberty of fixing his hair until every dark red strand fell perfectly into place. He scowled almost the entire time.

"Oh, Jesper," Kiara said, now raiding his closet when she changed her mind about the clothes she'd picked out earlier for him. "Don't look so despondent. Alavara is beautiful. And she's an elf. How many vampires can say they have a dark elf as a mate?"

He huffed and fell back onto his bed, gazing up at the ceiling with a dead stare. "Pick out the blackest outfit you can find. Today is a day of mourning, not of celebration." He squeezed his eyes shut but immediately regretted it. "*Oof.*"

A pile of clothes landed on top of him, and he tossed them aside and propped himself up on an elbow to glare at his sister.

"Well, I happen to think my future sister-in-law is lovely," she said and nodded to the clothes. "Put those on. And do hurry. Otherwise, you will be late for your own union ceremony."

He raised an eyebrow to say *does it matter*? But still, he dragged himself off the bed and behind the folding screen. The clothes she'd picked out for him were nice and slimming, and to his dismay, not a single speck of black. Too much red. Too much brown. Too much white. At least his crown was black. He took heart in that.

"The Diviner forced me to sign a document stating who my heir will be should I die," he mumbled as he stepped out from behind the screen and finished buttoning his shirt.

Kiara rolled her eyes at him. "And being the smarty-boots you are, I bet you named your future son as your heir."

He couldn't help himself as his eyes gleamed wickedly. "Precisely. It's a shame I will never have a son. Nor a child. In fact, I will keep Alavara's chambers on the very opposite end of the castle, and she will never have a reason to venture this way."

His sister smacked him in the face with a pillow, her vampire strength throwing him off balance. "To deprive your mate of children? You are awful. I ought to disown you."

In a mocking tone, he replied, "Oh no! Whatever shall I do without my annoying pest of a shadow?"

She hit him with a pillow again. This time, he deserved it.

"Come." She slid her arm through his and led him into the hallway where servants bustled to take care of the celebrations to be held tomorrow afternoon. "I am eager to witness your union, and I especially want to see how ravishing Alavara looks. I overheard one of the maids saying she was heart-stoppingly beautiful. Do you suppose she will stop *your* heart?"

The gloom of a shadow returned over his head once more. "The only thing that will stop my heart is an iron blade."

Kiara gave him a disbelieving sideways glance. "Have you no romantic bone in your body?"

"Not a single one."

"Likely because Sam stole it all and left nothing for you."

For many years, he'd worried he would never know what it felt like to love another. He stopped worrying long ago when he realized he wasn't capable of romantic love. When he was younger—much younger—he'd given courtship a chance. Again and again and again. But not once had he felt a flicker of feeling for any of the females he'd attempted to woo. It had quickly become discouraging and painful, and therefore, he'd stopped trying.

There was a permanent place in his heart filled with cobwebs and echoes, a place he couldn't reach.

A place no one could reach.

They arrived at the cathedral, and his stomach churned with nausea again when he scanned the filled pews. Each one of his guests held a candle, the flames flickering in a way that cast a brilliant sparkle on the stained glass lining the large room. Where people might have seen beauty, he only saw chains and misery. He would forever be shackled to the dark elf who had threatened to kill him and then led an army straight to his door. How could he ever forgive her for threatening his family?

"Let's get this over with," he muttered.

He ignored each vampire, elf, and human looking his way as he deposited Kiara at the front pew with the rest of his concerned family and headed to the front where the Diviner stood behind the altar. Although he wanted to frown and scowl and perhaps even scream, he forced his expression to remain neutral.

He knelt on one side of the altar and focused on taking long, deep breaths. And then he made the mistake of looking out over the guests in the room. He met Cybil's gaze, and she cringed as if he had lifted a hand to strike her. She looked so...melancholy. Heartbroken. Utterly defeated.

It was his fault.

But he had no choice.

Not wanting to look at her any longer, he stared down at the altar and counted to a hundred, his silent counting drowning out the low murmur of conversations throughout the room. When Alavara still didn't appear, he counted again. And then again.

Finally, the doors creaked open, and he glanced up to find Alavara on her father's arm. He couldn't help himself as his heart stopped for a moment before it resumed beating at a much quicker pace.

She was beautiful.

She was so very beautiful.

Her dark hair was pinned up in an elegant fashion as if to show off her long and slender neck. Hanging from her pointed ears were what looked to be droplets of water. Perhaps made of glass, but they shimmered and sparkled like prayers raining from the heavens. Her silver gown dipped low to show off the pendant of her golden necklace, with sheer fabric stretched across her collarbones. The rest of her dress was silver like the elegant sheen of a waterfall, the hem like a smooth, untouched river.

He narrowed his eyes at the dress, suspecting it might be made of unnatural elements using magic. But no. It was the way she walked, the way she moved, that made it appear so. He wondered for a moment if she would retain her unnatural grace after she transitioned, or if it would be stripped away the moment her eyes flashed red.

A chuckle nearly escaped him when he caught the faintest glimmer of silver beneath the sleeve of her dress, not to mention the pins in her hair that came to a deadly point. She was an assassin. Until they were fully mated, he had no reign over her, and therefore he still needed to be on his guard.

Ruvyn helped Alavara kneel at the altar across from him before taking a seat in the pews.

Jesper leaned closer to whisper in her ear, quiet so no one could overhear. "What do you suppose the Diviner would think if he knew how many weapons you currently carried on your person? In the cathedral of all places."

Surprise flashed across her eyes. "How do you know?"

"I can't help but notice everything. I don't know whether to be cautious or relieved that you chose to forgo your iron weapons today."

"I didn't want to appear rude. Besides, I need to get used to being without them for when you decide to turn me in the future."

His eyes gleamed wickedly, and he pulled away just enough to look her in the eye. He was well aware of the audience's captive attention, waiting to begin the ceremony, but there seemed to be a gross misunderstanding.

"The future?" He continued to speak quietly to prevent anyone from overhearing. "Are you thinking weeks from now? Months? Years? Oh, no. Right after the ceremony will do."

Her heartbeat quickened, music to his ears, her face turning a shade paler. "Why?"

"The mating bond won't take effect for you unless you are a vampire. I am *not* going to bed you twice."

He heard her swallow in the awkward silence that had descended upon the cathedral. "I'm not ready. I haven't had any time to prepare."

"Neither have I, but here we are."

This was the worst possible time and place to discuss this, but he was the shah. They would wait for him. Besides, no one could hear their hushed conversation, not even those who leaned forward as if to catch a sentence or two.

"The treaty states that the consummation must happen on the union night," he murmured quietly. "Therefore, you need to go through the long and agonizing process of transitioning before the night's end. There is no time for waiting. You can thank your father for that."

"I think I'm going to be sick."

"You and me both."

The Diviner cleared his throat, glancing with uncertainty between the two of them. "Are we ready to start?"

Jesper returned to his original position on his knees, taking her forearm in his, and motioned with his hand for the Diviner to begin. The holy man lifted his arms, his long sleeves draping down as he welcomed those in attendance.

He'd been to so many union ceremonies that the words the Diviner spoke about their religion and the sanctity of finding a mate flew over his head. He found his thoughts wandering, tuning out the words as he focused on maintaining a neutral expression. He'd tried hard not to think about Alavara's transitioning and the union night afterward, but now he wondered how best to approach it. Of course, he didn't delight in her misery as much as he made it seem. He wanted to make her transition as quick as possible to avoid extending her agony.

He internally shuddered as he remembered Sam's transitioning all too well. The screams. The hours of him writhing in agony. And then he remembered his mother's limited supply of venom. More venom would have made the transitioning process quicker. He could only bite Alavara so many times before he depleted his store of venom. He needed to bite her in the right places to quicken the process.

"Your Highness?" the Diviner said, and Jesper broke out of his own thoughts long enough to find the man holding out a goblet of blood.

He took it and sipped the thick liquid, still warm, the blood from a human criminal. Usually a murderer. When he handed it to Alavara, she stared at him in horror. Daggers... They should have discussed this earlier. Instead of speaking of the things they needed to discuss the other night, they'd spoken of Sam and his talent for wooing women.

Alavara's transition to Kumari wasn't going smoothly already as he'd promised it would. If he didn't act quickly, his people would never accept her by his side.

As he'd seen Sam do plenty of times with Natalia, he reached for her, his hand cupping her cheek like a loving caress. But in reality, the movement was to shield her horrified expression from the audience using his hand and arm.

A look of understanding passed across her face, and her fingers only trembled slightly as she lifted the goblet to her lips and took a sip. When the blood hit her tongue, she started to gag, but he kept his hand firm on her cheek to prevent her from turning her head for the entire congregation to see her adverse reaction. He forced her to look into his eyes and swallow. Steady. Calm. He may not be fond of her, but he would not have a kumari at his side that was not accepted by his people. Gagging on blood was a quick way to be scorned by other vampires.

Only when she got a hold of herself again did he drop his hand. Knowing the next part of the ceremony, his stomach churned again, but his skill of keeping a neutral expression kept up. The vow to seal them as One.

The Diviner looked to him first. "Do you promise to love and cherish your mate for the rest of your life and into the afterlife?"

The bond was forever. They would never be free of one another. But there was no other choice. He knew he could never love her, so that would be a lie. And to cherish her? This whole ceremony was a sham. He might as well chisel the word *liar* on his forehead.

"Yes."

Alavara answered the same way, and he wondered if they needed to chisel *liar* on her forehead as well.

Two vampires brought out both of their crowns sitting on red velvet pillows, and one after the other, the Diviner placed each crown over their brows. Jesper couldn't help but admit with some level of satisfaction that Alavara looked magnificent wearing the elegant but powerful black crown his sister had designed. It brought out the dark color of her eyes.

"Then with the blessing of our god and goddess, Ylios and Iqris, I join the two of you as mates in this holy union, Shah Jesper Degore and Kumari Alavara Degore, and send you forth into the world as mates, protectors, and rulers."

The Diviner smiled and gestured for them to seal the union with a nose nuzzle, something only vampires did for their mates, but Jesper raised an eyebrow in a challenge. He would *not* do it. Ever.

After a brief moment of awkward silence, the Diviner dropped his hands and said, "Vii si prospera," and the entire congregation echoed his words. The ceremony was over. They were officially bonded by law. The next part would not be so pleasant for either of them.

Everyone stood in the pews, a rumble like thunder after the quiet stillness only moments before. Jesper moved to stand, but Alavara grasped firmly onto his arm.

"Don't turn me. Please."

He gave her a cold stare. "I made it very clear from the beginning that I will not rule beside an elf. You and your father entered into this treaty knowing this. I cannot be held responsible for your decision."

"Perhaps you will reconsider."

Both now standing, he took her arm and pulled her close to make sure no one overheard his next words. "If I allow you to remain an elf, then Ichor Knell could be filled with and ruled by elves one day." Though, he didn't mention the fact that he didn't plan on having any children with her. "Do you understand the risk of not turning you? I will not take it. You agreed to this, Alavara. I did what was necessary to keep my people safe. You have absolutely no right to make any further demands of me."

True, genuine fear gazed back at him through her eyes. He had no desire to turn her, to see her in such agony. But what he said was true. Besides, if they had the audacity to march an army to his city, then they could suffer the consequences.

He sighed, allowing his stern expression to drop. But no words of encouragement or regret greeted his tongue. There was nothing either of them could do. They were both trapped in this agreement, and it was far too late to stop the boulder from rolling down the hill.

Offering her his arm, he said, "May tomorrow be a better day."

As he led her back down the aisle toward the door, those in the audience nodded to them or briefly expressed their congratulations. He avoided looking at Cybil again. He didn't want to see what lay in her expression. After the kiss they'd shared, they hadn't spoken a single word to each other. The silence cut into him like a knife.

Each step he took felt like walking through mud, each layer caking onto the bottom of his boot until he was inches taller than to begin with. The dread was too much to bear, and he knew Alavara felt it, too, though for an entirely different reason.

He waited in the hallway outside of Alavara's bedchambers while maids helped dress his new mate in more comfortable clothing. His heart thundering like a stampede of wild horses.

"Remember," his mother said as she joined him with his father and sister. He was glad Sam stayed away for this particular event, as he did not need any taunting. "Neck, wrists, inner elbows."

His hands slicked with perspiration as he nodded. He wiped his palms on his trousers, only to do it again when his nerves refused to ebb. His venom churned within his mouth, burning and eager to be released.

At last, the maids exited the room, and he slipped inside before anyone else uttered a single word. He softly closed the door behind himself and locked the bolt into place. When Alavara would inevitably start screaming, he knew everyone's first reaction would be to rush to her aid. The distraction might hinder his venom's release. It was best to do this alone until he saw it through to the end.

Dread clung to his every pore as he continued to face the door rather than his mate. He wasn't sure he could bear her cries of agony. The memory of Sam's transition flashed across his mind. Sam's ceaseless screaming. His mother's sorrowful wails. And the fact that no one could relieve his pain.

He didn't want to hurt her. But he wasn't about to allow anyone else's venom to rip through her other than his own.

"Please." Alavara's voice trembled. "Don't do this. Not yet."

Slowly, he turned to find her wearing a white nightgown with gossamer sleeves, which shimmered like sunlight on water as she moved to sit with her legs dangling over the side of the bed. Small, delicate toes peeked out from beneath the hem. Her long, dark hair trailed over her shoulders and down her back. Her dark eyes pleaded with him.

His heart caught in a surprising moment of anguish, and the transitioning hadn't even happened yet.

"I already told you why it needs to happen now rather than later."

Jesper approached slowly, each footfall sending Alavara's heart into a frenzy of fear. There was no use arguing with him. His reasoning was solid. He was not one to be swayed. But there were few times in her life that resembled the fear she felt now.

Neither of them uttered another word as Jesper climbed onto the bed with her. He placed a hand against her collarbone and lightly pushed her backward into the pillows until she found herself staring into his eyes. There was not an ounce of kindness in their depths, but there was not much other emotion, either.

No happiness.

No anger.

No nervousness.

No uncertainty.

She felt certain her eyes told a completely different story despite trying hard to contain her emotions.

I'm not ready. Please. I beg you to spare me this fate.

But the words died on her lips.

He slipped his hands into hers, pulled them closer to himself, and stroked her wrists with his thumbs. "I'm going to bite you three times," he said in a brusque, business-like tone. "It will be painful. Very painful. Like a fire raging through your body that you can't put out. But you will get through it." She watched his throat bob up and down, a flicker of regret in his eyes before it was replaced by the cold neutrality once more. "Are you ready?"

A couple tears escaped the corners of her eyes and soaked her hair. Still, she nodded. "Yes."

Her heart beat rapidly in her chest, and a small whimper escaped her mouth as he gently pushed her head to the side to expose her neck. Even in these last seconds, she begged her goddess to save her from this fate, to find a way to intervene. But no answer came to her silent pleas. She squeezed her eyes shut and whimpered again when she heard Jesper's fangs sprout from his gums like swords sliding out of their sheaths.

The bed shifted quickly beneath her before his sharp fangs pierced her neck.

Fire slithered into her bloodstream, so intense that her eyes burst open, and she gasped. Her body thrashed, and she might have head-butted Jesper if he had not been pinning her down as if he'd anticipated her to buck at the pain. He bit one of her wrists, more fire spreading through her blood, and then he bit her other wrist.

She could not handle the fire anymore. She screamed.

CHAPTER 11

JESPER CHOKED BACK sob after sob as he hopped off the bed as Alavara thrashed against her sheets. His hands trembled as her cries of pain attacked his ears. Her screams. Her *screams*.

He stumbled toward the door, his hands trembling as he unlatched the bolt only for several maids to come scurrying in to see to her welfare. His knees trembled. His blood ran cold as if ice entered his bloodstream.

Her screams!

Although they weren't even physically bonded yet, his emotions slammed into him like an iron arrow straight through his heart. He hadn't anticipated turning someone to completely destroy him and rebuild him and destroy him again. His legs shook, his entire body trembling, and his breaths came in short gasps. The agony she must be in… He couldn't bear it. He couldn't take it anymore.

He couldn't have been more grateful when his father entered with a couple of female servants in tow, one carrying a basin of water and fresh cloths, and the other carrying a goblet of blood and a change of clothing.

Still, his legs refused to work correctly, and his teeth began chattering.

"An adverse reaction to turning someone," his father grunted, helping him toward a chair at a round table. Alavara released a half-elf, half-vampire wail.

"Wh-wh-what?"

"The shaking. I doubt you've ever expended every last drop of your venom before. It happened to your mother too when she turned Sam."

On the bed, Alavara shrieked again and writhed in the sheets, tossing back and forth. Her back arched, and she cried out again. Alavara… He could not handle her distress, her pain. He wanted to run. He needed to run. But part of him needed to be near her as well.

When she screamed again, he shook his head, and he didn't realize he was crying until he swiped a strand of his hair out of his eyes only to find his face damp with tears.

"I-I-I can't." His voice quavered along with every part of him. "I c-c-can't."

He couldn't sit, not when she was in so much pain. On trembling legs, he threw open the window and allowed his vampiric transformation to wash over him. His skin turned to scales, his serpent body clinging to the side of the castle as he slithered out into the fresh air. He climbed higher and higher until he reached the roof, and only then did he return to his vampire form.

With his body still trembling, he laid down on his back, the sound of her screams still echoing in his mind. He hid his face in the crook of his elbow, and he did something he hadn't done in years, not even at Dracula's funeral—he wept.

Alavara's cries had stopped hours ago, but Jesper didn't dare go to her yet. She needed to rest as long as possible.

He bit his nails as he paced across the private drawing room. Sam sat in a chair beside the hearth. His father leaned against the wall, inspecting his knife. How was Alavara faring after the transition? He kept telling himself he didn't care, but he just wasn't sure anymore. Today had been an exhausting, emotional day, and it wasn't even over yet. But the clock had not yet struck midnight. There was still time to fulfill the treaty.

A servant knocked and poked his head inside the room after receiving permission to enter. "Sire, Her Highness is ready for you."

The moment the servant disappeared, he crossed the room and drank one glass of liquor, then another. How many more would it take before he could forget this night ever happened?

"I'm going to be sick."

Sam stood and clapped him on the shoulder, giving him a mischievous grin. "I can come for moral support."

Although his brother's words were tinged with humor, an uneasiness sprouted in his eyes.

He shoved the hand off his shoulder. "Not under any circumstance will you be allowed in there."

He paced back and forth in the room, glancing toward the window for the dozenth time, tempted to jump. If he managed to hurt himself badly enough, perhaps they could put this off for a while, and maybe by then, all their would-be witnesses would be long gone.

"Who cares about the witnesses? You can still have a little fun."

"You are unbelievable," he snapped at his brother.

His father, watching the exchange silently as he leaned against the wall, said, "Any one of Ruvyn's witnesses could claim the consummation never happened, which would be a breach of treaty, which would bring war anyway. You need witnesses of your own."

"I've already thought of that. I asked Leif."

Snorting, he replied, "Leif is a spineless coward, and who knows if he could be bought for his silence. I can't be bought. I'll be there as well."

For a moment, he hesitated. There was no one he trusted more than his own father, but it was *his father*.

Still, he found himself nodding before he slumped into a chair, his face in his hands. "Oh, daggers. I want to die."

"Humans do this sort of thing all the time," Sam said as if in an attempt to sound reassuring.

"Alavara is not a human. She's an elf."

"And? It's customary in her culture. None of them would bat an eye at this."

"*This* is a mockery of *our* customs."

No one had anything to say to that, likely because they agreed. It was a slap in the face, but one he needed to take. So, he would push away his thoughts, his emotions, and he would hold his head high.

He stood slowly, his eyes smoldering. "Ruvyn better watch his back, because the next move on the chess board is mine."

Alavara was overly aware of all the pairs of eyes on her, one of them being her own father, but she refused to meet them. Not now. Not tonight. Instead, she kept her gaze on the soft red and white diamond-checkered bedspread. She sat on her ankles in the middle of the bed, a pale blue, silky robe the only thing covering her. Her entire body ached, and she didn't dare think about what it meant.

It seemed as if far too much time had passed, and Jesper still hadn't come inside to meet her. Instead of dwelling on why, she listened to the candle flames whispering around her, all while her head spun. *Crackle. Whoosh. Slip. Pop.*

At last, the door opened, and despite her pulse thrumming far too quickly, she kept her gaze fixed to the bed. She felt rather than saw Jesper stand beside the door, his gaze on her. But he didn't approach. He simply stood still.

She dared a glance toward him only to find him frowning, his gaze darting toward the door. He didn't want to be here. Then again, neither did she. Not like this. But what else did she expect when her father managed to entangle them with a powerful monarch? Powerful, deadly, and far too cunning for his own good.

Jesper's hand clenched, unclenched, clenched, and finally unclenched once again as his entire demeanor changed. Gone were the tense shoulders. His gaze turned to her instead of the door. And then he approached. It was as if no one else in the room existed except for her, and she forced her gaze to remain on him to help her act the same way.

As if on their own accord, her gaze dipped to take in his entire body, and her mouth suddenly became dry. She was not supposed to be attracted to him. She was not supposed to hope for happiness in an otherwise hopeless future. She was not supposed to care.

Yet, she cared.

And caring was dangerous.

Her head spun again as weariness washed over her. Everything felt different. So many changes she had no desire to explore.

"I can't watch this," the vampire named Leif muttered, but when he tried to flee toward the door, Adam Degore grabbed him by the collar of his shirt and pushed him back into his original position.

Jesper swallowed, his throat bobbing up and down as he glanced toward her father. "Look at her. She can hardly hold her head up. Give us a few more days. She needs more time to recover."

Her stomach churned. Her dizzy head spun. Her entire body ached from her head to her toes. Not able to keep herself upright any longer. She allowed herself to lie back on the bed and close her eyes.

"And give you time to weasel out of this?" her father scoffed. "The treaty states the consummation must be tonight—"

"Jesper," she murmured. Her voice croaked. Her mouth felt funny when she spoke. "It's all right."

"No, it's not."

She opened her eyes and attempted a reassuring smile. "I am tired. Not incapacitated."

He paused again before fury flashed in his eyes. He approached her father, each an unmovable boulder facing one another. "Leave us."

Her father's fury smoldered right back, and she could almost see the black wisps of his magic curling in his fingers. "No. A treaty is a treaty."

"This," Jesper gestured to the audience in the room, "is not in the treaty. You have insulted me enough. I will not stand for this."

Tension crackled in the torches lining the room. It seemed as if everyone held their breath. No one stood up against her father without repercussions.

To her surprise, the darkness in her father's eyes dissipated as he dipped his head. "I will respect your customs, Shah Jesper." He gestured to his entourage, who followed him out the door.

"Thank the stars," Leif murmured before he darted away. Adam Degore was the last to leave, shutting the door resoundingly behind him until only she and Jesper remained.

A sense of relief filled her with the lack of audience, but it was short lived when Jesper turned to face her, fury still crackling through his eyes.

"Let's get something straight," he hissed as he climbed onto the bed and straddled her, pinning her to the cushions. Despite her fatigue and his contempt, excitement pooled in her belly. "This means nothing. I still hate you."

She fluttered her eyelashes at him and enjoyed watching his scowl deepen. "Hate is such a *passionate* word." She wrapped an arm around his neck and attempted to pull him into a kiss, but he placed his hand over her mouth and pushed her away, all while a smirk spread across her face.

His hands rested on either side of her head as he leaned closer. "Let's get something else straight." Menace leaked from his voice as he whispered in her ear. "I will never kiss you. And this will never happen again."

"Never?" Her fingers made quick work of the buttons on his shirt. He didn't stop her. "Another strong word." His body shuddered beneath her touch as she ran her hands up the muscles of his torso and smooth chest.

His scowl wavered momentarily as his eyes became unfocused. But it quickly returned, accompanied by greater disdain than before. He smacked her hands away. "Don't touch me."

She ran her fingers up the length of his thighs. His control seemed to lapse again as he sighed, his eyelids fluttering closed. At least until he smacked her hands away again.

"Where's the fun in that?" she asked with a mock pout.

"This is not meant to be fun."

"How unfortunate for you. Because I'm having a lot of fun." Despite her playful words, a sense of dread constricted her heart as he unraveled the laces on her nightdress. They were about to become mates. And her father would finally win.

But the moment she thought it, black fog swirled in her mind, pulling the words away from her as she tried to latch on. What would her father win? Why was he making her do this? She couldn't remember.

So, instead on focusing on the frustration of the holes in her memory, she focused on Jesper's strong, warm hands on her and how surprisingly safe he made her feel when the world around her had long ago burst into chaotic flames.

CHAPTER 12

EVERYTHING ACHED.

Alavara groaned as she sat up in bed, squinting against the light shining through the window. Not direct sunlight, but a light filtered through layers of clouds.

Everything seemed brighter, sharper.

And that *smell*.

Her gaze darted to the goblet on her nightstand, and she took a deep breath through her nose. Whatever was in that goblet smelled delicious, especially to her parched throat.

She sat up straighter, only for her face to blanch. Inside was a thick red liquid, and she didn't need to inspect it further to know what it was.

Blood. Human blood.

"No," she whispered.

Squinting her eyes shut, she tried to recall what had happened. She remembered the union ceremony, Jesper's refusal to allow her to stay an elf. She remembered Jesper's fangs in her neck.

Heat churned within her, smoldering in her core. The feeling was so intense that it startled her backward into her pillows, her breathing ragged. Only when the shock wore off did she dare venture into the feeling. No, it was hardly a feeling but an intense desire. A need. She needed Jesper. She needed to be near him, to touch him, and by the heavens, she *really* wanted to kiss him despite his refusal of the act.

"Is this the bond you spoke of?" she mused to herself. Some of those feelings had already existed, but to this degree?

Dread draped over her like a midnight blanket. With trembling fingers, she lifted her hands to her mouth and touched two sharp fangs. It was as if her entire mouth had been reconstructed to fit the fangs, which certainly explained the indescribable pain.

Despite the blood calling to her, a desire to drink nearly too intense to handle, she ignored the call and located her handheld mirror on the desk to get a good look of what had happened to her the other night. She lifted the mirror and cried out. The mirror slipped from her fingers and shattered into several large pieces on the floor.

"I don't have a reflection," she gasped.

She dove to the floor and picked up a shard of mirror. A surprising animal-like hiss escaped her when it cut her finger.

But before she managed to find a cloth to press to the wound, the cut began to reknit as her body healed itself. For a moment, she stared at her finger in shock.

Her hands now shook uncontrollably as she held the shard of mirror again, but no matter which way she angled it, she still had no reflection. It was gone.

And it took a little piece of her heart with it.

Alavara blinked once, twice, to restrain her tears. "I am a vampire."

How awful. How utterly awful.

Out of the corner of her eye, she spotted a sliver of white parchment on her nightstand, and familiar handwriting stared back at her. She'd seen Jesper's handwriting once before when he'd signed the treaties.

Alavara,

Meet me by the bronze statue down the hallway just before noon. Dress well. Wear your crown.

–J

She still didn't know how to tell time in Ichor Knell just by the amount of light seeping through the clouds, so she allowed a couple of female servants to help bathe and dress her, even as her body ached tremendously. One of them fashioned her hair into an updo, one she couldn't see because of her lack of reflection. The other tried to convince her to drink the blood, and when she refused, they slipped shoes onto her feet where she sat in a chair.

Queen of vampires, she thought to herself. The idea terrified her. Becoming a vampire had never been a part of the plan. Now she had impeccable hearing and sight, no reflection, and everything in her body hurt.

What plan? she asked herself as she fought through the black fog in her head. She vaguely remembered her father telling her. And then…

Nothing.

Her fingers subconsciously reached for the golden chain hanging around her neck. She ran it through her hands again and again as she walked on silent feet down an empty hallway and stood in front of what she assumed was the bronze statue stated in the note.

"You're late."

She jumped at the voice and spun around to find Jesper glaring at her on the other side of the hallway, his arms folded over his chest.

"Would you imagine that," she replied dryly.

"You didn't drink the blood."

"I don't want it." Though, how he'd known as much baffled her.

He raised an eyebrow at her, not a stern look but one of curiosity, and perhaps of concern. But the concern disappeared a moment later as if he hadn't wanted her to see it.

Slowly, he stalked forward until he stood in front of her, close enough to touch. She wanted to touch him. Badly. And his scent… By the forest, his *scent*. Earthy. Masculine. Beckoning. Intoxicating. She wanted nothing more than to breathe him in, to bask in his scent as if she were a feline basking in the sunlight.

"Do you feel the bond?" he asked.

Somehow, she managed to keep her hands at her sides as she nodded mutely.

"Good." He leaned even closer. "I will tell you this right now. The bond *lies*. It may tell you that you want me more than you've ever wanted anything in your life. It's a lie. My scent, my touch, my voice." She shuddered at the pleasant timber caressing her ear. "All a lie. It would do you good to remember as much."

A part of her heart closed off to him at his blatant dismissal, but it was just as well. It kept her focused, and it helped remind her that her *mate* was an evil bastard. Would she be punished if she punched him in the face? If only to punch his glare back into his brain?

"Why are you looking at me as if I'm the enemy?" she snarled quietly. "We're mates."

He took a step closer, and she wondered if he could hear her heart quicken just like how her new hearing picked up his. "True, but I don't trust you. Not for a single second. Let's take a look and see why, shall we?" He counted on his fingers. "You tried to attack me. You spread a glamor throughout my kingdom to hide five armies on the horizon. You brought said five armies to our doorstep. You *forced* me to take you as my mate. And you still have secrets swirling around in those eyes of yours. So yes, as far as I am concerned, my mate is also my enemy."

A low growl sounded in her throat, surprising her enough for it to cut off abruptly. She didn't used to be able to do it, and she didn't like that she could.

Before she could answer, he continued speaking. "There are a few things you need to know about being a vampire, so I will give you a quick overview before we enter the Great Hall together, and I will present you as my mate. First, your eyes are blood red."

She gasped in horror, her fingers flying to her eyelids. How long had they been like that? "Tell me how to change them back."

"You can't. New vampires have little control over their red eyes and their fangs. It could be weeks before you start to gain control, before your eyes become dark again and your fangs are able to retract. This is normal to vampires. No one in Ichor Knell will bat an eye. I just thought you should know what you look like and how humans and elves might perceive you."

Utter humiliation was an understatement.

"However, there are a few things vampires *will* bat an eye at. Don't even think about trying out your new vampire transformation yet, because you *will* get stuck in it and vampires *will* scoff at you."

"What do you mean *vampire transformation?*"

As if to demonstrate, his tongue flicked out of his vampire mouth, but it wasn't his tongue. It was the tongue of a serpent. But moments before it disappeared, it returned to normal.

Her eyes widened and she jumped backward, staring at his mouth where his tongue had disappeared. "What…what…?"

"Every vampire has their own transformation. Some felines, others canines or birds. Mine is a snake. Because I was the one who turned you, your transformation will likely be a serpent as well. Like I said, don't try to transform. Not yet. Moving on…" He trapped her chin in his fingers and turned her head back and forth, looking into her eyes. "Bloodlust. Don't be a pig about it. Don't slurp it down, gobble it up, spill all over yourself to get a taste. Learn to control your craving for blood."

"I don't want to consume blood."

The thought made her shudder, and she gagged at the memory of swallowing the small bit during the ceremony.

Again, he looked at her with that same confused curiosity. "You have to. You don't have a choice."

"I do have a choice, and I won't do it."

He said nothing, but the strange look he gave her made her stomach churn uncomfortably. Was it wrong to not have a taste for blood? How revolting.

"We'll see how long you last. But when you snap, I truly hope you don't do it when our human guests are still here. We have a treaty to uphold after all. This is important, Alavara."

"Noted," she said dryly, though he seemed to ignore her tone of voice.

"Things will no longer be the same as when you were an elf." Though she supposed she was part elf because her long, pointed ears were still there. "You no longer have a reflection. Iron and sunlight will burn you and can even kill you. You will need permission to enter a room beforehand. Some rooms are a given, such as the Great Hall, music rooms, and many rooms in the castle if I'm honest. You'll know when you can't enter a room—you will detect a sort of shimmering barrier. If you venture toward my bedchambers, you will find the barrier will always be there for you, and you will never gain permission to enter."

The snide remark was as clear as day. He didn't want anything to do with her. "A poor way to treat your mate, don't you think?"

It was the wrong thing to say, judging by his dark glare. "You and your father wanted the vampire throne? Well, you got it. And through very underhanded means, I might add. But believe me when I tell you that you won't see an ounce of power throughout your lifetime. I will make sure you have absolutely no control. No power. Nothing."

Her nose twitched in anger to match his. "Anything else, Your Kingliness?"

"Yes." His snarling expression fell into a look of vulnerability. Her stomach churned uncomfortably at the sight. "Why? Just tell me why. The only demand you and your father made was for me to take you as my mate. Why didn't you just come to the castle as a show of peace and *offer* yourself as a potential mate? Why the army? Why the treaty? Just *why?*"

Jesper's question surprised her, taking her completely off guard. "Because...because..." But when she opened her mouth to tell the truth, her tongue froze and fog claimed her mind, making her forget what she wanted to say. So instead, she asked, "Would you have said yes?"

He didn't answer for a long moment, but instead looked into each of her eyes, his gaze roaming over her face, to her lips, to the crown on top of her head, and he finally replied.

"I would have considered it. Daggers, Alavara. I would have considered it. I very well might have agreed under friendlier circumstances. But now I can't even look at you without seeing the betrayal, the trickery, the cruelty. There will never be anything between us. Whatever we had together ended the moment I left your bedchambers, and there *will be no more.*"

She wasn't sure what to say. Against her better judgement, her heart ached from his words. In her small amount of time in Ichor Knell, fondness for Jesper had tugged at her. His taunts. The spark of connection between them. The pull of attraction she felt for him. When they'd put this plan into fruition, she hadn't expected to care for the person standing before her. Therefore, his words stung, and she didn't think it was the bond making her heart ache.

Reaching for the necklace around her neck, she clutched the pendant in her hand. Tight enough for her fingers to ache along with her poor, wretched heart. She deserved this. She knew she did. It was best to tuck away any feelings for him before they grew like weeds in a garden of roses.

"Is my father still in the castle?" she asked.

"Yes."

He didn't sound happy about it in the slightest.

"Come with me," he muttered. "I want to get this over with. Then we won't have to see much of each other."

When he offered his arm to her, she took it, and once again, his scent caressed her nose. Her grip tightened on him as she tried her hardest to keep herself from leaning in and taking a breathful of him.

They arrived before the closed doors of the Great Hall, and her footsteps slowed as she found three others standing in front. From her spying around the castle, she recognized them as Adam, Willow, and Kiara Degore. Willow wouldn't even look her way. Adam regarded her with caution. But Kiara...

"Oh, look at you two!" Kiara threw her arms around Jesper, then Alavara, much to her surprise. "What good-looking mates you make. I wanted to officially meet you before everyone else did." She grasped her wrist in greeting. "Kiara Degore."

"Alavara Elroris."

Jesper cleared his throat, and only then did she realize her mistake. "Oh." Her surname was no longer Elroris but Degore.

A *human* surname, as it had come from Jesper's human father. She liked her last one much better.

"Careful," Jesper growled, positioning himself between her and his sister. "She bites."

Alavara bared her new fangs at him and glowered. Oh, she would bite *him* if she had any idea how these things worked. She wished she could retract them, as they felt far too strange and foreign in her mouth.

"I thought you had a brother," she said, not seeing him anywhere.

"Yes, and a sister-in-law. But no one seems to know where they end up."

Kiara snorted. "I think I have an idea."

Was that a personal jest? Because she didn't understand it.

Beside her, Jesper took a deep breath and let it out slowly, and then a couple of guards opened the doors to them. Her jaw nearly dropped at the hundreds of people within the Great Hall. It was as if the entire court was in this very room, along with her own father and a few people from his court. Everyone stood, and all talk ceased as the two of them walked forward.

An awful stench hit her nose, and she shied away from it. "What is that horrible smell?" she muttered, keeping her voice quiet.

"That, Alavara, is roasted mutton for the elves and humans to eat."

"Stop jesting. I love roasted mutton."

"I never jest. I am completely serious. Why don't you try a bite? I think I might actually laugh when you retch."

Evil bastard.

It was strange that something so seemingly simple could fill her with such sorrow. Her senses seemed to have altered, and now food she used to enjoy held no appeal.

Jesper led her to the front of the Great Hall, and she was aware of the numerous pairs of eyes on her back. Her heart dipped low in her stomach when he turned to face her and knelt on one knee at her feet. He gently took her hand and pressed it to his forehead.

"Long live my mate. Long live my kumari," he murmured.

As if every other vampire in the room heard him, they shouted in unison, "Long live the kumari!"

Her eyes misted as she stared out over the hall to her new people and back to Jesper who still bowed to her. He may hate her, but this was his gift to her, nonetheless. To show his devotion to her in front of his people. *Their* people... It would help them accept her.

And despite his dislike of her, she was immensely grateful.

So, he actually did it.

Cybil watched as Jesper knelt at the elf's feet, lowering his head in complete devotion to her. There was no doubt about it. They were mates. Truly mates, not just in law, but in body and soul as well.

Her heart broke into a thousand shards of dull glass. She had loved Jesper for as long as she could remember. She had waited in hopes that he might someday regard her as more than just his friend. But in the blink of an eye, someone else had swept in and stole everything from her. Absolutely everything. Did the elf even want him? Would she even care for him? Love him?

He deserved all of that and so much more.

But looking at him now... He did not appear to be happy. Yes, he seemed devoted to his new mate, but certainly not happy.

I only wish I could have been enough for you. I wish I could have been enough to save you.

However, she wasn't enough. She'd had nothing to offer him except her heart, and he had not wanted it.

Not waiting until Jesper had a chance to stand, she slipped out of the room, unshed tears pooling in her eyes. She wrote him a note and slipped it under his bedroom door. After she packed her belongings, she stepped foot out of the castle, and she never intended to return again.

CHAPTER 13

JESPER SAT IN the commons, his body rigid and still as he stared down at the small piece of parchment in his hands. The edges were worn and crinkled, showing just how many times he'd read it.

They couldn't be true. They couldn't. But he had pounded on Cybil's door in the soldier's barracks hard enough to break it down, only to find her room empty. He had approached the captain of the guard and asked after her. He had followed her scent to the very edge of the city, only for the trail to grow cold. And then he hadn't made it more than ten steps into the castle before his legs wobbled and he slumped into this very chair.

Dearest Jesper,

I think you already know how I feel about you, how I've felt about you for a long while now. Therefore, I hope you'll understand why I'm leaving Ichor Knell. I don't plan on returning. I only wish I'd had something more to offer you, something to make you happy.
Yours,
Cybil

He tried to rub the ache from his temple, but it remained. If he didn't have Cybil, who did he have? They'd spent so much time together. At the tavern. On the training grounds. On the battlefield. He already missed her laughter, her teasing, her hotheaded temper.

This wasn't fair. This just wasn't fair.

"Do you love her?"

The voice behind his shoulder startled him, and he reflexively crumpled the parchment in his hand and spun in his seat to find Alavara standing behind the chair. Her eyes were still red. As a brand-new vampire, how she had gone this long without drinking human blood baffled him. And she hadn't even batted an eye at the blood from the feast earlier.

"Don't sneak up on me. I am in no mood for your shadow feet."

She repeated, "Do you love her?"

The mere thought of Cybil made his shoulders sag, the weight of missing her too much to bear on his already burdened shoulders. "Yes. Not romantically. But I love her all the same."

"I'm sorry," she said quietly, and then after a pause, she added, "I know you shared a kiss with her."

"And?" he snarled. The kiss was none of her business, nor was it any of her business to have spied on them. How much more had she spied on in his ignorance?

"And I'm sorry. I saw how much she loved you."

There was no judgement, no disdain or mockery. Only true, genuine regret. His scowl disappeared, and he turned back to stare at the crumpled note. He chuckled humorlessly. "Cybil would have made a terrible kumari. She would have put Dracula's temper to shame."

"Tell me something, Jesper." Alavara rounded the chair and sat on the table across from him, their knees only inches away from touching. "Would you really have risked bringing a war to Ichor Knell if you had even a sliver of romantic feelings for her?"

He lifted his gaze to look into her red eyes, deep red as if her dark brown eyes factored into their coloring. Against his better judgement, he liked the way the red contrasted with her dark hair.

"There is something you don't understand about vampires finding their mates," he replied quietly before glancing around them briefly. He was all too aware of the two females up on the balcony watching them, the maid dusting on the other side of the commons while trying not to get caught with her eavesdropping, the group of men covertly glancing their way as they conversed. Privacy didn't seem to exist when one was the shah.

"And what is that?" When she shifted slightly, he caught her berry scent and tried his hardest not to shudder with pleasure. The bond pulsed alive, begging him to taste her lips, her skin. It took most of his restraint to keep himself from reaching for her and taking her in his arms.

It's a lie. It's a lie. It's a lie.

But the lie smelled oh so good.

"When you find the right mate, you will live and die for them. Vampires take selecting a mate very seriously. I would have risked absolutely everything for Cybil if she had been the right mate. But she wasn't." He lowered his voice and stared at the parchment again, a not-so-gentle reminder of what he lacked in himself. "I don't think anyone is."

Alavara shifted again, and this time their knees brushed. He squeezed his hands closed as he repeated the mantra in his mind. *It's a lie. It's a lie. The bond lies.*

"Why do you believe you never would have found a match of your own?"

Jesper snorted and stood, not able to bear her touch any longer. It tempted him far too much. "Because this," he placed a hand over his heart, "is incapable of loving anyone romantically. Even Cybil." His past attested to as much. No matter how hard he'd tried to fall in love, the very emotion had evaded him. "Now stop asking questions when I'm so vulnerable. I can't...I can't..."

He didn't finish his sentence before he strode away without looking back.

He took a couple of personal days from his duties, which was very unlike him, and he avoided Alavara the entire time.

This castle was too large, Alavara decided. Although she loved to sneak around undetected, she hated how easily Jesper managed to evade her. She'd hardly seen a single wisp of his dark red hair the entire week.

She slipped farther into the castle vault, holding her breath when her ears picked up faint footsteps in the corridor above. Darkness caved in on her when her lungs screamed for air, but the moment the footsteps receded, she inhaled quietly. This was the truest, most difficult test she'd faced with her nimble skills in a long time. Avoiding the notice of both Jesper and her father was no easy feat.

Her gaze roamed across the shelves upon shelves in the room, full of trinkets, treasures, and gold. An ancient, woven map hung from the wall, depicting a foreign land, a world that had existed over a thousand years ago even before Dracula's reign. Her fingers hovered over the tapestry, desperate to touch yet not willing to take the risk. She'd rubbed gold and silver coins all over her body in an attempt to mask her scent, but she didn't dare push her luck.

So many things depended on her success today.

The thought of the glowing orb around her father's neck sent her fingers reaching for her necklace. She treasured what memories of her mother remained in her head, and she didn't want to lose anymore.

She took a deep breath to steady her nerves and let it out slowly before she continued to peruse the shelves.

An entire row of shelves housed many different colors of vials, ranging from an invisibility potion to shapeshifting to healing. Farther to the left lay a table filled to the brim with neat rows of weapons. Bows. Arrows. Swords.

And daggers.

Her careful gaze scanned every dagger. Most of the sheaths were plain, though she didn't doubt for a single second that each held its own enchantment. The weapons hummed with power, tempting to lure her into the depths of their song.

She moved to the next table, a frown forming on her face before she approached a wall displaying a variety of weapons. Most were swords and bows. Each held a significance even she couldn't decipher. But none were the one she was searching for.

A sharp breath entered her lungs when she spotted a display case between two bookshelves. She approached on silent feet, her slippers making nary a sound on the carpeted floors.

Triumph sounded its trumpets within her soul as her gaze roamed along the foreign inscriptions inlaid in the bronze sheath. The Dwarven language. Akretti. Yes, this was her prize.

With careful fingers, she lifted the glass, but winced when the hinges squeaked. After a minute's pause without anyone storming into the vault, she lifted the weapon from its velvety cushion and replaced it with a replica hiding in the bodice of her gown. Though, the replica didn't have the same magical properties as the real dagger.

She carefully placed the dagger into her bodice. A single scratch could kill someone, and she didn't want to be that someone. The weapon only had a single use, and it needed to be used wisely.

Not wanting someone to catch her, she lowered the glass lid and slipped back out of the vault, down several hallways, and hid the dagger beneath the mattress in her bedchambers.

When she exited the room, her heart squeezed with panic when she found her father staring at her across the hallway with disapproving eyes. Had he seen her? Did he know?

But the jerk of his head in the direction of Jesper's council chambers eased her worry. No, he wasn't privy to her little theft in her mate's vault.

The plan with Jesper was not going as smoothly as they'd hoped. He was an uncrackable boulder, and no matter how hard she slammed the hammer down on it, not even a fissure formed.

Thoughts of her mother drove her forward with determination in each step. The darkness of evening descended upon her every stride, her own shadow following in her wake as she made her way down torch-lit hallways while her father stayed behind.

"I am your mate," she whispered under her breath after several nobles rounded the corner, leaving her once again by herself. "You can't keep me out of your private council room for much longer."

Glancing down each end of the hallway to make sure she was alone, she opened a window and slipped out onto the ledge. Two dots of fire from torches moved in the opposite direction down below as guards made their rounds. She cocked her ears, having practiced her newfound vampire abilities. A chorus of noises greeted her from laughter somewhere in the town to the squeaking wheels of a cart to a barking dog in the distance.

And then she heard them. Muted voices coming from the building opposite her. The room was soundproof enough to muffle their words, but she recognized Jesper's lilt.

The strange sensation of heat crawled through her heart at the mere sound of his voice.

His voice...

It was enough to undo her. He'd been correct in regard to the bond between them. She loved the sound of it, easily picking it out in a crowd.

She shook her distracted thoughts away, and as a habit, she rubbed her hands together as she drew upon her magic. Magic had been her constant companion throughout her lifetime, never once failing her.

Only too late did she realize her hands didn't glow blue as she jumped the small gap between the buildings with the intent to latch on with her palms. Instead of sticking to the wall, her hands slipped. Her feet scrambled for a foothold, only to skid over dark stones.

A cry escaped her mouth as she fell downward, the entire two stories flashing past in a blur before she landed with a *thud* on cold, compacted earth. Air whooshed from her lungs, heat flaring alive in her shoulders, legs, and arms.

The pain burned hotter when she gasped in a breath, her ribs aching fiercely down her entire right side. But the fire was quickly doused by cool relief as her vampire body began healing.

Vampire body...

Her head pounding, her mind spinning, she stared up at the dark clouds above as her heart shattered, breaking into a hundred pieces as her own boulder cracked within her. She willed her magic to seep into her fingers. She dove headfirst into the pool of magic reserves...only to come up dry. The once full lake of shimmery magic was now a barren wasteland.

"My magic." She released a strangled sob. "It's gone."

The wound of Cybil's departure started to ebb. Jesper understood why she left. Surely, if he had been in a similar predicament, he likely would have done the same thing. More than anything, he hoped she would find the right mate for her, and then she would be glad nothing had come of their relationship.

But he still missed their friendship something fierce. Sparring with his father just wasn't the same. His father had absolutely no temper, nothing to taunt and tease and laugh at. He suspected Cybil's absence would leave a permanent hole in his heart.

He sighed and rubbed the strain from his eyes. Working too late often gave him headaches, especially when the candlelight hardly did the words on the pages in front of him justice. When squinting through the strain proved too much to handle, he filed his papers away, snuffed out the candles, and left his office. The entire castle appeared to be asleep save for those on guard duty for the night.

Running a tired hand across his face, he thought of everything he still needed to do over the remainder of the week. At the top of his priority list was to try to get King Ruvyn to leave his city. Against his word, he still had a few of his troops camped out several miles away. They would leave when Ruvyn did, he'd said multiple times. But when would the elven king go back to where he came from?

Jesper froze when he realized he hadn't been walking in the direction of his chambers, but toward Alavara's chambers instead.

A scowl pulled his expression downward. Ridiculously absurd mating bond. It was leading his feet now, too? It was bad enough to have to fight feelings not his own, but to have to fight the very ground he walked on?

He turned in the opposite direction and only took a single step before he faltered. His ears twitched as he detected a strange sound. Despite his initial repulsion at being led toward Alavara's chambers by an unseen force, he turned back around and followed the sound.

Weeping. It was weeping he heard.

But who would be up at this hour?

On silent feet, he continued forward, following the noise to the very end of the hallway. The corridors were still, not even a flickering shadow across the wall. The weeping became louder with each step he took, hollow and filled with so much pain that it hurt him like a physical blow to the stomach.

He turned the corner and stopped dead in his tracks when he found a tall figure wearing a blue cloak standing beside a window. Her scent hit him first, a sweet berry aroma mixed with something tangy and metallic.

Another low, pained sob escaped her.

"Alavara?"

She gasped as if surprised to have been caught crying. But when she turned to flee, he lunged forward and grabbed onto her arm, only to inhale sharply in surprise when he touched something thick and sticky. He withdrew his hand to find it covered in blood.

His eyebrows drew together in a mixture of shock and concern. He grabbed onto her arm again and turned her to face him.

"Alavara," he gasped.

He took in the cuts and scratches along her arms, neck, and face. Her blood soaked into her clothing and smeared across her skin. And then he noticed the grime beneath her own fingernails. She had done this herself.

Even as her cuts began healing right before his eyes, she jerked her arm away from him, more tears falling from her eyes. "I don't want to be this vile creature."

Without another word, she strode away from him, and he watched her leave in shocked silence. It was as if she had been trying to rip the vampire out of herself, but he knew it wasn't possible. There was no cure, no transitioning back.

If she truly hated being a vampire so much, then why had she agreed to it in the first place?

He couldn't help himself. Bond or no bond, his heart ached for her. She certainly wasn't happy here. She seemed to be miserable in her new vampire body. And he wasn't making anything easier for her by shunning her and keeping his distance.

Tomorrow.

Tomorrow, things would change. It was time he brought her into his circle.

CHAPTER 14

THE DOOR ON the opposite side of the room clicked open, but Alavara had no strength in mind or body to sit up, let alone lift her head. She felt the room stir, heard a rustle of clothing and quiet footsteps before someone stopped in the middle of her room. Somehow, she managed to open her eyes just a crack to find Jesper standing in her bedchambers, looking down at her with an unreadable expression. He looked awful, with dark circles beneath his eyes, his face a shade paler, and his eyes were red, though she had no idea why. Wouldn't he of all people have more control over his eye color?

She closed her eyes again, her body too weary and too dejected to interact with him.

His footsteps moved away from her, and just when she thought he left the room and wouldn't return, her ears detected a second pair of footsteps, but these ones reached her bedside.

Dried blood still covered her clothing from the night before, and she hadn't bothered to change before falling into bed and crying herself to sleep. Someone began wiping her down with a warm, damp cloth and peeled her stiff clothes off. She cracked an eye open to find a maid wearing a concerned frown.

Was Jesper still in the room? She didn't particularly care.

Once dressed in a cream and lilac gown, the maid started to wash her hair, gently tugging and rinsing and drying, all while she lay limp. She did not want to move this vile body or feel her vile fangs or give thought to the dry scratchiness of her throat.

With surprising strength, the maid propped Alavara up in the bed, and only then could she see Jesper sitting in a chair beside the window with a book in his hands.

The maid dipped into a curtsy before Jesper. "Anything else, sire?"

He lifted his head. "No. That will be all. I petition you for your silence."

"You have it, sire."

The door clicked shut upon her departure, and Alavara closed her eyes again. She did not want to witness Jesper's likely furious or disappointed or cruel expression.

For a long moment, he said nothing, and she wondered if he would say anything at all. But knowing him, he would.

"Do you think I am a vile creature?" he asked finally.

She didn't answer.

"I don't understand, Alavara. You seemed so willing to spread that glamor through the kingdom. You didn't object to the proposal of becoming my mate. What I can't decide is if you're only just realizing what a horrible, *vile* creature I am... Or if this wasn't what *you* wanted all along. This was your father's wish."

The vampire king was too sharp for his own good. He seemed to realize she was just as much of a victim of her father's game as he was. "My magic is gone. I feel like I have a severed limb." Her voice sounded hollow to her own ears.

Jesper rose from his chair, his book closing in his hand but with his finger inserted into the pages as if used as a bookmark. He stopped at the corner of her bed but came no closer.

"I don't believe you have met my uncle, Zachariah. I would like to introduce you."

Her eyebrows twitched only slightly at the abrupt change of subject, but she looked toward the door to find a young-looking man wearing a physician's coat. His hair and eyes were brown, his face clean shaven, and he looked startlingly familiar. Had she seen him before?

Wearily, she said, "I don't need to be looked at by a physician."

"I'm not here to examine you as a patient." Zachariah came closer, and with a nod of his head, Jesper left the room, and the two of them found themselves alone.

"Then why are you here?"

He pulled up a chair and sat beside the bed, only a couple feet away. Again, the familiarity of his features struck her. Where had she seen him before?

By now, she'd learned the difference in smell between vampires, elves, and humans, and Zachariah was most definitely a vampire. How old was he? He looked to be in his late twenties, but he could be a thousand years old for all she knew.

"Do you know who I am?" he asked.

Of course. Jesper had just introduced them after all. "Zachariah."

"Zachariah *Degore*. I am Adam's brother."

Her mouth fell open as she looked him over. The brown hair, the brown eyes. The reason he looked familiar was because he looked like Adam. "But...you are a vampire. Adam is a human."

"Yes," he nodded. "I am all too familiar with the agony of transitioning. I have experienced the foreignness of a new, stronger body, the grief of losing the person I was before I was bitten."

"H-h-how," was all she managed to say.

"Vampires attacked my village when I was thirteen years old, around a hundred years ago. I escaped with my life, but I was never the same person again. I was disgusted with what I was. My lust for blood disgusted me. My fangs... My eyes... My senses were too sharp. There was too much to take in all the time. And the sunlight..." He sighed and leaned back in his chair. "I missed being able to feel the sun's warmth without getting burned."

In all honesty, she hadn't thought about the sunlight. She was sure she would miss it, too.

Alavara managed to prop herself up further, turning more fully toward him. "And then what?"

He gazed back at her, and her stomach squirmed at the genuine concern in his eyes. "I refused to drink blood. I only made it three weeks before I snapped. I almost killed someone, but my brother stopped it. I managed to feed off animal blood for two years. *Two years,* Alavara. And then my body shut down without human blood. I became feral, something between a beast and a rabid animal. I was lucky. Most vampires don't come back from that."

Becoming feral was something she had never even considered. Her throat burned, begging to be quenched, but *drinking* human blood?

A tear escaped the corner of her eye, startling her. She was never one to allow anyone to see her tears, and besides, she thought she'd cried them all out last night. "I don't want to be a vampire."

Zachariah scooted closer, the empathy shining brilliant in his eyes. "I didn't, either. I spent a long time fighting it. But it was a waste of effort and a waste of my life. Live your life, Alavara. You can do a lot of great things for this kingdom."

"Jesper won't give me any power."

He leaned even closer as if to keep Jesper from overhearing if he was anywhere near the door. "Then find a way to get some. Jesper is angry. Fuming mad. And the easiest person to punish is you. I'm sure if you reconcile things with him, you will find more reasons to enjoy being a vampire."

"I could never enjoy it."

He smiled and stood, giving her hand a squeeze. The contact surprised her—one of the only bits of kindness she'd received since her arrival. "I thought so at first, too."

She watched his retreating back as he walked toward the door and exited the room. The metal of her necklace seemed much warmer than only moments before as she ran the length of the chain through her fingers.

The door opened again, and when she found Jesper standing in the hallway with not only his book but a stack of papers as well, she stuffed her necklace back into her blouse. Had he actually been concerned enough for her to fetch his uncle?

What was she supposed to make of it?

"My family is taking their meal in the drawing room. Care to join?"

Yes, she most certainly cared and wanted him as far away as possible. She'd made a spectacle of herself in a moment of weakness. Her pride was in need of immediate restoration.

But...

Thoughts of the blue, swirling orb entered her mind, and she internally cringed as she envisioned her father crushing it in his palm with his dark power, obliterating the memories he'd trapped. Suddenly, she vaguely remembered why she was here and what she needed to do before grasping at the information proved difficult as it slipped away. It would be a much easier task if Jesper hated her, but hate didn't allow her closer to him.

Despite herself, her tone turned to ice. "You haven't allowed me within a league of your sister. Are you going to bring a few bodyguards to separate us?"

He pointed to himself and gave her a wicked grin. "One is all I need."

"You still think you can outmatch me in combat, vampire?" Miraculously, her limbs moved when she willed them to. She ignored his watchful stare as she tucked a thin blade between her breasts, placed a few lethal pins into her hair, and for extra measure, she strapped a dagger to her thigh. She did it slowly, smirking when his gaze trailed the action as she lifted her dress high up her leg and fit her weapon into a holster. As if embarrassed from getting caught looking, he cleared his throat and turned his head. A flush climbed his neck.

Lies, indeed.

"I would prefer you leave your weapons behind when you are around my family."

"*Your* family?" She took a step toward him and then another, and soon he was within arm's reach. "Last I heard, you and I were mates. Doesn't that make them *my* family, too? *My* uncle. *My* father. *My* sister."

A low growl sounded in his throat at the mention of his sister. Ah, so Kiara was his bane then?

"If you hurt any of them, I will kill you."

"But I thought mates couldn't kill each other. Besides, I have no interest in hurting any of them. You think too lowly of me, Jesper."

"And you of me." He leveled a stare at her—challenging dominance.

She breathed in deeply, and her teasing grin widened. "I think I am getting better at this scenting game. Why am I not allowed to have any weapons on my person when you have almost a half dozen on you?"

His body stiffened.

However, she was not done teasing. "There's the obvious dagger on your belt, a couple of knives in your boots, the thin blade in your bookmark, and..." Her hand skimmed his side and rested on his hip where a dagger lay hidden beneath his shirt. Her eyes gleamed with humor when he batted her hand away.

"Don't touch me," he growled in her face.

"Why? Are you afraid the *bond* will keep whispering lies in your ears?"

Not giving into her teasing, he strode toward the door. "Well? Are you coming or not?"

She followed, keeping up with his long strides with long legs of her own. "How were you able to enter my chambers? I thought you needed permission first."

He gave her a sideways glance before he bared his teeth at her. "You tell me, elf."

The rest of the journey to the drawing room was quick and quiet, and when they entered, nearly all the Degores were already inside. Adam sat at the head of the table, eating cheese and bread. Although he didn't glance her way, she felt his eyes on her all the same. Willow and Kiara sat on either side of him sipping from goblets of blood, and Jesper's supposed brother was still missing. A part of her wondered if he even existed.

Jesper sat between her and Kiara as if reminding her to stay in line.

Kiara leaned around him all the same. "I was beginning to wonder if you would ever show your face, Alavara. I thought I might have scared you away."

"You?" she snorted against her better judgement. There was nothing menacing about Kiara in the slightest. Jesper's mother on the other hand…

Willow watched her with cold eyes, like a mama bear ready to protect her cubs. If Alavara made one wrong move… It was possible she would find dagger-like fingernails in her neck.

A servant entered quietly with two goblets of blood and set them in front of them on the table before retreating out the same door. Jesper didn't hesitate as he started on his while keeping half of his attention on the stack of papers he spread out before him. She refused to touch hers, though her dry throat begged for it.

Feral...

The last thing she wanted was to turn feral.

Jesper kicked his feet up, and the moment he did, Willow scowled. "Get your feet off the table." His feet came down with a *thud*, and Alavara hid her amusement at seeing the king of vampires ordered around by his mother.

The door opened again, but this time, a handsome male with brown hair and light brown eyes entered the room, tugging along a pretty strawberry-blonde female. The two of them were otherworldly beautiful, and she couldn't help but gape. Who were they?

"Sam," Jesper greeted through clenched teeth.

"Jesper," Sam returned the greeting with a wide grin, his eyes sparking with mischief as if preparing himself for battle. The moment they sat down, his gaze turned to her, and he took her in with interest. "You look more beautiful close up, Your Elfliness. I heard about what you did in the throne room. What an exciting fight that must have been. It's a shame you ended up with this boring prick." He jerked his head toward Jesper. "He doesn't have an exciting bone in his body."

"Or a romantic bone either," Kiara chimed in. When Jesper glared, she added, "What? You said so yourself."

Jesper muttered something under his breath and continued glaring, but this time at his work spread out on the table.

"Oh come, Jesper. You know we love you." Kiara patted his cheek. Alavara stopped breathing when Jesper put his arm around his sister and kissed her forehead. She'd had no idea he was capable of affection of any sort.

Her attention snapped away from them when she heard a smacking noise, only for her eyes to widen when she found Sam and Natalia kissing, their hands all over one another as if there was no one else in the room. Uncomfortable awkwardness pricked at her when they didn't stop. Was no one else affected?

Judging by the heaving sigh from Adam and the annoyed expression from Jesper, it likely happened quite a lot.

"I swear you do that just to make me want to throttle you," Jesper finally blurted. "Can you stop *always kissing* your mate?"

"Not again..." Willow muttered under her breath. "Everyone run for the hills."

The two pulled away, but rather reluctantly. Sam snorted and pointed to Jesper. "I'll stop always kissing my mate when you stop *always working*. I mean seriously, Jesper. Who knows how long we'll all be together as a family again. We're here enjoying each other's company, and then there's you, a big old bag of boring bones hunched over your papers."

"Better than being hunched over a pair of lips."

Sam inhaled a hiss through his teeth. "Oh, it sure isn't. Have you even kissed Alavara yet? Just try it and we'll see who's hunched over whose lips next time."

"Leave her out of this."

Sam rhythmically pounded his fist on the table and chanted, "Kiss her. Kiss her. Kiss her."

She blushed at the directness and gasped in shock when Jesper jumped over the table and tackled Sam right out of his chair and onto the floor. They started punching and biting and scratching each other, growls and hisses filling the room.

No one else moved. No one else tried to break them apart.

"Is anyone going to stop them?" she asked, shocked further when Jesper rolled on top of his brother and punched him in the jaw.

The others looked at her as if she were mad. She couldn't help but wonder how often this sort of thing occurred. She'd rarely seen Jesper's temper, but it seemed as if his brother easily coaxed it out of him.

The hissing and growling grew louder.

Well, if no one else planned to stop the fight, she would.

Calmly, she approached the brawl, pulled back her sleeves, and when Jesper rolled on top of Sam again, she struck with her fingers. Shoulder, shoulder, side, side. He cried out in surprise as his body stopped working, and she took the momentary pause to kick him off Sam. Her brother-in-law's eyes only managed to widen before she struck out at him as well. Shoulder, shoulder, neck.

Each vampire lay on his back, moaning and groaning with limbs rendered immovable. She used Jesper's stomach as a step on her way back to her seat, a sense of satisfaction at his "oof." Gaping stares followed her, but she ignored them and swiped the top paper from Jesper's pile of documents. She leaned against the wall and scanned the content depicting Ichor Knell budgets, at least until a deep rumble of laughter filled the room.

Adam's chuckle turned into full-blown laughter, and he said through gasping breaths, "I think our bickering problem has officially been solved."

"Oh, Papa." Kiara rolled her eyes but smiled herself. "Be nice." Then she turned and clicked her tongue at Sam. "You know better than to taunt a newly mated vampire. Emotions run a little high at the beginning."

"A little?" Willow laughed as well. It seemed as if she could find amusement in her son getting attacked, after all. "I believe that is the quickest Jesper has ever lost his temper."

"I can hear you," Jesper said from the ground.

The conversation continued, but Alavara tuned out the voices as she read over the budget reports. Her eyebrows furrowed more and more with each section she read. To say the kingdom's income had decreased after Dracula's death was an understatement. Many of Ichor Knell's trading recipients had cut ties with them, not to mention the previous war they were still trying to recover from. Jesper had literally been backed into a corner when her father proposed the idea of Alavara becoming his mate.

It had been his only option.

Someone snatched the paper from her hands, and she lifted her head to find Jesper glaring down at her. "These are not for your eyes."

"Why not? I am Kumari, aren't I? I should be aware of these things."

"I already said you will have no power here."

She scowled right in his face. "Why?"

"Because I don't trust you."

The verbal slap hurt, despite how much she deserved it. She wanted to deliver one right back at him, but he shuffled up his papers and stormed out the door before she found the chance.

He must have really been upset enough to leave her in the same room as Kiara without his protection. Or perhaps he was confident the people in this room could flay her alive should she lay a single hand on his sister.

Not that she wanted to. Kiara was one of the only people who was actually kind to her.

"Stubborn, that one," Sam said, wiping a trickle of blood from his healing lip. "Once he makes up his mind about something, he doesn't change it."

"How can I get him to trust me?"

"Blind his senses. Tap into your bond." A grin spread across his face. "Seduce him, maybe."

Kiara kicked him beneath the table, and he grunted. "Do you always have to center everything around wooing and seduction?"

"I'm not wrong."

Turning to Alavara, Kiara chimed in with her bit of advice. "Make yourself valuable to him. What can you give him that no one else can?" Sam snickered, and she kicked him again.

Her sister-in-law's words followed her as she left the drawing room and made her way back to her chambers. Locating parchment and ink at her desk, she scrawled a note to Jesper to meet her early tomorrow morning in the training room, and to wear something comfortable.

Out of the corner of her eye, she spied another goblet of blood on her nightstand. She swallowed an uncomfortable lump in her throat and approached, dipping her finger into the thick red liquid. Cold. But it smelled fresh.

Live your life, Alavara. You can do a lot of great things for this kingdom.

Feral...

Feral...

Feral...

She didn't give herself time to overthink her decision as she downed the contents of the goblet in a couple seconds. She hated that she drank it. She also hated that she liked it.

CHAPTER 15

JESPER STOOD OUTSIDE the indoor training arena, leaning against the wall with his arms crossed. He'd been in this position for a few minutes already, nodding to those who entered and listening to the clamor of steel from within. When the corridor was empty, he turned his face toward the wall and inhaled Alavara's scent again, as if she had touched the wall on her way inside.

"What am I doing?" he muttered to himself.

Quickly, he snapped his head in the direction of the open double doors and scowled. Why did he linger when he knew Alavara was inside? He had absolutely no idea. A part of him wanted to return to his office, but another part of him wanted to know what she had planned for him.

He peeked around the corner and easily located her lithe form on one side of the room. His mouth dried when his gaze raked down her body. She wore a two-piece elven outfit. Tight, dark blue leggings, thick, embroidered strips that draped over each shoulder and tucked into a belt before draping nearly to her ankles, and a long-sleeved blouse as tight as her leggings.

Alavara's long, dark braid reached her lower back, swaying the smallest bit as she absently trailed her fingers across the wall as if deep in thought. He'd seen her do it before, though he refused to admit he'd watched her. He also refused to admit her scent drove him mad.

All too suddenly, her lips spread into a grin as she chuckled to herself before continuing her absent finger trailing.

He darted behind the corner again, his breathing ragged and his mouth dry. *The bond lies. The bond lies. The bond lies.*

"No. Absolutely not. I can't do this."

Whatever *this* was, he still had no idea.

But when he turned to leave, he jumped when he found himself face to face with Alavara, a smirk on her lips.

"Where are you going, Your Highness?"

"I-I-I have work to do." By the dark clouds raining from heaven above, she'd startled him out of his skin. Those shadow feet of hers…

"So I keep hearing." She twisted a dagger between her fingers and used it to motion him inside. "Go on. I'll try not to bite too hard."

"I have too much work."

She dared to press the knife to his side, though not hard enough to draw blood. Her dark, thin eyebrow lifted. "I just changed my mind. I will bite *just a little* hard."

He growled and batted her knife hand away. "Find yourself another sparring partner."

"Sparring? Is that what you think I want from you? If I recall correctly… You asked me what my fighting style was called. I thought you were interested in learning. Seems I was wrong."

When she turned, he snatched her elbow. "Wait. What *is* your fighting style called?"

"*Erbrumthin.*"

The way she said the word was like water gliding along her tongue. If he tried to say it, he would likely bungle it. "And you will teach me?"

"It depends."

"On what?"

A wild grin grew across her face, and he knew he wouldn't like what was about to come out of her mouth. "Why don't you grovel to me? Ask for my forgiveness for being so rude just now. I was simply trying to do something nice."

He drummed his fingers against his arms, irritation poking at him like a thorn in his side. He wanted to learn. He truly did. But to grovel?

"I will meet you halfway and ask nicely," he finally said, holding out his hand for her to shake. "Please teach me."

"You drive a hard bargain, my vampire liege," she laughed and slid her hand into his. The moment their fingers made contact, a jolt of lightning shot through his stomach, warping it right and left, up and down, and he quickly jerked his hand away. It wasn't the first time it had happened. The first time was in his office before the union ceremony, which told him this...*feeling*...was real. Genuine. Not influenced by the bond.

But he refused to acknowledge it.

Besides, he didn't even know what the feeling was. He hadn't experienced it before.

"Right, well, let's find a place to practice, shall we?" He entered the training arena with Alavara at his heels. Far too many pairs of eyes followed them to the empty space near the window she had occupied only a minute earlier. The rhythm of clashing weapons faltered, telling him where people's attention had turned to.

Honestly, was there no such thing as privacy? Could he not go somewhere without the entire Ichor Knell population watching him? Was this how it was for his grandfather?

When he turned to face her, his mouth twitched.

"What?" she asked cautiously.

"Nothing." He cocked his head to the side and continued to stare. "Your eyes are—"

"—red, I know."

"No, they're brown again. You finally fed. I'm pleased."

Relief filled her entire expression, her finger touching her eyelid. "Yes, well, I didn't want to become feral. How long would it have taken? If I hadn't consumed any blood at all, even animal blood?"

He shrugged. "Far too quickly, I'm afraid. If you would have snapped and still not received the sustenance you needed, you would only decline from there. Your mind would tear itself apart until there was nothing left but bloodlust."

A grimace.

Quieter, he asked, "What would you have chosen? If you could have decided your own fate?"

"A dangerous question to ask." Silence followed when she turned her back to him, and for a moment he thought she wouldn't answer. Finally, she said, "To live in the forest, just me and my mother."

"Did you and your father leave her behind? Where is she?"

Another pause. "Dead."

"Oh." He blew out a long breath, wishing he'd kept his mouth shut. He and Leif had poured over the records of Varesia, and nothing he'd read said anything about the elf queen's demise.

But what more could he say? If it had been his mother, he wouldn't have wanted to talk about it at all.

In the blink of an eye, her entire demeanor changed as she spun on him and jabbed those lethal fingers of hers in his direction. He instinctively dodged the first jab, ducked when she lunged for his neck, and jumped backward when she tried for his side.

"Stop moving so fast!" Alavara laughed. "At least allow me to hit you so I can teach you what I know."

She reached over her shoulder and took hold of her own braid. He eyed it cautiously as she twirled it as if she might use it to whip him. He'd never been whipped by someone's hair before. From what he'd seen of her fighting in the past, he knew she wasn't below using it.

Raising an eyebrow at her, he asked, "I'm supposed to let you beat me up? How is that any way to teach?"

In his momentary distraction, she lunged forward and jabbed her fingers into his shoulder. A terrible tingling sensation burst through his arm, and for several horrifying moments, he lost all feeling from his shoulder to his hand. It hung limp at his side.

When she attacked again, he grabbed her wrist to block with his only working hand and kicked her in the stomach. She stumbled backward and landed with a *thud* on her back, rolling out of the way just before he struck out with his fist and hit the ground instead of her jaw.

Breathing heavily, whether from exertion or surprise, or perhaps even exhilaration, she started circling him with an amused smile on her face. "You would punch your own mate?"

"You're a vampire now. You'll heal fast enough."

The feeling slowly returned to his arm like pins and needles pricking his skin. Once again, her clothing drew his attention and the way she moved fluidly in them. Water. She always seemed to move like water.

"You don't wear this kind of outfit often."

"Ah." Her eyes sparkled mischievously. "You like?"

Yes.

But out loud, he just scoffed and rolled his eyes. "An observation is all. I wonder why you usually wear our clothing and not yours."

The comment seemed to give her pause. "I am simply trying to blend in."

His gaze roamed over her dark hair, her dark eyes, and lingered a bit longer on her pointed ears. "You will have to do a lot better if you want to blend in."

"Do *you* want me to blend in?"

He straightened and folded his arms across his chest. "I thought you were teaching me *Eroombrumathoon.*" Yes, he completely slaughtered the pronunciation, but she only smiled. "Sounds more like we're having a conversation."

"Just answer my question."

Sighing, he glanced toward the other fighters in the arena—soldiers training for the battlefield. Most were older than himself. Some were younger, but not by much. All were impeccable fighters worthy of serving in his army. A part of him couldn't help but wonder if they and their mates and their families...what would happen to his people if—*when*—their culture mixed together with Alavara's? Would it be a good thing or bad?

Inevitable.

He answered honestly. "You are my mate. I don't want you to blend in with the wall. Now stop talking and start teaching me or I will go find other, more useful things to do."

"Of course." A flicker of emotion flashed across her face before it disappeared. Uncertainty? Remorse? "Come closer. And stop looking like I might eat you alive. I won't attack you again. Yet, at least."

He willed his heart to stop beating so quickly when she touched his bicep, but it didn't listen. Her hands were so gentle. "I will start by showing you the pressure points on the body you will want to attack to render someone useless."

Her gentle hands touched a couple places on his neck, shoulder, and arm. Heat followed in their wake, burning, smoldering, a desire to return her touch nearly too great to handle. And when she moved lower, he caught her wrist and twisted only enough for a slight amount of pain.

"Stop touching me," he growled.

"*Erbrumthin* is a very high-contact fighting style. No weapons. Only hands. Do you want to learn or not?"

He released her wrist. "Show me on a dummy."

"Why?" she whispered knowingly, moving close enough for her breath to caress his skin. "Can't handle your mate's touch?"

A scowl settled into his forehead when he realized she'd backed him into a corner. To practice on a dummy meant to admit her touch affected him. To practice on her meant to risk the bond's influence.

"Fine. But there is *nothing* between us, Alavara."

She flipped her braid over her shoulder. "I never said there was."

Another trap, and he'd fallen straight into it. Could his touch possibly affect her as much as hers did to him? Ridiculous mating bond. It served no purpose other than to frustrate and lie.

So, he stifled the heat, he stuffed down his discomfort, and he allowed her to show him where each weak point was located on his body. Neck, arms, torso, legs. When she squeezed a pressure point, his body protested at the sudden pain, but when she jabbed her fingers into it instead, he lost all feeling. Not for long, but enough to render him useless.

If he could master this new fighting technique...

A slow, dark chuckle escaped him, which earned him a questioning look from Alavara.

When he didn't answer her look, she said, "Now practice on me. Try to find the pressure points on your own."

He started at the neck, which was a *really* bad idea. Her scent was strongest there, and he couldn't help but breathe it in. Silver in color. Berry in scent. Intoxicating and powerful. His eyes soaked up the silver brilliance, like stars twinkling in the midnight sky. Sweet berries filled his nostrils, reminding him of calm walks through the forest. Or perhaps not so calm. His pulse thrummed in his neck. And her skin... Smooth. Perfect. Deliciously taunting. He wanted to sink his fangs into her and taste the berries for himself—

"Jesper," Alavara rasped. Her hand lay against his chest, pushing him away. "What are you doing?"

Until now, he hadn't realized he'd sprouted his fangs. His fingers stilled on her neck where they had caressed it a moment earlier as if readying it for his bite.

"Huh?" He dropped his hand faster than her scent fled his nostrils.

"Were you...were you..." Another ragged breath. She pushed him away even more. "Were you going to bite me?"

"What? No. *Daggers, no.*"

His pulse still thrummed with each denial. *Lies. Lies. Lies. The bond is nothing but lies.*

"What..." Her throat bobbed when she swallowed. "What would happen if you did?"

He shook his head and searched wildly for a bucket of freezing cold water to douse himself with. He couldn't do this. He couldn't spend time with her like this. It was dangerous.

Unfortunately, he found no such bucket.

"I don't know," he rasped. "Ask Sam."

"Why Sam?"

"Because he's the supposed expert in..." He couldn't finish the sentence. He didn't know *how* to finish the sentence. There was nothing between him and Alavara. Nothing. Yet, his fangs desired her blood.

Somehow, he managed to retract his fangs, which helped cool his desire, if only slightly. He turned to leave when Alavara struck out with her fingers. His body reacted on reflex to dodge. Skin transformed into scales, his body coiling on the ground in his cobra form. One moment he lay on the ground in a heap, and the next moment he flared his hood wide and hissed at her. If she tried to attack again, he would lunge for her ankles.

However, instead of attacking, her own skin became the shimmering white scales of a python, and she dropped into her own pile of coils. Her tongue darted out of her mouth and slithered back in. Her black, beady eyes stared back at him as she lay still. And her scales... They glistened like the luster of a full moon in the night sky.

Was it possible to be attracted to a snake? She was beautiful. And it was unnerving.

Jesper surprised himself by laughing out loud as he returned to his vampire form. "You *are* a serpent. You better get comfortable in your scales, Alavara. You could be stuck in your transformation for weeks. Or two months if you are anything like my sister."

Turning on his heel, he started toward the exit but cried out when something tackled him from behind. He reached behind himself and grabbed his attacker in a headlock, flipping them over his head, but shock slammed into him when he watched as Alavara gracefully landed on her feet. *In her vampire form.*

"What?" he gasped. "How?"

"Do you think I'm a fool?" The grin on her face was a look of pure, evil delight. "What do you *possibly* think I do all day in your absence? Sit around and mope? I mastered my transformation last week."

Clearly.

She spun so quickly that he only just barely managed to catch her elbow before it slammed into his stomach, but he hadn't anticipated her braid to come at him like a leopard pouncing on its prey. Her knotted hair whipped his face, and he stumbled backward in his momentary blindness. She tackled him again, and this time, he was thrown backward onto the floor. Those deadly fingers of hers lunged at him, and he dodged his head to the side to avoid the attack. He hooked his leg around her and flipped them again, this time finding himself on top of her.

His legs straddled her stomach, her chest rising and falling with each heavy breath. And her eyes... They captivated his very soul, freezing it so thoroughly in place that he wasn't sure anything could melt it again.

The space between them calmed into a deeper quiet, the clamor surrounding them disappearing. He slid his fingers into hers. Overwhelming desire suffocated him. His hands started to shake as he fought it, and the tremors continued up his arms.

No!

In all but a few moments, the clamor returned. He jumped to his feet and didn't look back as he rushed toward the exit. But just before he left, he spotted a figure on the top level of the arena, staring down at him as if he'd just witnessed everything that had happened between him and Alavara.

King Ruvyn's expression gave away nothing, but the cold calculation in his eyes sent shivers down his spine. He hurried from the training arena before he could dwell on it.

CHAPTER 16

LIKE ALAVARA SUSPECTED he would, her father intercepted her on her way to her chambers. He pulled her into the shadows of a hallway corner that looked as if feet hadn't touched it in years. The red rug was still bright from the lack of trodden feet. The candles in the sconces might have looked new if it hadn't been for the thin layer of dust coating the wax. The heavy emerald drapes lay still against the window as if they hadn't been drawn in a century.

"Well?" her father asked, raising an eyebrow.

She shook her head. "Not yet. Patience, Father. You knew this would not be easy."

"But I see it is possible."

She forced her expression to remain blank, not daring to show a flicker of emotion. "Yes. Give me a little more time."

Her father slipped his hand into his pocket and pulled out a bracelet made of pure silver, each bead intricate and weaved with powerful magic. Dark magic. "It's almost time. Do you think you will need it?"

Swallowing the lump in her throat, she whispered, "You know I will, Father."

He placed the bracelet into her palm, the metal cool against her skin. "Be vigilant. You can't dare to miss the moment you need to slip it on."

She paused as she stared down at the bracelet with metal beads engraved with dwarven symbols. Emotion pricked her eyes as she thought of her mate. The potential of a bright, happy future lay within reach. She just knew it. But if she wore the bracelet?

"No," she whispered as dread climbed up her spine. She dropped the jewelry to the floor. "I will not do this."

Her father's expression contorted with dark rage, and moving faster than anyone had any right to, he grabbed a hold of her head, dug his fingernails into her skin, and squeezed until pain throbbed from his sharp nails.

"I won't," she sobbed. "I won't."

"You. Will."

And then his dark power struck her mind, clouding her thoughts and masking her free will. She fought against the ebony vapors, trying in vain to push them away. But they seeped into her and claimed her entirely.

When at last the vapors dissipated, Alavara swayed dizzily as she tried to remember her last thought, as she tried to recall where she was and why she'd ventured down this hallway. She stood alone in the corridor and gazed back at dusty emerald drapes. Her eyebrows furrowed, and she blinked sluggishly as confusion swirled in her mind.

Something solid turned her attention to her hand, where she found a metal bracelet in her palm. She recognized the dwarven symbols as some sort of enchantment, but otherwise, she wasn't sure how she came to pick it up.

She meant to ask around to find out who lost it, but somehow, she placed it inside her pocket instead. For safekeeping. A vague warning in the back of her mind told her to throw it out. But she couldn't help but hold onto it.

Seeking out Sam certainly was not a good idea, especially when his and Jesper's relationship was so rocky. But Jesper had been avoiding her for a couple of days, and she wanted answers.

Alavara found him in the library by following his scent—something she'd been practicing lately. He stood by a window while writing what looked to be a letter, a book beneath the parchment to keep it steady. His expression was wistful, longing.

"Good evening, Sam," she said, and when he glanced up, he beamed at her. How were he and Jesper brothers? They were complete opposites. "Where's Natalia?"

Sam sighed. "I sent her back home to our coven in the east."

"Why not go with her?"

"Because I love to miss her. Makes our reunions all the sweeter."

What a romantic. The thought made her smile.

"I have a question for you. Jesper told me to ask you because he didn't know." She wrung her hands. "What happens when a vampire bites another vampire?"

"Ha!" he cried. His face split into a wide, amused grin. "Did Jesper try to bite you?"

"Yes, though he denies it."

He set down his quill, and it seemed as if the more seconds that passed, the more amused he became. "Alavara, dear sister. When a vampire bites another vampire, it is a show of deep affection. Desire, even. Vampires *only* bite their mates. Or potential mates, for that matter. It feels like..." He sighed with longing. "*Ecstasy.*"

Her heart thundered in her chest like a stampede of wild horses. "Oh." She swallowed. Although she wanted more answers, she wondered if Sam was the best person to ask, especially because he and Jesper did not get along.

She asked anyway. "Jesper is convinced any feelings he might have for me are a direct influence of the bond."

"Jesper is a fool," he snorted. "He wouldn't know love if it smacked him in the face."

"Jesper doesn't love me."

"Maybe. At the very least, he *is* incredibly fond of you. Protective, too. He liked you *before* the union even happened. I'm not sure he knows it, though. He can be embarrassingly dense at times."

Dense, indeed. She'd known of her own feelings for him before the union, too. Though, she wanted to stuff them away to never see the light of day again. It was dangerous to fall for the vampire king.

One more question. "Why are you two always at odds with one another?"

Witnessing for the first time, Sam's mood darkened, but only momentarily before his expression lightened. "Between you and I, Alavara, and no one else..." His fingers absently tapped his arm. "He got everything I wanted, and I got everything he wanted."

"What do you mean?"

He glanced back and forth in their small nook of the library before responding quietly. "I always wanted to be noticed. I wanted power and influence. But Dracula chose *him* as his heir. And not me. Jesper was twenty-four years old when our grandfather chose him, and I had been eighteen."

Her voice lowered. "And what did Jesper want?"

"He wanted to fall in love."

Surprise shocked her heart. Jesper? In love? But he always acted cold toward her. He'd never looked a female's way during her spying before the union. Although…

She recalled the look of hope, of desperation, moments before he'd kissed Cybil. Desperation had quickly turned into devastation. Perhaps he still wanted to fall in love. It made complete sense now why he would have thrown away the safety of the entire kingdom just for a little taste of love.

"But…he's eighty-five. Surely, he has fallen for a female by now."

Sam shook his head. "Not a one." He sighed and leaned against the windowsill, his gaze on the comings and goings outside. "It wasn't for lack of trying. He tried plenty. I wouldn't say he courted females, per say. Rather strategically pursued. When his fourth attempt at courtship fell flat, he wanted to give up, discouraged as he was. But I convinced him to try one more time."

She leaned closer, clinging to every word. "What happened?"

"I found a good match for him. A really good match. I was so sure things would work out in his favor this time. She was head over heels in love with him. And he felt…nothing. But he was desperate this time. Desperate to love. He didn't give up." Sam frowned. "He was miserable. I'm sure being near someone you can't seem to catch feelings for is difficult. He ended his pursuit, and in the backlash, she called him an unfeeling monster. He swore off courtship afterward, and he'd been true to his word. Until..."

His stare seemed to go right through her to her very soul. She shifted uncomfortably and played with her necklace to give her hands something to do.

Sam continued after a few moments. "I would never say this to Jesper's face, so you better keep your mouth shut. I had hoped things would change for him after finding a mate in you. But it seems he is determined to ruin his only chance at finding love."

Only chance...

"Do you think you can love him, Alavara?" he asked.

She stared at the floor as she fiddled with her necklace. If only things were so simple. It didn't matter what she wanted or what he wanted. In the end, nothing mattered at all. When her father's plan came to fruition...

An ache rushed through her head, followed by confusion as she lost her train of thought.

"I dare not hope for a future filled with happiness," she replied at last. "This stays only between you and me, of course."

"I care for my brother despite our differences. If you break his heart..." Sam's expression darkened. "It's not something I can forgive."

Alavara looked away when her eyes misted. She would not break Jesper's heart.

She would rip it to shreds.

Alavara focused on breathing slowly as she waited outside Jesper's office. She dared not breathe too loudly nor move an inch to alert him to her presence in the hallway. He usually left the office around this time, and she hoped to catch him before he managed to evade her again.

Finally, the door clicked open, and Jesper emerged. Her breath caught in her lungs at his disheveled appearance. He looked dashing with his hair standing on end and the beginnings of stubble on his face. The moment the door swung wide, his scent washed over her like birdsong on a young, crisp morning.

His breath hitched, and he lunged for the dagger in his belt, but he lowered the weapon when he noticed her in the shadows.

"Do you *want* a blade in your neck?" he snapped. "It may not be iron, but it will hurt all the same."

"What would happen if you stabbed me with an iron blade? Would I die?"

"First, I would never do such a thing. The bond would prevent me from killing you. Second, you would likely die, yes. It is in your best interest to steer clear of iron of any sort."

She moved closer, and she wondered if he could hear her heart hammering in her chest. He watched her warily, but still allowed her to approach. Slowly, she lifted her hand and caressed his arm, his muscles strong and capable beneath her fingers. He quickly snatched it away and jumped backward.

"Stay away from me," he snarled. "I don't want you touching me again. In fact, why don't you just leave the city altogether? Then we wouldn't have to run into each other, either."

His rebuff hurt more than she liked to admit, and she watched his retreating back with a heavy heart. His own heart seemed to be closed tight, chained with every lock imaginable. Just when she thought she managed to unlock one, another quickly replaced it.

As soon as he disappeared, she waited another minute to make sure he wouldn't return. A clear, shimmering barrier stood between her and the office door, barely detectable with her strange new vampire senses. She tentatively reached out and touched the door handle, only to hiss when an invisible fire singed her skin. The red flesh didn't heal quickly like other injuries would. Instead, it throbbed and festered and warned her against a repeat offense.

A set of footsteps alerted her to someone's presence, and she wasn't quite fast enough to slide back into the shadows before a female rounded the corner, carrying a pile of linens in her arms.

The female stopped short, her eyes wide. She dipped into a curtsy and murmured, "Your Highness," under her breath.

Alavara adopted a look of innocence. "Oh, I am glad I ran into you. Jesper is sleeping and I don't dare disturb him" The lie slipped easily from her lips. "You see, I'm in a bit of a bind. He asked me to retrieve something from his office, but he forgot to give me permission to enter. He's been worn ragged this past week, and I truly don't want to interrupt his rest. How can I get inside?"

The poor female didn't even bat an eye at her deception. "I am the head maidservant. His Highness gives me permission to enter to clean, and he gives me permission to give others permission as I see fit. Go on in. I wouldn't want to disturb his rest, either."

The shimmering barrier sputtered out moments before the woman unlocked the door with a key. Interesting... How did she come to earn Jesper's trust enough to enter his office?

She dipped her head. "Thank you."

Giving her another curtsy, the maid scampered off, and Alavara slipped inside.

Guilt gave her pause. Her lies kept stacking higher and higher, and soon enough, they would cave in on top of her and crush her. But she had no choice. She had to do this.

Neat piles of papers lay on top of the desk next to a candle low on wax, the ashy aroma indicating the flame had only recently been snuffed. The inkwell and quill lay next to a purple quartz heavyweight on top of a small stack of papers. Everything within the room was neat and orderly, not a single paper or wax dripping out of place.

And the royal seal...

She picked up the stamp and inspected the wyvern inlaid within the seal, its teeth bared as if to mimic fangs. With this seal, she could do a lot of damage. Or a lot of good. It was a means to an end, and she needed to be swift lest Jesper catch her in the act.

She moved fluidly on silent feet, her fingers shuffling through paper after paper. She memorized every piece of information she read, careful to leave everything where she last left it. Though, she wasn't sure if it mattered. Her scent would likely be all over this office by the time she was through. She'd be long gone before Jesper found out.

"Ah, there you are," she whispered.

The document in her hands had notes scrawled across it in Jesper's handwriting. Ironfell—Ichor Knell's most influential trading partner—had cut ties with them the moment they'd heard of Dracula's death. The kingdom was where the human emperor resided. Their loss of allied partnership had devastated Ichor Knell the most financially. Alavara planned to regain them as allies behind Jesper's back.

Perhaps only then would he begin trust her.

Using the notes from the document as well as others she found scattered throughout the office, she dipped the quill in ink and carefully crafted a treaty in elegant script, one that would benefit both kingdoms, but she dared to demand a bit more than the last treaty. If the emperor signed this, Ichor Knell would find its footing again.

After the last stroke, she forged Jesper's signature and added her own below his. They looked completely different— no one would be the wiser.

For the finishing touch, she poured a glob of wax below their signatures and pressed the seal into the red mixture. The wax gave off a similar appearance as blood, which reminded her that she needed to be careful. In a city full of humans, she didn't want to lose control should her throat become dry and scratchy with bloodlust.

She wasted no time. After the remainder of the treaty dried, she returned to her chambers, gathered up a few provisions, and threw a hooded cloak over herself. In the dead of night, she snuck out her window, scaled the palace walls, and dropped to her feet on the northeastern side of the palace where the guards didn't bother to include for long stretches during their rotations.

She stood still and cocked her ears, listening for any activity and found none other than muffled laughter from a group enjoying a game of cards and the *clinking* of swords against armor as the palace guards moved in the opposite direction.

On lithe feet, she crept toward the stables, and only when she was inside did she allow her movements to become a little louder. The stable boy gasped from his chair beside the wall. He leaped to his feet and bowed low.

"Your Highness. Forgive me. I was not expecting anyone."

"Saddle a horse," she commanded, and he obeyed quickly. When a chestnut mare wore a bridle and saddle, he handed the reins to her. "Tell no one I was here. At least not until morning."

"Your Highness?"

"Did I stutter?" She cocked her head to the side and smiled at his flustered reaction. "Your shah is not to know of my departure until morning. If anyone comes after me before then, I will know exactly who ratted me out."

The boy's face blanched, but he nodded and bowed hastily once more.

She led the horse outside into the night, and after she mounted, she pulled the hood of her cloak over her head. With a firm kick to the horse's flanks, the creature started forward at a slow pace to start, and then she urged it faster as soon as they reached the trees bordering the city.

A grin spread across her face. Her only regret was not staying to witness Jesper's furious reaction when he learned of her departure.

CHAPTER 17

A POUNDING KNOCK sounded on his bedroom door, and Jesper rolled over with a groan. He covered his head with his pillow, intent on getting a few more minutes of sleep. At least. Couldn't someone else solve whatever this problem was? There were other people in this castle. It seemed like no one was aware of the fact.

"Your Highness!" a male voice bordering on puberty screeched. "Your Highness! Your Highness!"

The urgency in his tone made Jesper leap out of bed. He threw the door open only to find a red-faced, breathless stable boy hunched over, looking like he might retch.

"She…she…she…" The boy gasped and reached for the wall to steady himself.

All the blood drained from Jesper's face. Ice crawled up his veins. He grabbed the boy by the lapels of his shirt and lifted him off the ground. "What happened to Alavara?"

"She's gone! She ordered me to tell no one until morning. Your Highness, I waited until the crack of dawn. Our kumari took a horse and left the city. She's gone."

He dropped the boy, a surge of shock striking him in the face like the slap he deserved. He'd told Alavara to leave the city last night. Of course, he hadn't meant it. He'd only been flustered by her touch.

Without another moment's hesitation, he strode down the hallway, the stable boy at his heels. The light of dawn only just began to filter through the windows. "When did she leave?"

"Last night, sire."

Discomfort churned in his stomach, and he urged his feet to quicken their step. Panic nipped at his heels. Even his coolheadedness couldn't keep it at bay. His mate. *His mate.* Gone. Without a word.

"How far could she have gotten on the horse she took?" he asked while simultaneously barking orders at his soldiers to ride out after Alavara with him.

"Fifteen miles. Maybe more. But she's an elf. They are known for their affinity with animals. Vampire or not, that horse would carry her without stopping to rest until it dropped dead."

He swore under his breath.

The moment he stepped outside, he regretted not thinking to bring a cloak with him. The wind bit at his face, foretelling of a coming storm. There was no time to turn back now. He stamped his feet impatiently as he waited for someone to saddle a horse for him, his mind whirring all the while of where she might have gone. Her scent lingered in the stables, heading east. Varesia was west, not east. She wasn't returning home. So where was she going?

A horse now saddled, he stepped into the stirrup and swung his leg over. He led the search on horseback while several soldiers in their aviary forms flew overhead to cover more ground.

They would find her. They would.

Alavara's scent led them through the forest, the trees becoming thicker and thicker with each passing moment. His horse breathed heavily as it jumped over protruding roots and hobbled across uneven stones. Jesper ducked a few times when the boughs of pine brushed too low.

Her scent became stronger and stronger until...it disappeared.

The trail went cold at the river. Alavara had *wanted* them to lose her scent. She hadn't wanted to be followed.

He ran his hand across his face as he only barely held his panic at bay. A cold trail meant nothing. They would find it again.

"Come on, boy." He clicked his tongue and led the horse into the stream. Frigid spray splashed upward to claim his trousers, sinking into the fabric to his very bones. He led the horse up the river, down the river, and up again in hopes of catching even a glimmer of a berry scent. His entire group of soldiers thoroughly covered both the ground and the skies on either side of the river, but her scent had long since disappeared.

They searched for hours until water soaked his entire body. His teeth chattered. His body shivered. He had no choice but to call off the search after their efforts yielded them nothing but withered vines and dry earth.

His mate had left him. And it was his fault.

Rain pattered against the window, thunder shaking the entire castle with tremors. Fire crackled and popped in the hearth, followed by a *hiss* when a piece of a log crumbled. Jesper stared out the window, straining his eyes against the darkness of evening. He watched for any sign of movement down below, for the grace and stealth only an elf could muster.

But the streets were empty. Alavara hadn't returned, and three days had already passed. The rain hadn't let up, either.

Scratch, scratch, scratch.

He turned his head slightly to find Kiara gazing intently at him before turning her attention back to her drawing, only to glance up at him once more. She drew him often enough that he usually thought nothing of it, but this time, he didn't want these moments of misery captured by her chalk.

"Kiara, please," he asked quietly.

"But I'm almost done."

"Kiara," their mother said, also sitting at the table grinding herbs for their father, who was helping Uncle Zachariah in the infirmary.

His sister sighed and set down her chalk. She flipped the page in her notebook and held it out to him. "She will return." From this angle, he recognized the image of Alavara. "Here. Perhaps this will make you feel better."

He scoffed and crossed his arms. "Of course not. Because I'm not worried." But he still paused momentarily before giving in. "Let me see it."

The lines of ink came together beautifully to depict an image of Alavara. One where she was smiling. He hadn't seen her smile very often unless it was directed at him in a teasing or mocking manner. Her likeness made his heart sink in despair.

"Am I truly so awful?" he whispered hoarsely. "My own mate doesn't want to be around me. What does that say about me?"

"Jesper…" It wasn't Kiara who spoke but his mother. She pushed away from the table and pulled him into a comforting embrace. "Don't think such things. You are wonderful just the way you are."

"That is the most fictitious thing I have ever heard." He broke away from her and stared out at the rain pounding against the windowpane, wondering if Alavara had been caught in the storm or if she'd found shelter from the elements. "I am *me*. I am not exceptional mate material."

The truth hurt. It had always hurt.

Cobwebs and echoes. His heart had never been able to care for a female before, and therefore, he didn't deserve one in his life. Yes, the bond lied. But he'd never been so close to giving into those lies than in that moment.

Just for a day, he wished he could have Sam's expansive heart, if only to know what it felt like to love another.

And to be loved in return.

"I didn't like Alavara," his mother said, joining him at the window. "Not until I witnessed how much she means to you."

"She means nothing."

Then why did his heart ache so fiercely?

He felt rather than saw his mother and sister share a look before Kiara squeezed his hand. "Word of her whereabouts will turn up eventually. I'm sure of it."

"And then what? Drag her back to Ichor Knell? She left for a reason."

"Have you asked her father where she might have gone?" his mother questioned.

Jesper shrugged, then nodded. "I felt dirty groveling to him like a puppy. He doesn't know where she is. He also doesn't seem concerned. But I'm worried." There, he said it. "After she hurt herself so badly last week… Oh, daggers…" He ran his hand down his face. He could hardly breathe at the thought. "What if something happened to her?"

"You never told me she hurt herself," Kiara whispered. "What happened?"

He'd forgotten he'd kept it a secret. It just slipped out.

He told them about his encounter with her in the hallway and then cleaning her of her own blood the next morning. Speaking of the incident only amplified his distress.

Kiara held him tight, her face hidden in his chest. "I will light a candle and say a prayer for her."

He swallowed and found himself unable to speak for a good few seconds. Finally, he said, "I think I will, too."

Alavara's hair slicked to her neck, her breath heavy in her lungs. Her hair had escaped its braid long ago and now fell in sheets down her back, likely tangled into a thousand knots. She eyed the five men approaching her warily, each carrying a spear. Steel. The spears were made of steel. They'd nicked her a few times, and although blood seeped into her sleeve, her injuries had already healed over.

A spear from one of the fallen in her hands, she snapped it in half against her thigh and held each end of the weapon in either hand. Sharp spikes of splintered wood faced her competitors, threatening to cut them to ribbons.

Emperor Geraint clapped his hands once to call off her combatants, and she lowered her weapons a fraction as he stepped down from the dais, his long red robe melting off each stair like molten copper. His amused expression amplified with every footfall, and he stopped several yards away with a guard on each side of him.

He thought she was dangerous. Good.

"Do you know how Dracula maintained an alliance with Ironfell?" Geraint asked, not taking his gaze off her for a single moment. "He fought for it with his bare hands. My ancestors would not become allies with a weaker party, and therefore, he had to earn it. And earn it, he did."

The emperor rounded her as if taking her in, his guards keeping close by his side. He continued, "I am impressed with your endurance, I will give you that. But you are a *female*. What right do you have to come in your shah's stead?"

"I am sure word has reached you about the armies in Jesper's kingdom. In *my* kingdom. He does not dare leave should he need to declare war. He sent me here to represent him in this alliance. If I must fight my way through every one of your soldiers to prove myself, I will."

He frowned. "Is Shah Jesper so much of a coward to send his kumari to fight? How do you expect me to make a treaty with someone so weak?"

Alavara knew coming here would be a gamble, but it was a gamble she needed to see through. "Jesper can best me in combat. He is much more skilled than I. If I can fight my way through your men, he could do it ten times faster with strength that far outmatches mine."

Intrigue filled his expression as he returned to his place on the dais. He raised a hand to order his soldiers to resume the fight. "Show me."

She threw down her two pieces of splintered spear and surged forward with nothing but her hands as weapons.

A week.

An entire week had passed since Alavara's departure, and there was still no word of her whereabouts. The longer she was gone, the increasingly worried Jesper became. He knew servants whispered about him, about what he might have done to drive her away. He only prayed that the maid who had cleaned Alavara's blood would keep her promise to keep her mouth shut. He didn't need anyone thinking he'd beaten his own mate.

Despondently, he leaned back in his office chair and slowly breathed in her lingering scent. He had no idea how she'd managed to get into his office nor what she'd seen, but her scent coated everything—stacks of parchment, his quill, the royal seal. It even clung to the walls, the desk, and his chair. Only one piece of blank parchment was missing, and he'd first thought she had written him a letter to say goodbye. However, after a long and fruitless search, he came up with nothing. No letter. No goodbyes. Nothing.

"I'm not even worth a farewell," he muttered to himself.

The thought didn't sit well with him. They were mates. Didn't he deserve at least that much? Then again, he *had* driven her away.

He groaned into his hand. Since when was his every thought plagued by an infuriating female? He could hardly focus on his work.

Not able to stare down at his work any longer, he left the office and made his way down the hallway, only to jump when a hawk flew through the window and transformed into his captain of the guard, Cornell.

"Sire," he said with wide eyes. "Her Highness has returned. She's riding toward the palace as we speak."

Jesper's heart stopped beating for several moments before it resumed at a faster pace than it had ever beaten before. His feet couldn't move quickly enough as he rushed down the hallway. Cornell easily kept up with him.

He ordered the captain, "I want her followed. Until she is safe inside the palace, I want eyes on her every movement."

"I have scouts flying overhead."

"Good. I ask you to escort her personally."

Captain Cornell nodded and flew out the window in his hawk form.

The palace suddenly suffocated him, caving in on him in his desperation to see Alavara well and unharmed. His quickened pace turned into a jog, which became a full sprint. Nobility and servants stared at him as he passed, but he ignored them. The walls closed in on him more and more until finally, he burst outside, the afternoon air fresh after a thorough rainfall.

Alavara rode in on a chestnut mare with Captain Cornell trotting beside the horse, her form graceful as if she had been born to ride such a creature. Their gazes locked, and she visibly flinched as if she thought he might be angry with her.

Angry? No.

Relieved? Absolutely.

The moment she hopped from the saddle and landed on her feet, he jogged down the stairs. Each stride took him closer to her until he was near enough to see the uncertainty shining in her eyes. She opened her mouth to speak, but he cut off her words as he grabbed her arm and pulled her into an embrace.

He buried one of his hands into her hair and breathed in her scent with his nose pressed against her neck. Holding her ebbed his worry and pushed away his fears. With her enfolded in his arms, the entire world stood still instead of tilting with each passing minute of her absence. His relief at her return magnified tenfold as she tentatively lifted her arms and returned his embrace.

He didn't dare lift his head because he knew she would witness every flicker of uncertainty, every morsel of fear, every ounce of anxiety.

Never again.

Never again would he allow her to leave as she had.

"Where did you go?" he growled into her neck. *I worried about you.* "Why didn't you tell me you planned to leave?" *I missed you.* "You purposely hid your trail from me." *I thought something might have happened to you.*

"You would have stopped me." Her fingers tightened on his shirt, and in turn, he tightened his grip around her shoulders. He had never held a female like this, but it felt so right, like a breath of clean, fresh air after a wilderness fire.

"No." He shook his head, the ache returning to his chest when he remembered the reason she'd left in the first place. "If you didn't want to be by my side, I wouldn't have stopped you from leaving."

Her body became rigid against his, and she pulled away just enough to look him in the eye. "Is that why you think I left?"

"Isn't it?"

She shook her head and dropped her arms. The loss of contact filled him with need, but he couldn't decide if he should encourage the feeling or stuff it away until it disappeared completely.

"Let's go somewhere private so you won't be furious at me in front of an audience."

Indeed, an audience had gathered in front of the castle, each a witness to their reunion. An embarrassed flush crawled up his neck, and he refused to look anyone in the eye as he led Alavara up the stairs, down the hallway, and into his office.

He opened the drapes to let in more light. He usually kept them closed because he hated the feeling of being watched. Keeping the drapes drawn gave him the small bit of privacy he craved day after day.

"You are going to be very angry," Alavara began. "Please try not to shout at me."

He held still, waiting for her to speak.

Taking a deep breath, she said, "I went to Ironfell to negotiate a treaty for Ichor Knell."

His eyebrows drew together. His mouth curled into a snarl as he took a step closer and glared down at her. "You had no right! Absolutely no right, Alavara. How could you do such a thing behind my back?"

She also took a step forward until she glared straight into his face, only a few breaths away. "You weren't going to do it. I read all the documents. You didn't think it was possible to regain their alliance."

"We didn't have the resources to risk it."

"No?" She reached into the pack on her back and pulled out a scroll, waving it in his face. "But it went so well."

He narrowed his eyes at the scroll. "What is that?"

"It's the treaty. Don't you want to know what we agreed upon?"

"Emperor Geraint signed it?" His heart stumbled in surprise. He was speechless, especially as he snatched the scroll from her hands and unraveled it. The words stared back at him, a list of agreed-upon demands. And there at the bottom of the page was the emperor's signature.

But...but she had done this behind his back. The sting of betrayal warred with the elation of a newfound alliance. An improved alliance.

"Why did you not consult me beforehand?" he asked, a lingering hurt in his eyes. "You cannot do something like this behind my back, Alavara."

She had the decency to give him a guilty grimace. "I didn't think you would allow me to go."

"I don't know what I would have allowed. You did not give me the chance to make this decision with you!"

Her gaze dropped to her feet. "I'm sorry. I thought you would be happier."

He released a long breath and looked over the treaty once more, this time with a more careful eye. With each section on the parchment, the tension in his shoulders released little by little. Ichor Knell would thrive again. Alavara had made it so, despite her betrayal.

Voice hoarse, he said, "Do you know what this will do for Ichor Knell?"

She nodded. "I know very well. I had to resort to underhanded means to find out as much. Perhaps you should stop being so stubborn and allow me more rein in kingdom affairs. I'm quite good at diplomacy. As you can tell."

"I don't..." He swallowed and lifted his gaze. "I don't know what to say."

"How about thank you?"

Instead of saying the words, he returned his attention to the treaty, only to find his own signature above the emperor's, a signature he hadn't signed.

"You forged this."

"Another one of my many skills." She arrogantly flipped her hair over her shoulder. "If you don't agree, then it's up to you to return to Geraint and tell him of the forgery. But I thought you would agree."

He couldn't fault her for the forgery, especially after such a much-needed alliance. And he didn't dare expose it lest the emperor retract the alliance forever. He set the treaty on top of the desk and looked at her with appreciation in his eyes. "You must promise to never do something like this again. But...thank you, Alavara."

She laughed and touched his arm, and this time, he didn't tell her off. "You can do better than just a few measly words, can't you?"

Not really. "What do you want?"

"Give me a few minutes of your time. Just me and you. How would you like to join me for a game of chess in the courtyard?"

Not a good idea. "It has rained a lot recently."

"I don't feel another storm in the air for a good while."

Was that an elf thing? Could she predict the weather, too? Honestly, he didn't put it past her, especially after hearing what a simple horse would do for her if she willed it.

"Fine." It was the least he could do after what she'd accomplished for his kingdom. "Tomorrow afternoon will work. I have a little time to spare before my meetings."

She trailed her hand down his arm and gave him a sultry smile before making her exit. "I look forward to it."

Even long after she left, he wondered if he'd just agreed to something far more dangerous than a simple game of chess. Spending time with her was never a good idea.

CHAPTER 18

A NERVOUS DRUM beat wildly inside Jesper's chest with each step he took through the palace. The courtyard was too close but not near enough at the same time. Spending time with his mate was a bad idea. A very bad idea.

Yet, the idea excited him.

What was wrong with him?

"Where are you off to?" Sam laughed behind him, and he internally cringed as he slowly turned to find an enormous smirk spread across his brother's face.

"It's none of your business."

"I heard Alavara returned. I also heard she's a sight to see."

He clenched his hands into fists at his sides, doing his best to rein in his temper. Just being near his brother boiled his blood. "And? It's none of your business."

Sam shrugged, his smile remaining. "What else do I have to do but taunt you when Natalia is gone? My work here doesn't take nearly as much of my time as I want it to."

With a roll of his eyes, he continued on his way. "For all our sakes, I'm hoping you go home sooner rather than later."

A chuckle followed him before he finally stepped into the courtyard.

And froze.

Alavara looked stunning, enough to freeze his blood in his veins. A collared necklace of sheer blue fabric connected by a silver brooch lay at her neck, with more blue fabric dripping from the collar and down her arms to expose her bare shoulders. Ornamental beaded flowers lined her blue and silver heart-shaped bodice, and the rest of the fabric dripped elegantly to her feet. Silver metal cuffs hugged her pointed elven ears, strands of simple crystal earrings brushing her shoulders.

He stared at her bare shoulders again, a flush rising to his neck. "What are you wearing?"

"You said you wanted me to wear the clothing of my people. You also said you wanted me to stand out." She twirled a strand of dark hair around her finger and looked up at him from beneath her lashes. "You like?"

Yes.

"On second thought, maybe you *should* blend into the wall."

She laughed, the sound sending shivers down his spine. "You are Jesper Degore, and I am Alavara Elroris. We were not born to blend in. Come. Sit with me. You promised me a game."

The situation seemed harmless enough. There was no physical contact involved in chess. There were plenty of others either in the courtyard or inside the castle walking past windows. He could leave at any time by making up some excuse or another.

Warily, he lowered himself onto the seat across from her while surreptitiously scenting the weapons on her person. Two daggers beneath her dress and a hidden knife in her hairpiece. She always carried a weapon no matter what she wore or where she went. He'd be disappointed otherwise.

He didn't know why he was worried she might spring one of those weapons on him. She was his mate, and therefore, she would never be able to hurt him with one of them.

But trust was still hard to come by. What she had done with Ironfell… She'd gone behind his back. She'd pursued a treaty without his permission. Yet, Ichor Knell benefitted from her actions.

What was he supposed to think?

Clink. She made the first move on the chessboard, white glass on a black and white glass checkered table. A silver-beaded bracelet on her wrist caught the light with the movement, snagging his attention. Etched into the metal beads were symbols that looked dwarven in nature.

"That's a new bracelet," he commented.

"Yes." She smiled as she ran a finger over the metallic beads. "I wanted to tell you—" Her smile slowly melted into a look of confusion. "I don't remember what I was going to say. I believe my father gave it to me as a union gift."

He furrowed his eyebrows as he tried to remember if he'd seen her wearing it before. No, he hadn't. Not until today. Why would Ruvyn give it to her several weeks after the ceremony rather than on the day or week of?

"I heard you were frantic while I was gone," she cut in suddenly, distracting his thoughts. "The entire guard searched for my trail."

A scowl glared daggers into the black glass piece he moved forward. "I was simply protecting my investment. And no, I certainly was not frantic. I cared not one whit about your absence."

"Ah." Her eyes twinkled. "My mistake." She moved a piece forward and added casually, "Our embrace was nice."

Yes, it had been nice. He didn't know how to explain it, however. "Just a result of the bond. It lies, remember? I wish I didn't have to keep telling you as much."

"Telling *me*? Or trying to convince *yourself*?"

He pushed himself away from the table and crossed his arms, continuing to scowl at her. "Why did you ask me to play with you? I don't want to talk about this, and if you insist, I will leave right now."

"Fair enough. I would like you to stay. Let's find another topic of conversation."

They resumed the game, but not their discussion. Instead, as they traded turns back and forth, his ears picked up on a hushed conversation between two male vampires near the large oak, one named Renwick and the other Alec.

"—sitting idle while we work so hard," Renwick said.

Alec seemed to agree judging by his grunt of affirmation before he muttered something about dallying with females.

As the seconds ticked by, he became more and more glum, his movements sluggish. He tried hard to not allow his shoulders to hunch. Invisible. For once in his life, he just wanted to be invisible. Or perhaps even go somewhere far, far away where no one could watch his every movement.

"Jesper?" Alavara asked, and his gaze shot up to meet hers. Only then did he realize he'd been staring at his game pieces for a couple of minutes without making a move. "Are you all right?"

His mouth tightened into a thin line. He contemplated whether to tell her or keep his mouth shut, but he finally relented and used his finger to circle the courtyard around them. "I just hate *this*."

"What?"

"People watching and listening. For example, the two nobles talking behind my back." The vampires' conversation hushed immediately. "Ah, it seems they are listening to us this very second. Come here, please."

Renwick and Alec approached with shame evident in their eyes. Jesper didn't look up to acknowledge them, but rather averted his gaze to make them feel inferior.

"Alec," he said, his finger touching the top of his knight before he decided against the move and touched a pawn, contemplating. "You have a mate, right?"

"Yes, sire," Alec replied in a husky tone.

"And how long did you court her?"

"Two and a half years, sire."

Finally, he decided to move his bishop forward and take one of Alavara's pawns. "I have courted my mate for all but twenty minutes. Why should I not have the same privilege you did?"

The vampire ducked his head. "Forgive me, sire."

"The next time either of you have a grievance with me, I would appreciate it if you came to me directly rather than speak in hushed whispers. You are dismissed."

Even as the two vampires trudged away, he didn't look their way once. It was such a waste of effort to turn his head even a fraction for their benefit. Besides, it was a good way to remind them of their station.

"Courting?" Alavara asked in a sly tone. "I thought I was nothing to you."

He rolled his eyes and rested his chin against his hand. "Don't read into it."

"How did you know they were there?"

"I can't help but notice everything. Those two by the oak. A trio of females on the upper balcony watching us and giggling. Your father staring deviously down at us from the north side of the castle."

She glanced in the northern direction, and he followed her gaze in time to see a flicker of movement as someone darted out of sight before all was still. If he wasn't mistaken, a prick of annoyance creased her forehead. While it might seem like they had all the privacy in the world, they truly didn't. They were being watched on all sides.

"Is there anywhere you like to go where people *won't* scrutinize your every action?" she asked.

Other than leaving Ichor Knell entirely? Not really. "My office. And the gardens. It's usually quite private."

"Let's go on a walk then. In the gardens. Just the two of us."

"Why?" he scoffed, trying to ignore the anxious strain in his shoulders. Ever present and seemingly permanent. "We don't have a reason to be alone together. Ever."

His point came across loud and clear—he never planned to mate with her again. Spending time with her in the courtyard was pushing it as it was. Each one of their encounters were dangerous—the training arena incident was indication enough.

"Then why did you tell those vampires you were courting me?"

"To get them off my back."

She stood, and his entire body tensed as his gaze followed her short journey around the table until she stood directly behind him. She gently touched his shoulder and spoke softly. "I'm not asking you on a walk to spend time alone with you. I'm trying to get you away from *this*." She placed her other hand upon his second shoulder and squeezed. He groaned when her massaging touch seeped deep into sore muscles. It was as if eighty-five years of responsibilities had formed layers upon layers of ache.

When she kneaded his shoulders with her gentle hands, he closed his eyes and arched into her touch.

"What are you doing?" he grunted.

"Easing your sore muscles."

"No, no. *How* are you doing it? It feels good."

Her light, feminine chuckle sounded far too close to his ear, but he didn't want to pull away just yet. "*Erbrumthin* may be my fighting style, but there's so much more to the pressure points on the body. We don't just use them to hurt, but to heal. Elves who have perfected the art are some of the best healers in the world."

"Seems like..." He grunted again when she tackled a knot near his neck. "Seems like you have perfected the art."

"Far from it. I am a fighter, not a healer. But I know enough."

"Do you miss it?"

"Miss what?"

"Your home. Do you miss it?"

Alavara dropped her hands from his shoulders, and he was both grateful and disappointed at the same time. "Very much. The forests in Varesia are spectacular. Giant sequoias. Plants that glow like moonlight. Magic singing in the breeze."

Silence echoed in the space between them, and he turned just enough to catch a glimpse of the sadness in her eyes. A desire to take the sadness away surfaced, and he gave in all too easily.

"I'll take you up on that walk."

They strolled side by side into the enormous Ichor Knell gardens, plants of all shapes and varieties spread out before them. Although flowers other than red nettle blooms didn't grow in the vampire city without sunlight, the gardens were still beautiful. Jewel trees shot up sporadically throughout the gardens with gems ranging from sapphires, rubies, diamonds, and more. They sparkled in the afternoon breeze. On impulse, he reached up and snapped a sapphire off the branches and handed it to Alavara.

"What is this for?" she asked, her eyes wide in surprise.

Jesper shrugged. "Females like pretty things. At least Sam says Natalia does. Maybe you are an exception."

"No female is an exception." A smile graced her lips, and when she began studying the jewel, he looked the other way to make it seem like he didn't care. Because he didn't.

Something warm slipped into his hand, and his stomach tied into a thousand knots when he glanced down to find

Alavara's fingers threaded through his. He snatched his hand back and glared.

"Don't touch me."

"Why?"

Did she always have to challenge him about *everything*?

"Because it makes me uncomfortable. My stomach hurts, and it feels as if pins and needles are in my chest."

She grinned slyly, and he certainly didn't like it.

"What?" he asked.

"I've heard you've never courted before. Nothing serious, at least. What you are describing is infatuation. The excitement of being near a female companion."

He looked at her as if she had gone mad and took a step away to put a little distance between them. He didn't speak until he was certain they were alone in the gardens. "What? No. It's anything but pleasant."

"You don't allow it to be. Give me your hand, and I will show you."

"I'd rather not."

"Stop being so stubborn. It's only your hand."

Memories of the training arena flickered in his mind, when she had pressured him into allowing him to practice *Erbrumthin* on her. Her blood had called to him then, singing songs of desire and beautiful promises.

Touching her at all was a dangerous game.

"I don't want to hold your hand, Alavara." He glanced toward the garden's exit, and it suddenly seemed so far away. Entering the gardens had been a bad idea.

When he turned his attention back to her, she held her gaze steady. Enticement swirled within the dark depths of her eyes, and for a moment, he couldn't breathe.

"Just ten seconds," she said quietly, her voice as smooth as velvet and as rich as cream. Once again, she slid her fingers into his, and his stomach reacted as if a drone of bees attacked him from the inside. Her slender fingers fit nicely in his hand. Warmth traveled from his fingertips, to the base of his wrist, up his arm, and enveloped his entire chest. She continued to hold his gaze as she lifted their conjoined hands and kissed his knuckles. Surges of heat slammed into him in waves, and he jerked his hand away as if he'd been burned.

"What are you doing?" He moved away from her again and walked backward even as she advanced slowly toward him. "I told you there is nothing between us. The bond lies."

"But what if it doesn't?" She smiled with that nicely shaped mouth of hers, and his gaze followed her movement as she trailed a strand of her hair through her fingers. He tripped over a root and only just managed to catch his balance. "You must feel some regard for me, bond or not. Isn't there at least something you like about me?"

Swallowing, he looked away and admitted, "Well, there may be a few things."

Why did he just confess? It was those eyes, he decided. Alluring. Bewitching.

"Like what?"

He glanced toward the garden exit again, contemplating running away like a coward at this point. What would his grandfather think of him? A coward?

The thought of his grandfather gave him the courage to face her head on and speak the truth. "I should hate that you're stealthy and have a knack for spying, but I actually like it. No one sneaks up on me the way you do."

She raised her eyebrows as if surprised before a smile lit up her expression. "Well, about the spying… I like the way you chuckle to yourself as if you thought of something funny when you think no one is watching."

"Someone is always watching."

"Yes, I have learned as much today. Your turn."

"I like watching you when you reach for something up high. You are graceful."

"I like the way your hair stands up after you've had a particularly long day."

"Bad habit of mine, I suppose."

The distance between them had grown shorter and shorter with each confession, and he found himself backed against a tree. Alavara was close. Too close. The dark depths of her eyes were endless, as if he stared into a shadowy abyss.

Dark elf.

Vampire.

His mate.

And then she spoke two words, a demand, that set his heart racing.

"Kiss me."

He frowned and scrunched his nose as if she had asked him to eat a dirty worm. "No."

She touched one of her slender fingers to his chest, stroking over his frenzied heart. "You keep saying the bond lies. I keep hearing there is nothing between us. Prove it to me. Prove it to yourself. Kiss me."

"I'm not going to—"

A grunt of surprise escaped him when she grabbed him by the shirt and pulled him toward her. Their lips crashed together. At first, he tried to escape the contact, but then his eyes widened in shock, his hands hovering over her shoulders at the trickle of warmth that entered the darkest recesses of his soul. Nothing had ever reached it before. No one had ever touched it. It felt as if the kiss blew a layer of dust off his heart.

When the kiss broke, he continued to stare at her with furrowed brows. All his life, he had only hoped to feel a sliver of that warmth. All his life, he had longed to know what it felt like for this part of his heart to begin beating.

And now it did. Slowly, but surely.

"I didn't..." He swallowed, daring himself to place his hands on top of her slim shoulders. "I didn't feel anything. Maybe we should try again."

Her lips parted, eager for more. He lowered his mouth to hers and breathed in sharply when it felt as if the second kiss struck a match to burn away every last cobweb in his heart. The fire didn't stop there. It traveled through every inch of his body like roots holding fast to the earth.

When they broke apart, the loss of contact left him wanting for the burn.

"Feel anything yet?" she breathed.

"Not a thing."

"Me neither."

They collided for a third time, and a river of feeling poured inside, slamming into each wall of his heart. He didn't know what to do with the rush of emotions. Fondness. Desire. Not just a trickle of emotion but an entire flood.

He needed more, more, more.

A low, possessive growl escaped his throat. He pulled her closer, his fingernails digging into her back but not breaking the skin. The desire to bite her grew as the heat built up between their lips. He growled again and pinned her against a tree. His fingers fumbled to unclasp the collar around her throat, and the moment it fell free, his fangs shot out from his mouth. He clamped down on her neck, and she cried out at the sudden pain. But instead of pushing him away, she clutched tighter, her breathing ragged with desire as he both sipped at her blood and allowed his venom to mingle with it.

If the bond lied, this was the greatest lie he'd ever been told.

With his fangs still in her neck, he pulled them into a vacant gardening shed and slammed the door shut behind them. After feeling that warmth in the darkest part of his heart, he knew he'd never let Alavara go again.

197

CHAPTER 19

ALAVARA WAS SPEECHLESS as if struck dumb. She hardly remembered a thing about the first time, but this…

Her fondness for Jesper left her trembling in her bones, her heart aching but so full at the same time. Each beat of her heart thundered words she dared not speak aloud. *Stay with me. Kiss me. Love me. Hold me.*

It was too soon to demand more. What they had was too fragile to risk breaking.

"What did you do with my collar?" she laughed as she finished buttoning his shirt for him. Although her fingers brushed his skin, she wanted to be even closer, to breathe his air, to taste his lips.

"What did you do with my belt?"

She glanced up to look into his face. The dim lighting in the shed made it difficult to see his features, but she didn't fail to notice the wildness in his eyes or the way his fingers grazed her waist as if he couldn't stand to be far away. She felt the same way.

By the forest, she felt the same way. She knew she shouldn't, but she did. Being near him made her heart flutter like silver butterfly wings. She wanted to step into his arms and never leave.

They located his belt slung over a rack of gardening tools, and when he secured it in place, she took him by the hand and led him outside to retrieve her collar. Footsteps neared them, a couple of voices echoing closer. They hastily clasped her collar around her neck, and he pulled her down onto a bench so suddenly she nearly fell off. She only barely managed to right herself as a male and female rounded the corner. She ducked her head as heat flared in her cheeks, though she noticed Jesper watching them from the corner of her eye.

The two bowed hastily and murmured, "Your Majesties," before scurrying away far too quickly to be ignorant about what had just happened between her and Jesper.

Was it so obvious?

When she glanced up at him, she snorted in amusement at finding his hair in disarray, dark red strands sticking up in all directions.

"What?" he asked.

"Your hair. You have clearly been up to something naughty."

His hands shot toward his hair, his fingers combing through to bring order back to his locks. Endearment toward him took a hold of her, and she cradled his cheek in her hand, his skin soft against her palm. He ceased his fussing and gazed back at her with his beautiful eyes. Green like the forest leaves bathed in the afternoon sunlight. She caressed his cheek with her thumb, soft and tender. Gone was the distrust from his eyes. Gone were the hatred and disgust. Instead, she enjoyed the fondness in his gaze, the hope, the admiration.

It felt wonderful to no longer be frowned at like she was the enemy.

"Daggers." Jesper leaped up from the bench and continued his attempt to flatten his hair. "I forgot about my meeting. I'm so late." He smoothed his rumpled clothing and started toward the palace but turned back to her momentarily. "Alavara?"

"Yes?"

"I recommend you stay here for at least a few more minutes. The love bite hasn't healed all the way."

Love bite...

Her fingers lightly brushed the tender spot on her neck where he'd bitten her. The first time he'd ever bitten her, she'd only wished for death, whereas this time... She'd never wanted it to stop.

When she glanced up again, Jesper was gone.

Without him nearby to see, she smiled softly as she repositioned her collar to better hide the love bite as she slowly made her way back to the castle. His scent was stronger now than ever before, and her smile turned smug when she realized his scent lingered all over her.

Her mate. *Her* vampire. *Her* shah. He belonged to her, and she wouldn't let him or anyone else forget it.

For so long, Jesper had kept her out of kingdom affairs, but she felt confident he wouldn't kick her out this time. She followed his scent through the castle before she entered the council chambers. Jesper stood at the front of the room addressing the council members, but his words cut off the moment she entered. Everyone quickly stood in her presence.

"A-A-Alavara," he stuttered before clearing his throat, a mask covering his initial surprise. "Why are you here?"

"I simply wanted to learn more about our kingdom and our people." *Our.* "Thank you for allowing me to join you."

Before he had a chance to dismiss her, she asked Leif to give up his seat so she could sit at Jesper's right. The vampire quickly scrambled out of her way.

The meeting resumed, though she didn't fail to notice the strain in her mate's shoulders.

Time for a little teasing...

"And if they bring iron weapons across our border?" someone asked. "What then?"

She picked up a blank sheet of parchment sitting on the table and adopted a look of innocence as she used it to fan her face, angling the movement to fan her scent in Jesper's direction. With growing amusement, she watched his nostrils flare when he picked up the scent, and he stopped speaking entirely to turn his head toward her.

The corner of her mouth twitched. *Check mate.*

He squeezed his eyes shut for a moment as if trying to eliminate her from his nostrils, and by some miracle, he continued speaking. "Let them have their weapons. But if they bring an unreasonable amount, we'll just send them back across the bed and tell them to not come back."

Sam snorted, and Jesper turned to glare.

"What's so funny?"

"You said *bed* instead of *border.*"

A visible flush crept up his neck, and he glanced sideways at her. Her own blush heated in her cheeks at the way he looked at her. Dark. Smoldering. Full of desire.

He cleared his throat. "What I was saying was this is our land and our rules. Let them have means to defend themselves, but if they go on the offensive, we have every right to strike their name out of our treaty. We want to avoid a bite if possible."

Now the entire room chuckled at Jesper's slip-up. Sam seemed to make it his job to correct him, "You mean *fight* instead of *bite*, right?"

Jesper ran a hand over his face, and her mouth twitched in amusement when he turned his back to her completely. She glanced in Sam's direction to find him smirking right at her as if he knew exactly what was going on.

"What's the next item on the list?" Jesper asked.

Leif answered, "Misty Loch wants our lumber in exchange for copper ore. We have already started the trade, and we're better off for it. We have more trees than we know what to do with."

"Good. Though, I'd prefer a steady supply of silver ore myself. We have to replenish our pretty eyes somehow." He breathed in sharply and snapped his attention to his brother when he started to guffaw along with everyone else in the room. "*Knives.* I said *throwing knives*, you useless waste of council space."

Sam wiped a red-tinted tear from his eye. "Do you need a bit of time alone with your mate? I'm sure we can all agree that we can schedule this meeting for another day."

"We'll reschedule for tomorrow, but only because you are all being a bunch of big-headed idiots."

Alavara's face warmed as Jesper took her hand and pulled her into the hallway, and he didn't let go for a single moment. Instead, he threaded his fingers with hers, met her gaze, and then looked away as if he wasn't sure what to say. She wasn't entirely sure, either. She wanted to follow his lead, but he wasn't leading at all. He simply needed a little push.

"So...that was a boring meeting," she said, smiling knowingly at him when he glanced her way again.

"Very boring. They're all equally boring. You haven't been missing out."

Silence again aside from their footsteps in sync down the hallway.

She asked suddenly, "Do you want to go to my room?"

"Daggers, yes," he breathed.

Laughter erupted from her mouth when he tugged on her hand and veered off in the other direction, and she delighted in seeing a smile spread across his face. He practically dragged her to her own chambers, and she was more than happy to comply.

CHAPTER 20

JESPER HAD NEVER been happier in his life. Everything had changed for him. Absolutely everything. His heart thrummed with life. It whirred with birdsong and burned with warm embers from a fire's glow. Places recently covered in cobwebs now teemed with joy and elation.

So, this was what the beginnings of love felt like. He'd waited eighty-five years for the smallest taste, and he'd found more than a mouthful in the most unlikely place. A dark elf. His enemy. A female he was supposed to hate with his entire being.

He smiled with fondness as he waited with folded arms, his back leaning against an obsidian archway. He took in the red nettle vines climbing the wall as if reaching for the clouds looming over the castle. Beautiful blooms dotted the wall, as red as Alavara's eyes when she'd first become a vampire. He hadn't seen them red since, and he was glad for it. It meant she made feeding a priority.

The scent of sweet berry taunted his nostrils, and he turned his head to watch as Alavara exited the palace doors. She lifted her midnight blue skirts and descended the stairs. Her body moved with admirable grace from the gentle curve of her wrist to the soft footfalls of each step.

She seemed unaware of his presence beside the archway as she walked by, but before she moved out of reach, he grabbed her by the waist and pulled her into the shadows with him.

A shriek of laughter escaped her mouth, and he quickly silenced it with a kiss. And another. And soon his hands tangled themselves in her hair. He breathed in the scent of her, tasting the sweetness of her lips.

"Jesper," she laughed, pushing him away while simultaneously attempting to fix her hair. "We're meeting your family in just a few minutes. I can't have you ruining what my maidservant painstakingly pinned up."

A long-suffering sigh blew out his mouth, and he reluctantly relinquished his grip on her, though he kept one hand firmly on her waist. Out of all the days his family planned an outing to the lower town...

Pushing the disappointment away, he stood on his toes and plucked a red nettle flower from a vine and tucked it into the dark strands of her hair. He bit his lip with uncertainty at his fumbling fingers.

"I don't know if I'm doing this right."

"Tucking a flower into my hair? It can't be that hard, Jesper."

He shook his head, vulnerability seeping into his normally calm and collected mask. "Courting you. I've never had anyone to practice on."

"No one? Not even Cybil?"

Cybil's sudden departure still stung, but not quite as much anymore. He snorted. "Cybil would have gutted me if I had come within ten feet of her with a flower in my hand. No. Not even her." He paused. "Do you like flowers?"

His heart seized at the bright smile she gave him. What was wrong with him? He'd never been softer in his life. "Yes. Silver petals are my favorite. They only grow in Varesia."

They relinquished the privacy of the shadows and started toward the square where horses and servants and soldiers went about their work for the day, and where they would meet his family.

"If I were Sam," he continued, smiling when his fingers brushed hers momentarily, "this is the part where I'd say I'd scour the entire world to find a silver petal for you."

"But you're not. You would never do such a thing."

Probably not. It seemed like such a waste of time for a measly little flower that would only die before he managed to get it back to Ichor Knell.

"Would you scour the entire world to find me a dragon scale?"

She glanced sideways at him, surprise lighting her eyes. "You want a dragon scale?"

"I certainly do."

A beautiful, silvery laugh lifted into the air. "Dragons haven't existed in a very long time. Finding a scale, especially a preserved one, would be next to impossible."

"How disappointing. I suppose you will have to wait on that silver petal then."

"Boar-pig," she muttered before bumping her hip into his.

He pushed her right back in the shoulder. "Toad-spotted elf."

When she attempted to return the favor, he dodged and grabbed her by the wrist, pinning it behind her back while simultaneously bending her backward. He bathed in her shriek of laughter, in her tantalizing breath on his cheek. Not able to help himself, he kissed her yet again. Her lips were soft against his, a warmth spreading through his entire being and shrouding his heart in a cloud of pure happiness.

Deep, throaty laughter sounded behind him, and he momentarily froze. Quicker than he knew he could move, he pushed away from her and dropped his hands to his sides, only to find his entire family staring with slack jaws as they sat in a carriage while Sam laughed on.

His brother hardly managed to speak through his guffawing. "*Who's* hunched over *whose* lips now?"

A searing hot flush spread from his toes to his neck to his ears. It must have been visible because Sam entered into another laughing fit, and Jesper died inside. Of all the people…

He coughed into his hand in an attempt to hide his embarrassment at getting caught, but it was too late. His family had witnessed everything.

"I never thought…" Sam wheezed. "I never thought I'd see the day."

"Oh, come now, dear brother," Alavara said, gracefully stepping into the carriage and sitting beside Kiara. "Jesper had to come to adore me eventually. I'm almost disappointed it didn't take me as long to earn his favor as I thought it would."

Jesper wanted to die. He wanted to hide away in his office under a pile of parchment and die. Courting was normal—he knew that. Kissing one's mate was normal—he knew that, too. But it wasn't normal for *him*. And now he wanted to die of embarrassment. Judging by the secretive grins his parents exchanged, it seemed everyone could guess he and Alavara had shared a bed at least once under friendly circumstances. Although they had never spent all night together, and they still slept in separate rooms, they were mates in every sense of the word.

"Oh dear." Kiara clicked her tongue. "He's still blushing."

Alavara leaned backward against the carriage to shoot him a teasing smile. "Are you coming, darling? Or shall we leave without you?"

Darling?

He glared at her over the use of the word. He was nobody's darling, not even hers. A few sweet kisses and several passionate encounters gave her no right to give him a name of endearment, especially not in front of his family.

I'm going to gut you, his expression implied.

She simply smiled back, though the look in her eyes posed a challenge. *I'd like to see you try.*

Despite his glare—and his raging flush—he stepped into the carriage and sat on Kiara's other side to avoid the temptation of touching Alavara in any way, shape, or form. The last thing he needed was his family to witness him showing affection toward his mate again.

The carriage jolted forward, the horse's hooves clomping on the cobblestone path. Jewel trees flew past in a blur of yellows, oranges, greens, and blues, reminding him of when he'd given Alavara a sapphire as a gift.

Smug satisfaction set in his jaw when he glanced at her out of the corner of his eye only to find the very same sapphire dangling from her neck by a silver chain, inlaid in a silver oval setting to match the cut of the jewel. They hadn't spoken of the sapphire since, but he would never tell her how much it meant to him that she wore it.

"Can you hear really well with those ears of yours?" Kiara asked. "As both an elf and a vampire."

Jesper perked up and listened despite his concentration on the road ahead.

Alavara answered, "I'm still learning to hone my hearing. Jesper is much better at picking out sounds than I am."

"He's better at it than all of us combined," his mother cut in. "He's always had a knack for detail."

"So I've learned."

His mother watched Alavara with interest that hadn't been there only a week before, and he wondered if she accepted his mate because he had come to care for her and accept her himself. She asked question after question as if wanting to learn more about her daughter-in-law. They spoke of the forests in Varesia, of the plants and wildlife that resided there, and even of elven customs.

Jesper turned his head to more fully take his mate in as she spoke of her favorite wedding custom. Two elves would stand in a languid river, the frigid water washing over their toes. They would wear wreaths of sticks and flowers in their hair and face each other while holding hands. After the ceremony, elves would use their magic to rain silver, sparkling droplets over them to bless the union.

The way she spoke of the custom... The life in her eyes ebbed. Her shoulders drooped. Her broken heart leaked through her voice. There was no mistaking the cloud of somberness she stepped into when speaking of her homeland. She clearly still didn't enjoy being a vampire. Would she ever?

A prick of guilt traveled up his spine. He had done this. He had taken the life from her eyes by turning her. But what else could he have done? An elf could not sit on a vampire throne. He had taken small victories where he could with five armies on his doorstep.

But looking at her now... Turning her didn't feel quite so much like a victory anymore.

The carriage pulled to a stop in front of the foundling home. A wooden sign with those words hung from the building, coated with fresh white paint. As if anticipating their arrival, children ran outside, laughing and shouting. Some surrounded the horse to stroke its sleek coat. Others waited on their toes as if eager to get a glimpse of the royal family. Jesper's gaze drifted to the few children with bare feet, noticing several others who wore shoes with holes in the toes or heels.

"Oh my," Alavara breathed, her eyes wide as she picked up a small girl who couldn't have been more than three years old. "Jesper, I want them all."

He searched her face for any trace of a jest but found none. It took all his self-control not to scrunch his nose in distaste. At least not in front of the children.

Only one word deflated the spirits right from her expression. "No."

Ignoring her downhearted stare, he forged a path through the children, but stopped short when a boy, perhaps five years old, tugged on his tunic. The boy's wide eyes took in the sword strapped to his belt, and he took his thumb out of his mouth momentarily.

"I want a sword like yours."

What was he supposed to say? He didn't know how to speak to a child.

Kiara urged him to reply with a nod of her head toward the boy, and he tried not to sigh. "When I was your age, I practiced with a wooden sword. Join the army one day and you can get a real one."

A smile blossomed across the boy's face moments before his thumb popped right back into his mouth.

Already, he wanted to leave. He felt so out of place here, but Dracula had made visiting the orphanage once a month a priority because his mate had done it, too, a long time ago. Now Jesper continued the tradition, and he would feel awful if he stopped. Last month, he'd visited with Cybil, and the children had gawked at her when she'd showed them a few fighting techniques. He wasn't half as good with children, and Cybil wasn't even good with them to begin with.

"What are you reading?" Alavara asked once inside, and he craned his neck to find a child sitting on her lap with a book in her hands.

The girl ducked her head shyly. "I'm not very good at reading. Lady Degore taught me my letters, but I don't get to practice very often."

Lady Degore as in his aunt Laurel, Zachariah's mate.

New books, new shoes, new tutor volunteers. He made the list in his head, considering whether or not they could afford the expense at this time. With the new treaty in place with Ironfell, he might be able to get them new shoes next month at the very least. Winter would approach soon enough, and they couldn't very well be walking around in their bare feet.

He watched from the shadows in the corner where he was most comfortable, his father at his side while the others interacted with the children. Despite having had three children, his father was almost as out of his element as he was.

A two-year-old held out a dirty cloth to him, snot dripping from his nose. He grimaced and searched for Alavara to do the deed for him, but she was buried in a sea of children.

Reluctantly, he took the cloth from the boy and wiped his nose before handing it back, but the boy scampered away and left him with the mess.

He grimaced again as he searched for a place to deposit the cloth and found a table on the opposite side of the room. Someone lightly touched his elbow, and he jumped when he found Alavara smiling at him.

"Do you want children one day, darling?"

His following glare said, *Call me darling one more time. I dare you.* He snorted. "No."

"Why not?"

He had grown to hate those two words. She asked them all too often.

Lowering his voice to keep anyone from overhearing, he said, "They are gross and loud and disrupt work that needs to be done." He lowered his voice even further. "You *are* still taking the contraceptive tonic, aren't you?"

She stared at him for several moments, the confusion on her face unnerving him. He nearly asked after her well-being when she answered, "Yes, yes. You don't need to worry. But I think I can convince you someday."

"You will only be disappointed, Alavara. I don't want any." And he didn't. Not only were children loud, he also feared his heart wouldn't be large enough to let one in. It was a miracle Alavara had been able to wedge her way into his heart, but a child? He was so scared he wouldn't be able to love one.

"People always say they don't want children, or they don't like children, but it all changes when you have one of your own."

"Which we won't have," he reminded her.

A look of faraway sadness entered her eyes. "Perhaps not." She trailed her fingers down his arm as she made her way back to Kiara, and he wondered for a moment if he should apologize. But for what? He had never wanted children, and he wouldn't change his mind anytime soon. Or ever.

When it came time to leave, Jesper couldn't get out of there fast enough. He swore trails of snot and dirt followed him to the carriage, and he brushed himself off as if trying to eliminate spider webs from his clothing. The trail only seemed to disappear after everyone clambered inside, and the carriage jolted forward up the road toward the lake.

Sam laughed, his arms draped lazily over the seat. "What you just witnessed, Alavara, is Jesper's fear of children."

He glared at his brother. "I'm not afraid of children."

"You wouldn't go near Kiara until she was at least six years old."

"That's not true. I held her as a baby."

"Yes. Once."

"And are you any better? You would think you and Natalia would have had a child by now after all your years of being mated."

His mother grimaced, and he realized his mistake when Sam's smile fell, his eyes becoming suspiciously moist. As if to hide it, he turned his head and stared at the passing trees.

"We have been trying to have a child for *fifty* years," he said quietly. "Natalia has lost four pregnancies in that time. I've wanted to adopt, but Natalia is holding out for a child of our own."

The despair in Sam's expression made his stomach churn as if a horse kicked him. He didn't know how to reply. There was likely nothing he could say to take away his brother's pain. He didn't know the heartache of a mate losing a pregnancy, nor would he ever understand it.

"Oh." Jesper stared in the opposite direction as his brother. "I didn't know. I'm sorry."

Kiara chimed in, saving him from an awkward silence. "Perhaps I can convince Natalia to adopt. And then when you eventually have your own children, you will already have plenty of experience."

Her suggestion brought the smile back to Sam's face. "Come back home with me for a little while when I leave Ichor Knell. I want her convinced sooner rather than later."

Jesper drummed his fingers against his knee and stared intensely at the shah ring on his pinky. He had named his firstborn son his heir with the knowledge that he would never have any children. Who would be next in line for the throne? Would the Ardelean-Degore reign end with him? Perhaps a Covaci would take the throne when he eventually died one day.

Thoughts of the future continued to race through his mind for the rest of the ride to the lake and even when he absently walked along the lake's edge. Someone slipped their hand into his, and he jumped in surprise to find Alavara at his side.

He pulled his hand out of her grip and glanced behind him to find Sam blatantly grinning at them. "My family is watching."

"And? Is it so horrible for them to know we're fond of each other?"

His heart thundered in his chest as he held her gaze. "You're fond of me?"

"Immensely."

He took to staring at his feet while they walked, but a small smile touched the corners of his mouth. He reclaimed her hand and pressed a kiss to her fingers. It was a strange thing to hate Alavara and everything she stood for one minute, and the next to never want to leave her side. These feelings were new to him—eighty-five years' worth of new. And he liked them. A lot.

Locating a canoe resting on the lakeshore, he helped Alavara inside and pushed it toward the water. The bottom of the boat scraped with the movement. Water lapped at his boots before he jumped in himself, rocking the boat as it cut through the blue-green depths. He dipped one oar into the water and then the other, and soon they were gliding across the lake.

Each beat of the oar was like another stroke of peace to his cumbersome soul. Birdsong lifted into the air and joined in with the melody. Clouds lazily rolled past above them.

"It's beautiful out here," Alavara breathed.

"Another place I can usually go to be alone for a while. Although people might be able to see me, they can't hear me think."

She studied him for a moment. "Vampires can't read thoughts, can they?"

He snorted. "No. But being out here helps even my thoughts feel a little more private."

"What are you thinking about right now?"

They reached the middle of the lake. He set the oars down and allowed the boat to float with the natural push and pull of the water. He gazed back into her eyes, wishing he could stare into them all day. They seemed endless, and a desire surfaced in him to reach the very end of the abyss.

"I wish you weren't so unhappy," he said at last, recalling the sadness oozing from her when speaking of her people and customs.

Her fingers fiddled with her necklace as she looked off to the side of the boat. "I'm not unhappy."

"And I'm not a fool. I think you managed to deceive my mother and sister, but you can never deceive me. You hate being a vampire. Do you still consider yourself a *vile creature*? Do you consider me one as well?"

"No," she whispered. "Not you. Never you."

"Then what?" He lifted her chin with his finger to look into her eyes. "You can tell me anything, Alavara. Anything at all."

His ears picked up her increase in heart rate, but after she took a deep breath, her heart slowed, and a smile returned to her face. "I find myself homesick at times. I miss my magic. I miss my friends. I miss my mother."

Still, she smiled. Something wasn't right. What was she hiding from him?

Then again, she rarely spoke of her mother. He thought he might try to convince her to open up. "What happened to your mother? How did she die?"

Her smile faltered.

Ah, she was hiding something about her mother from him. But what?

Once, she opened her mouth. Twice, she opened her mouth. Then she cleared her throat and tucked her necklace into the bodice of her dress. "She has been gone for some time now. I do not wish to speak of it."

"Fair enough. What would you like to speak about?"

"You never finished your list of things you like about me," she said a little too innocently.

"And it better stay that way." He glanced toward the lakeshore to find his father and Sam skipping rocks while his mother and Kiara walked along the water's edge. "If it ended anything like the last time, my family would wish to be anywhere but here."

Her laughter never failed to sprinkle his heart with silver windchimes. "Humor me, Jesper."

"You first."

With graceful, slender fingers, she tucked her hair behind her ear. "I love the way you treat your sister. She is obviously one of the most important people in your life."

Again, he glanced in Kiara's direction and smiled. "She only just turned eighteen. She's much younger than me, and I can't help but feel protective over her, especially because she's under my care."

"Only eighteen? But you and Sam are six years apart. Why is there such a large age gap between you and your sister?"

Sixty-seven years apart to be precise—as old as Alavara was.

He shrugged and leaned against the side of the boat as much as the slight lean would allow. "That's a better question to ask my parents. Though, they often speak of how awful it was to raise me and Sam together. I'm sure they never wanted to have any other children afterward."

"Just watching the two of you interact, I wouldn't want any children after, either."

He rolled his eyes and splashed water into her face. Instead of splashing back like he thought she might, she kicked him lightly in the chest with her foot. He caught onto her foot, his heart pounding when the hem of her dress fell away to reveal her bare ankle. Beautiful and slender and smooth.

"Careful there," she teased. "I thought the goal was to *not* have another repeat of last time."

"Then stop flashing your ankles." Heat rose within him as he set her foot down, and he splashed cold water onto his face in an attempt to cage the beast begging to be released.

"Your turn, Jesper. What do you like about me?"

Too many things. "I like that you can keep up with me in the training arena. If I had to be forced into a union, I'm glad it was with someone who wasn't boring."

"I wish I could say the same about you."

He snarled jestingly and splashed more water at her, but she only laughed.

Through her laughter, she said, "I love your dedication to your kingdom. Sacrifice is written into your every pore."

He blinked in surprise at the sudden shift in conversation. He never thought anyone noticed his sacrifices, and it felt good for someone to point it out. His brain turned off when he blurted, "I love the way you trail your fingers across the wall when deep in thought. Your scent drives me mad wherever I go in the castle."

"Ah." Her eyes twinkled with humor as she cupped the back of his neck and pulled him toward her throat where her scent was the strongest. "You like?"

Yes.

But his tongue refused to work correctly, his words strangled in his throat. A deep, aching warmth entered his heart as he stared back into her eyes, and he did something he'd sworn he would never do.

His fingers slid from her wrist to her forearm, and he grasped it lightly before moving in close to nuzzle his nose against hers. His mate. He was claiming her as his mate. Forever. Always. He wanted her by his side throughout the rest of eternity.

As if recognizing the intimacy of the gesture for what it was, she said nothing but rested her forehead against his. He closed his eyes and took in her sweet berry scent with each inhale. Their breaths danced a slow beat between them.

A trickle of love warmed his heart, and he sighed at the beauty of it. Not just friendship. Not just fondness. But love. Actual, real, incredible love. He was falling in love with Alavara. And oh, how he delighted in it! The frozen brook inside his heart had thawed into a rushing stream. The cobwebs and echoes had blown away as dust in the wind, only for sprouting trees to replace it. Roots took a hold of the tilled landscape, winding and weaving and healing.

"Jesper?" Alavara interrupted his thoughts.

"Hmm?"

He opened his eyes only a fraction to find himself staring back at a pair of playful dark eyes, but it only lasted a moment before she shoved his shoulder with both hands. He cried out, but the sound was smothered as he lost his balance and frigid water engulfed him with a splash. The water soaked his shoes, his clothing, his hair. When he kicked to the surface, water dripped into his face and into his sputtering mouth. Alavara's laughter lifted into the skies, and only grew louder when she noticed his scowl.

His own mischievous grin replaced his frown. He held out a dripping hand to her. "Help me up."

"Nuh uh. I know that trick. I'm not planning on getting wet today—"

He pushed against the boat, and she shrieked as she plunged into the water with him, dress, slippers, and all. She gasped and sputtered and splashed him, but he only splashed back.

"Stop it!" she laughed. "I'm losing my slippers!"

Taking a deep breath, he dove downward and snatched the slippers right off her feet before dragging her under the water. She stuck two fingers up his nostrils and pulled. Bubbles of laughter escaped his mouth and shot upward, and he only just managed to free himself of her grip when his head broke the surface. He took in a deep breath and wrapped an arm around her waist, pulling her closer and nuzzling his face into her neck. She was so warm. Much warmer than the freezing water.

Slowly, her arms wrapped around his neck, and he resorted to holding onto the side of the boat to keep them afloat.

"This dress is heavy," she murmured into his wet hair. "It will drag me down and I'll never be seen again."

"Drowning can't kill you," he murmured right back, his lips against her neck. "It would be one awful recovery, but you can't die from it."

"How strange…"

"Drowning?"

"No. Not dying from things everyone else would die from. There truly is very little that can kill a vampire."

Death was the last thing he wanted to think about when he held his mate securely in his arms. They each were immortal vampires. Neither of them would die anytime soon, especially when he took great pains to protect them from outside threats. He could smell iron from a mile away. He never ventured any place where sunlight might burn him. Salt couldn't kill him unless in large quantities. They were both safe.

He swore to protect her with his life either way.

He moved her closer to the boat. "Hold on," he instructed. "I'll get us back to the shore."

Swimming back was no easy feat, especially with her *and* a boat in tow. But eventually they made it, water dripping off their clothing as they emerged from the lake. Kiara immediately saw to Alavara, fretting over her well-being while Sam offered her his coat. Jesper watched his brother drape the coat over her shoulders, and he took a mental note and tucked it into the back of his mind as something he should do in the future.

The others walked ahead to return to the carriage, and he and his mother fell into step behind.

"You seem happy, Jesper," she said, and despite him being soaked from head to toe, she wrapped her arm around his waist, and he pulled her closer by the shoulders as they walked.

Not able to help himself, he smiled. "I am. Happier than I think I have ever been."

"I'm so glad." She squeezed his waist. "That's all I have ever wanted for you." Their footsteps crunched against the path for a few beats before she turned her head to look at him. "Your father and I agreed we have stayed in Ichor Knell long enough. You are happy with your new mate. Peace has once again settled over the kingdom. And we miss our home."

He swallowed but nodded in understanding. "When are you leaving?"

"By the end of the week. You know you can visit us anytime."

His parents lived in a cottage in a small town much farther east. He only wished he could have more time with them before they returned to their everyday lives.

"I hope your journey is safe."

She squeezed his arm. "It will be."

CHAPTER 21

AFTER THE FREEZING journey home in a topless carriage, Alavara spent far too long soaking in the warm bathtub in the washroom connected to her chambers. She sank lower, only her nose, eyes, and the tips of her ears poking out of the water.

A soft smile claimed her lips as thoughts of Jesper wrapped her in a warm embrace, far warmer than the water in the tub. Who knew that the cold, cunning, fearsome vampire actually had a soft side to his prickly heart? The moment she'd stepped through the thorny gate, his entire countenance toward her had changed. Instead of barbed words, he spoke to her with cautious kindness. Instead of glares and glowers, she often caught him watching her with fondness in those endearing green eyes.

It was too easy to love him.

And loving him was dangerous.

The sigh she breathed out through her nose caused the water to ripple and bend before it stilled into a calm, glassy surface. She fidgeted with both the golden chain hanging around her neck and the silver. She never took off her mother's necklace, and since she had clasped Jesper's sapphire around her neck, she hadn't taken it off, either. Forever a reminder of the vampire she had come to care about far too much.

Stepping out of the bathtub, she slipped a silky blue robe over her shoulders and reached for a drying cloth. She exited the washroom, only for her fingers to snatch the dagger on her dresser. She held it, ready for attack, a menacing snarl on her lips.

Three female servants froze in their tracks, eyeing her cautiously. It appeared as if they were packing her things up.

"What are you doing in my room?" Even more worrisome, how had they gotten permission to enter? How hadn't she heard them? Was she getting sloppy? Or were her ears full of cotton?

Water, more like it.

"If I may, Your Highness." One of them dipped into a curtsy and lowered her gaze to the floor. "His Highness ordered us to take your belongings to his chambers."

Her face blanched.

No. Jesper, no. Please, no.

Her throat clogged with panic, and when her fingers began to tremble, she sheathed her dagger and hid her hands behind her back. This was what she had wanted all along, but that was before she had started to develop feelings for him.

But now…

She cleared her throat and turned toward the window to hide the tears pooling in her eyes. But now, her father's plan was to set in motion. She wasn't ready. She didn't think she would ever be ready.

Stop! she screeched in her mind as black fog spilled through her thoughts, through her memories. All along, her father had wanted her to get close enough to Jesper to share his chambers. But why? And why couldn't she remember? She needed to tell him! She needed to tell him…what?

She didn't know.

Years of practice allowed her to clear her mind of all thoughts, her heart of all feelings. She emptied her entire being until she stared blankly out the window at the birds flitting overhead. Even when the servants finished clearing away her things, and another servant helped dress her and braid her hair, she forced her face into an expressionless mask.

However, the moment she stepped foot outside what was no longer her chambers, her fingers started to shake again. Hollow echoes of each footstep pounded against her ears like the drums of an execution. Vampires nodded, bowed, and curtsied to her as she passed, but she hardly acknowledged any of them. Not when her hands trembled, when sweat slicked across her forehead, when her stomach tied in horrible knots.

She was not nervous. No. She was afraid. For Jesper. He had no idea what he had just done by moving her to his chambers.

And he would not know until it was too late.

Because hard as she tried, she couldn't remember, and she knew the moment she tried to speak to him about it, the fogginess of her father's magic would cloud her mind.

At last, she stood in the hallway outside his chambers. The shimmering barrier to prevent her from entering no longer rippled across his doorway. She knew for a fact that *no one* had access to his chambers, not even the servants.

She stood rooted to the spot, staring at the door handle, but it never turned, almost as if Jesper waited for her to enter first. If she entered those doors, she feared something awful might happen.

She dragged the golden pendant up and down the golden chain of her necklace. Before she could contemplate her choice any further, she turned the door handle and entered.

A gasp of surprise escaped her when the candlelight from dozens of flickering candles greeted her, some sitting on a desk, others on the floor and dresser. Several bouquets of flowers stood tall in vases, and in the very middle of the room...

Jesper stood with his hands in his pockets, a look of uncertainty on his face. He seemed to be waiting for her to say something.

"Jesper, this is...this is..."

He ran a hand down his face. "I knew it. This was too much. Sam suggested it, and I knew I shouldn't have listened, but I did. I'll get rid of all of it, starting with these flowers, and then the candles—"

It took three strides to reach him. She cupped the back of his neck with her hand and stopped his words with a gentle but brief kiss to his lips. She wrapped her arms around his neck and buried her face into his chest. Horrible, heartbreaking thoughts whirled in her mind. Her chin trembled as she pushed them away and focused on the moment, on his scent she had come to love, on the comfort of his arms, on his even breaths.

And his beautiful, steady heartbeat.

"It's perfect," she whispered. "You should listen to Sam more often."

Just as she'd hoped, Jesper grimaced. "I don't think so. Otherwise, you'd be sitting on my lap through every meeting, every audience, and we'd certainly make a fool of ourselves."

She chuckled under her breath. "It can't be as bad as all that."

He grimaced again. "Then you don't know Sam as well as I do. Everything revolves around Natalia. *Everything.*"

After what she'd witnessed when she first met Sam and Natalia, she believed it.

A comfortable, enjoyable silence fell between them. All she wanted was for him to hold her. Forever and always. Now and well into the afterlife.

An acrid, smoky smell choked her nostrils, and she lifted her head from his chest to find flames licking their way up the bottom of his window drapes.

"Jesper," she gasped, pushing away from him. "Your drapes are on fire!"

He swore under his breath and attempted to use his foot to stamp out the flames. When the fire still climbed the fabric, he grabbed a blanket off the edge of his bed and smothered the fire. The acrid burn remained, but the flames sputtered out. He pulled the blanket away to reveal a black singe in the fabric like streaks of black paint on a canvas.

His eyes widened. "Don't you dare tell Sam what happened. I will never live it down."

"I won't." She laughed as she took in the black, ashy burns fringing the drapes. "You need to come up with a good excuse about the burn marks."

His expression turned sheepish—a vulnerability he only seemed to show her. "I think I might be a hopeless case. When I try to do something romantic, it literally ends in flames. What a disappointment our union must be to you."

Shaking her head, she gently held each side of his face and gazed into his forest-green eyes. Such a lovely, beautiful color. "I will take you as you are for as long as I can have you."

"You better settle in then. We have a long life ahead of us."

A response to his comment got lost on her lips, so she simply smiled and tried her hardest not to cry.

Over the years, Alavara had buried many sad memories. The day she had lost her mother. The instance when her father had threatened to mutilate her fingers if she refused to comply with his demands. The night she had wept more tears than there were stars in the sky over all the horrible, nasty things she had done in the name of her father. The person she used to be didn't exist anymore, nor would she ever see the light again.

Yes, they were all sad memories, but none held a flame to what she would face today. Oh, how she despised herself.

Dressed in her riding attire the day after moving to Jesper's chambers, she took a deep, focusing breath before pasting a smile on her face and making sure the smile reached her eyes. She knocked on the door of the council chambers and popped her head inside. The meeting ceased, and judging by the bored expressions of everyone in the room, the meeting wasn't particularly exciting.

Each male in the room stood in her presence like a rumble of thunder drifting across the sky. Twelve in all, with Jesper at the head of the table and Sam sitting near the middle. Sam only seemed interested in attending the meetings just to irritate his brother.

She spoke before giving anyone else a chance. "Jesper, love. I'm headed out for a ride with my father. I don't know about you, but I'm tired of him looking over my shoulder. I think I can convince him to take his army back to Varesia."

"Oh-oh-oh... I-I-I..." Jesper stopped, color rising to his neck. A delightfully wicked grin spread across her lips at his flustered stuttering. He cleared his throat. "How far are you going?"

"I am uncertain. Maybe escorting him back to his camp if I'm lucky."

The color on his neck deepened. He was clearly uncomfortable with others witnessing a personal conversation. "Take a cloak. The clouds will be sparse over there, and you will need protection from the sunlight."

"Don't worry too much. I will be sure to be careful." She smiled at Sam. "Good afternoon, Sam. Try not to vex your brother too much. I will need him in one piece when I return."

Laughter rumbled through the room, and to make matters even worse for Jesper, she blew him a kiss before darting out of sight. More laughter followed in her wake, and she easily imagined Jesper turning bright red from his head to his toes.

As soon as she turned the corner, her smile drooped, and her legs slowed. Her feet felt heavy as if she were trudging through mud. Her fingers brushed against the dagger hilt hidden beneath her dress, strapped to her thigh.

With each step she took toward the stables, her heart sank lower and lower until it rested in the deepest recesses of her stomach. Without a word, she climbed atop a horse her father handed to her, and together, they rode side by side through the forest. Neither dared to say a single word, not when Jesper's spies could be following them this very moment. A hawk flying overhead confirmed her suspicions. Captain Cornell never let her out of his sight when she left the castle. Since the last incident, it seemed Jesper didn't want to risk losing her again.

After nearly an hour of riding, they veered back toward his camp, an army of elven soldiers garbed in golden armor creating a path for them. She knew each face. She knew their names, their families, their stations. She also knew they were loyal to the crown. There would be no bribing any of them to help her out of this situation.

When they reared the horses to a stop, Alavara hopped down and joined her father inside his tent where her older brother, Thalanil, waited. Her heart jumped to her throat upon seeing him, as she hadn't seen him in months. But no recognition flashed across his eyes. Instead, they stared vacantly over her shoulder at the canvas of the tent. She counted herself lucky for having some degree of control over her own body. Thalanil was lost to her father's magical vapor. He had been for many years.

Now out of sight of even Cornell, her father's hand glowed blue, and a shimmering bubble surrounded them, preventing anyone from overhearing their conversation.

"Dealing with vampires is such a pain." He sighed and poured himself a drink at the opposite side of the tent, but when he offered her a drink, she declined. It didn't taste the same anymore now that she was a vampire. "They have eyes and ears everywhere. How can you stand being one?"

She said nothing. She preferred being an elf without the vampire mixed into her blood. But there was no going back now.

The weight of the dwarven dagger strapped to her thigh screamed for her attention. But she waited, watching her father's movements carefully. He, too, watched her closely, never turning his back on her. Besides, her brother could attack faster than an arrow, even under her father's control. If she managed to get past him to her father, it would be a miracle.

The black fog shrouding her brain lifted, and her thoughts and memories tumbled back to her, striking her like lashes to her skull. Emotion pricked her eyes, and it was all she could do to keep herself from weeping. She remembered. All of it. But how could she stop it?

Somehow through the lump in her throat, she said, "Jesper moved me to his chambers."

"I know." He smiled wickedly. "I have eyes and ears everywhere, too." He opened a drawer and pulled out a dagger with the hilt and sheath made of sea-green glass. The blade was visible through the glass, but even with her new vampire sense of smell, she only detected glass and nothing else.

Her father pulled the dagger free of the sheath, and she recoiled as the burning scent of iron smashed into her nose.

An involuntary hiss escaped her throat. Her eyes watered, and she hid her burning nose in the crook of her arm.

Respite from the smolder came only when he sheathed the dagger. The gleam in his eyes grew with every passing second. "The glass masks the scent of the iron. Hide it near the window in your bedchambers to keep him from finding it."

The lump in her throat grew larger. "You forget that mates cannot kill one another. The bond will prevent it."

"And you forget to hold your tongue," he snapped. Calmer, he replied, "I have found a way around the bond. Take this."

He held out a vial of deep purple liquid encased in the same sea-green glass as the dagger. Her voice escaped as a mere whisper. "What is it?"

"An elixir of sorts. It will only last sixty seconds, which should be more than enough time to finish the deed. It will suppress the bond by stripping away every last one of your emotions. You need to do it before your in-laws leave the city. You said they witnessed your *love* for each other. They can vouch for you on his behalf when he is dead."

No. I can't. I can't!

Slowly, her fingers moved closer to her concealed dagger.

"Killing him only two days after moving into his chambers will be suspicious. If they don't point fingers at me, they will point them at you."

Her father swallowed another mouthful of liquor and glanced toward the tent flap as if checking to make sure his magical barrier still held. "Take a closer look at the dagger."

She did. A sharp intake of breath. Movement rippled through the weapon like water, the iron forged in a way that was native to Tatteson. Understanding hit her, adding to the uncomfortable sensation already churning in her belly. "You plan to blame King Daudi for the assassination."

"Yes," he confirmed with a nod. "I think it will be far too easy to falsely incriminate him."

With every word spoken, her stomach churned and churned until she thought she might retch. A tear trailed down her cheek, followed by another, at the thought of Jesper covered in his own blood. To never hold him again... To never hear his rare laugh or see his uncertain smile...

Her father clicked his tongue. "Just like your mother. So quick to tears. You'll need them once he's dead."

He moved close enough to set down his glass, near enough to smell the liquor on his breath. Alavara moved quickly as she snatched the dwarven blade strapped to her thigh, unsheathed it, and plunged it downward. Just when her father cried out in alarm, Thalanil stopped the momentum of the dagger with a strong arm around her wrist. He squeezed hard enough for her to drop the weapon before throwing her onto the grassy floor on her stomach. He pinned her down by the neck and smashed her face into a mound of dirt.

Alavara bucked and screamed as she tried to throw her brother off her, as she fought against his superior strength. She thrashed harder as she noticed her father's boots approaching closer by the second until they stood only inches in front of her face.

"No!" she shrieked as she bared her fangs and tried to attack him with her hands alone, but Thalanil also pinned them to the ground beneath his knees. "I won't kill him! I won't!"

But her father only chuckled and stooped down to put himself closer to eye level. "I'm afraid you don't have a choice."

"Please, Thalanil," she begged. "You can fight him. Please!"

But her brother's eyes remained glossed over. And when her father reached for her, she shrieked as loud as her lungs allowed, praying for Cornell to hear her even through the magical elven barrier. But no one rushed to her rescue.

A wildness claimed her soul as she thrashed again, this time managing to free one arm. She twisted beneath her brother and smashed her palm against his throat. He stumbled backward, enough for her to roll onto her feet. Against her brother and father combined, she knew she would never win a brawl.

Instead, she sprinted for the opening of the tent. But instead of passing through the barrier, it threw her backward, and she landed hard on her side. Pain coursed through her entire body, stunning her enough for her father to place his hands over her head.

She lifted her foot to kick him. He dodged. And then his dark power slithered into her mind and pierced a hole through her free will. Slowly, her body became limp when his magical strength far outmatched her own, which was now nonexistent. Her elven magic had been the only thing keeping him from commanding her completely.

And now?

Her limbs fought for control, but no matter how hard she tried, she couldn't lift them.

"Jesper Degore must be dead before his parents leave the city," her father hissed.

A shudder ran through Alavara's body. Tears trailed down her cheeks as he thrust the glass-sheathed iron dagger into her palm.

"Go," he ordered. "Tell no one." The darkness slithered thicker, faster, as his power weaved through her mind like sturdy strings, and she was his puppet. "And forget this conversation ever happened."

The next few minutes passed in a blur until Alavara found herself on her horse, headed away from her father's camp and back toward the castle. Uneasiness crept through her soul as she gazed back at the numerous white tents pitched in neat rows with elven soldiers wearing armor and carrying golden weapons prowling the area. She vaguely recalled speaking to her father. And then...nothing.

"What did you do, Father?" she murmured as she placed her hands on either side of her head. She felt his power, barely perceptible, swirl within her mind. But it was as if it lay dormant, waiting for the right moment to strike.

With a frown, she turned her attention toward Ichor Knell and kicked her horse's flanks, spurring the creature into a gallop. She needed to warn Jesper about her father's power. She needed to—

Confusion spun her head until her train of thought dissolved like sugar in water. She wasn't sure what she needed to tell Jesper. But judging from the uneasiness in her stomach, she thought it best to keep her distance. At least, as much as she was able to.

CHAPTER 22

THALANIL'S FEET THUNDERED across crisp grass. Frigid air entered his lungs with each rapid inhale and left his mouth as a foggy cloud. Dark mists curled around him, blinding the path out of the dense, black fog. Confusion burned him as he turned every which way, only to find the mists nearly obstructing his view of towering pines, tall enough to reach the heavens.

How long had he been stuck within these forests?

Too long, his consciousness answered for him, though he couldn't recall exactly how long.

"Please, Thalanil. You can fight him. Please!"

He started at the sound of his name, at the desperation in the familiar voice echoing through his mind. He knew that voice. He'd heard it throughout his life but couldn't recall who it belonged to.

An intense pain shot through him, and he cried out as he sank to his knees, clutching his head. The agony persisted but he fought against it despite the discomfort rippling through his body.

He blinked once, twice. His surroundings brightened from foreboding woods to a white, canvas tent. His heart skipped at the sight of a woman with long black hair exiting the tent while his father intensely watched her departure.

Thalanil's jaw clenched as the surprise of controlling his own body struck him. But the longer he held onto his control, the more it bended, threatening to snap.

His gaze darted to the dwarven dagger lying on the soft grass, and while his father's back was turned, he snatched it up and sheathed it inside the waistband of his trousers.

And then his brittle control snapped in half. His eyes glazed over, and his body slammed back to cold, damp earth, black mists once again shrouding his vision.

Confusion crumbled around him as he tried to place his surroundings. But no matter how hard he attempted to break through the thick fog, it remained. And he quickly became lost within its dark depths.

CHAPTER 23

Alavara was acting distant, and it made Jesper uneasy.

Had he done something wrong? Or perhaps spending time with her father had set her off, as she'd avoided him since she'd returned from the excursion. When the elven king finally left the kingdom, only then would everyone be able to breathe easier.

Jesper entered his chambers at the end of the day, and relief spread through him when he found Alavara standing beside the window, her long, dark hair flowing like a waterfall down her back. She turned to smile at him, and the sight nearly melted him into a puddle on the floor. There was nothing better than coming home to one's mate after a hard day at work.

Yet… Aloofness still settled in her eyes.

"Won't you look outside? It's a bit dreary tonight." She looked at him expectantly, a fierce hope shining in her eyes.

He approached the window cautiously, eyeing her while trying to make sense of her strange behavior. Glancing out the window, he found nothing unusual. At least not for him. Dark clouds swirled lazily up ahead. Lanterns lit up the city below. A few drunks sang bawdy tunes and stumbled down the street.

"Umm…yes? It always looks like that, Alavara. If you want a different view, you need to visit the countryside."

"Look closer," she insisted. "I think the smudge on the window is distorting your vision."

"I have seen all I need to see. If you want to tour the countryside, I can make it happen. As soon as your father leaves the city with his army. He *is* leaving, isn't he?"

She faced her back to him as if upset. His eyebrows furrowed in confusion, but when he turned her back around to face him, she simply smiled at him.

"Are you all right, Alavara? Is something bothering you?"

"I just…" She swallowed, looking back and forth between his eyes. "I *really* would like you to take a thorough look out the window."

Heavens, was she about to cry? Over a window? He supposed it might be that time of month. He'd never had to deal with females in an intimate sense before, and therefore didn't have much experience with such things.

Just to appease her, he stepped closer to the window, wiped his sleeve across the glass to remove any smudges, and stared at every inch of Ichor Knell within sight. The forest. The buildings. The lanterns. The streets. The skies. The vampires out and about at the late hour. It was a peaceful night, like the stillness before a coming storm.

"Is there something in particular you would like me to see?" he asked. He turned to face her, only to watch her expression fall with disappointment. Honestly... Females and their monthly bleedings... He made a mental note to ask Kiara more about it to better understand his mate.

"I think..." Distress coated her eyes in a layer of stain. "I think you should send me back to my own chambers."

"Why?" The rhythm of his heart increased, and not in a good way. Panic. It started to rise within him, but he forced his expression into a neutral calm. "You have been distant all day. Have I done something to upset you?"

She shook her head. "No. Not at all. I just think it would be best."

Kiara's words from a couple of years ago surfaced in his mind when she had cried and sniffled as she painted. *Don't mind me, Jesper. If I say something terrible in the next few days, please disregard it. I don't mean it. These monthly bleedings are awful.*

Perhaps Alavara simply wanted to be alone during this time. She shouldn't have to go through it by herself. "I would rather you stay. Take your slippers off and lie down."

"Jesper—"

"Please. You gave me a nice massage earlier. I would like to return the favor."

Without another word, she did as he asked. He knelt on the end of the bed and took one of her feet in his hands, watching as she melted back into the pillows with a sigh.

He dug his thumb into the arch of her foot. "I would like you to teach me the pressure points to heal. At least as much as you know."

"You haven't even mastered *Erbrumthin* yet."

"Are you saying I must first learn to hurt before I can learn to heal?"

She lifted her head off the pillow to look him in the eye. "What I'm saying is you are too ambitious for your own good."

A smile tugged on his lips, and he put more focus into the task. Usually, he would stay up to odd hours of the night to work, but how could he do it anymore when he had someone waiting for him? He would never admit it to Sam's face, but he was right. Having a mate was better than working. *Far better.*

With the exciting reminder, he dropped her foot and plopped down on the bed beside her, rattling the mattress. The sadness in her eyes just wouldn't do. He gently took a hold of her face, leaned her head to one side, and moved closer to her ear as if about to tell her a secret. At the last second, he allowed his serpent transformation to wash over his tongue only. It darted from his mouth, and he hissed in her ear.

"Stop that!" She grinned and pushed him away.

"Why?"

"It's harrowing."

His eyes flashed yellow like a snake's. She shrieked with laughter and grabbed the nearest pillow to smack him in the face, which led into a game of tickling one another. Soon enough, they were both laughing and rolling over each other until he pinned her by the wrists and gazed down at her. Her dark eyes captivated him, churning his stomach with beautiful emotions, far more beautiful than he'd ever known existed.

With the tip of his finger, he traced the points and curves of her ears. He trailed his finger across her eyebrows, down her nose and lips, and along her jaw.

"I love you," he breathed.

The words escaped without his consent, but he welcomed them, nonetheless. The warmth of love embraced him from his toes to his heart to the loving gaze he directed at her. Never in his life had he loved a female. Never. But he loved Alavara. Daggers, he loved her. So much.

Her smile melted off her face.

She cried one red-tinted watery tear and then another, but she never broke his gaze. "I do not deserve your love."

Disappointment replaced the warmth inside him, and he fell onto one elbow as he continued to hold her gaze. She did not say the words back to him like he thought she might. Had he misinterpreted her feelings? Did she need more time? Did she not feel the same way?

"I'm sorry," he said quietly. "Should I have kept my feelings to myself?"

She shook her head. "I need to tell you something." She stared at him intensely, her mouth closing and opening and closing again.

"What is it?"

"I don't know." A sniff escaped her, followed by several tears trailing down her face. "I don't remember. It's important."

"Shhhh," he tried to soothe as he gathered her in his arms and held her close. "You'll remember in the morning."

"No!" she shrieked, startling him with the desperation in her voice, in her eyes. "I need to remember *now*. It has to do with...my bracelet." She squeezed her eyes shut. "Argh! I cannot remember."

He fiddled with her beaded bracelet and turned it around on her wrist as he studied it. Nothing seemed amiss. He paused, discomforted by the panic in her eyes. "Is it us?"

"No, it's my father. He's...argh! My head hurts. I cannot remember." Her weeping worsened as she clutched her head as if pained. Between breaths, she gasped out, "Jesper, I'm scared. This is important."

"Shhhh," he soothed again as he caressed her shoulder with his thumb. "Everything will be fine in the morning."

"But it won't. Because...because..." She squeezed her eyes shut, and he ran his fingers over her hair to try to calm her down. "You mean too much to me," she sobbed. "I never want to be without you."

"I'm not going anywhere." He frowned when she said no more but instead cried herself to exhaustion until she fell asleep against his shoulder. The visit with her father had set her off, he was sure of it. But what warranted such an explosive reaction?

He kissed the top of her head and pulled the bedspread over them to keep them warm. First thing in the morning, he planned to bring it up again. Until then, he wanted her to rest.

Alavara woke in a daze, her head foggy and her vision unclear. A hush descended upon the castle aside from the sharp breeze rattling the windows and rustling through branches outside. The darkness surrounding her indicated it was just after midnight.

What was she doing awake?

Hot tears startled her as they trailed down her face, and she turned to find her mate beside her, sleeping. For a few moments, she listened to Jesper's deep, even breathing, his face peaceful as he slept. She attempted to move closer, to tangle her body with his and hold him close, but it didn't obey her.

Her eyes snapped wide open when she slipped her legs out from the warm bed sheets and placed her feet onto the cold floor, moving away from him rather than toward. *No, no, no!*

she tried to scream, but the words caught in her throat, her father's magic not allowing them to escape.

Jesper's peaceful slumber haunted her as she approached the window and dislodged the vial and glass dagger from the corner of the windowpane.

She'd tried to get him to notice the dagger to get around her father's strong magic. But he hadn't. Even when it had been mere inches from his face.

A quiet sob of heartache threatened to rise to her throat but was unable to get past the thick wall of black magic.

She fought against her body, but her movements were no longer her own. Her lips refused to move, to warn him of the danger. Her legs worked on their own accord as if a puppeteer controlled her from somewhere out of sight as she slowly approached Jesper's side of the bed.

Stop! she screamed at herself. But it was as if someone else controlled her body rather than herself. *I just need to unsheath the dagger early. To wake him with the potent smell.* But her hand shook at the effort at fighting her father's magic.

Her hands trembled as her grip tightened on the vial of elixir, as she fought against unstopping it. Heartache slammed into her as if she were a fragile straw cottage weathering a turbulent storm. Straw crumbled around her bit by bit until nothing remained over her head to protect her from the howling winds and ferocious rain. Large droplets of water pounded down on her and leaked from her very soul in the form of tears, the only thing her father couldn't seem to control.

She fought with every fiber of her soul, willing herself to unsheath the dagger, to wake Jesper with the stinging scent of iron.

But instead of accomplishing the task, she lost the battle as she unstopped the vial of elixir. Her hands trembled as she lifted it to her lips. And then without her willful consent, she drank its contents.

Within moments, her tears stopped, her eyes hardened, and not a sliver of emotion claimed her heart. The fierce winds stilled. The rain ceased. Her heart hardened into a block of cold steel. When she looked in Jesper's direction, she felt nothing. No remorse. No heartache. No love. Only steel emptiness.

Her fingers tightened around the glass of the dagger. Even through the veil of the emotionless void inside her heart, she fought like a ferocious beast trying to break free of its cage.

You. Do not. Control me! she screamed in her mind as she battled her father's influence. But in a quick movement, almost as if her father fought her back, she unsheathed the iron dagger and grasped the glass handle with both hands. She fought with all her might, mind, and strength but only managed to delay herself by a single second before she plunged the dagger downward.

Jesper awoke with a start as something burned his nostrils, strong like smelling salts. He spotted the glint of metal, and his hands shot upward as a defensive reflex. The movement shifted his body just a fraction before the scorching dagger pierced his chest. He cried out as fiery pain erupted, seeping through his ribs.

Years of defensive training kicked in. He grabbed the assassin by the wrist, hooked his leg around their torso, and together they flipped over the bed, and he landed hard on top of them on the floor. But instead of scenting a human or an elf or a dwarf, he distinguished the familiar sweet berry scent of an equally familiar vampire.

His eyes widened as he found himself staring down at Alavara, except it wasn't her. Her eyes were glazed over, no flicker of recognition in their depths. She didn't try to wriggle free from beneath him. Her tears trailed from empty eyes as she stared at him.

Shock wore off, and he fully felt the agony of the wound, the dagger sticking out of him. Blood gushed from his chest and soaked his shirt, and only then did the panic set in. It didn't heal. It didn't heal!

Iron. Alavara had stabbed him with an iron dagger.

Pain roared through his chest, spreading like a wildfire in a dizzying breeze. He felt like a helpless animal trapped in the flames, unable to escape. He gasped in air, each breath harder to draw into his lungs than the last.

Fear took a hold of him. True, agonizing fear. She had just tried to kill him. His own mate. And by the surge of pain spreading through his chest, he thought she might still be successful.

"Captain!" he choked. His own weight was too much to bear, and he collapsed onto his side. "Captain!"

Moments later, as if keeping watch in the hallway, Captain Cornell burst into the room. His eyes widened as he took in both their blood-stained clothes. "Your Majesties!" He rushed toward Alavara as if she was the victim.

"Don't help her!" His voice was a shriek. Of pain. Of fear. Of bitter betrayal. Cornell stopped in his tracks. "Take her…" Blood filled his mouth, drowning him from the inside out. "Take her to the private dungeons. Now! Tell no one…" He coughed and sputtered, and when his chest burned with the dagger lodged inside, he ripped it out of himself. His own screech sounded foreign to his ears, and he breathed heavily through the pain. "Tell no one she is there. Tell no one what happened."

As if suddenly loosed from the spell that had seemed to take a hold of her, Alavara started to weep as Cornell dragged her to her feet, the captain now realizing what had happened. The spell on her seemed to have broken, but when blood continued to gush from his chest, it was the least of his worries.

"Sire," Cornell argued. "Allow me to treat your wound."

"Get her out!" he shouted. His next words came in slurred, panting breaths. "Send for Zachariah. Send for my family."

The captain nodded, and his grip tightened on Alavara as he dragged her weeping out of the room.

A choked sob strangled him, cutting into the silence of the night. It was too much. Too much pain. He couldn't handle it. His body shivered. His hands trembled. And he was covered in his own blood.

He didn't know how much time passed of panting, sobbing, pained breaths. Too much. But then the door slammed open, followed by frantic footsteps. More than one pair. He couldn't lift his head enough to look.

"Jesper!" his mother screeched, suddenly at his side. She grabbed either side of his face, but his gaze couldn't focus on hers. "No, please, no!"

His chin trembled as he opened his mouth. It hurt so much to speak. "It-it-it was Alavara. Sh-sh-she's in the dungeons." He gripped her hand with what little strength remained, his eyes frantic. "H-h-her eyes were wrong. F-f-find out why she did it. Promise me!"

She only continued to sob.

"I-I-I'm going to die. I can't s-s-survive this one."

"No," his father growled at his other side. "You won't die. Zach, help me lift him onto the bed."

A guttural screech escaped his throat as he was lifted from the ground by his legs and arms, the blinding, searing pain almost knocking him unconscious. He wished it had—then he wouldn't be forced to endure this agony.

Each breath cut into him like a knife, each panting sob gutting his chest. He only barely registered the bed sinking with weight beside him moments before a gentle hand smoothed back his hair.

Kiara.

"Jesper," Zachariah said in a professionally calm manner, still wearing his night clothes. Although he tried to turn his head in his uncle's direction, his neck refused to obey him. "By the fact that you're still conscious, I'm hopeful your heart is untouched. This is what we're going to do. I'm going to clean out the wound as much as possible to clear it of iron. Next, I will stitch it up." Hands began to cut his shirt off his body, and while they worked, his uncle continued to speak. "You are losing too much blood, and the iron wound will make it impossible for your body to heal as quickly as usual. There is no coming back from a wound like this if we don't hurry. You need to be cooperative."

"Sam, Willow, help me hold him down," his father ordered, and they pinned each of his limbs to the bed.

Zachariah touched a white cloth to his chest, and Jesper's body thrashed as if scalded with a brand. He screeched louder than he had ever screeched before, the sound promptly muffled by a pillow that someone smothered into his face. The searing lightning continued to strike his chest like ripples of bolts stretching across the sky. He sobbed. He screeched. He thrashed. He begged his god and goddess to make it stop.

The pain turned from intense fire to an aching throb. His hands trembled uncontrollably, and as if satisfied he would no longer screech, someone removed the pillow from his face. Tears covered his sister's cheeks. She held onto his trembling hand while simultaneously stroking his hair. Everything hurt. Everything.

Prick. Tug.

He winced. The sting of the needle was nothing compared to the burning hell of iron.

Prick. Tug. Prick. Tug. Prick. Tug.

His eyelids drooped, his body feeling far away. Heavy. He felt heavy like an invisible thread pulled him down, down, down. This was it. This was what moments before death felt like, like sinking to the bottom of a lake to never again surface.

He gave in to the gentle pull, and darkness consumed him.

CHAPTER 24

INTENSE, HEART-WRENCHING agony ripped through Alavara as if she had been the one to get stabbed. The look of betrayal in Jesper's eyes had undone her. His blood. So much blood. It covered her, soaked her nightgown. Drops of it smeared across her chin and neck, mingling with her unceasing tears.

"Jesper," she sobbed as Captain Cornell dragged her into the dark depths of the private dungeon. "Jesper!"

He roughly threw her into a cell and locked it behind him. Her knees scraped against the hard stone ground, but her minor wound started to heal, unlike her mate's mortal wound. She wasn't sure if he was dead.

And not knowing destroyed her.

A scream burst out of her mouth as she clawed at her head, trying to dispel her father's magic. But it stuck fast to every pore in her body.

The thought of losing her dear mate ripped her apart to shreds from the inside out, an intensity she hadn't expected even after she'd fought against her father's plan. It was like jumping into a burning building, her body fighting to heal itself as fire seared her skin.

She wasn't sure how long she cried in a fetal position when footsteps alerted her to someone's approach. In the flickering torchlight, a head of red hair came into view, followed by a head of brown hair. An anxious pit formed in her stomach. Sam and Willow stopped short of the cell. No tears spilled from her eyes. Only the hazy smoke of self-hatred escaped.

She hated herself for not being stronger. She hated herself for what she'd done.

Willow uttered three words that crumbled her world into a pile of shriveling dust. "Jesper is dead."

Alavara's tears fell fast and hard, and the deep, black chasm of pain within her heart opened up until she could no longer see the bottom. Her mate. Her beautiful mate. She had done this. This was her fault.

Her mother-in-law remained where she stood but watched her carefully. "Why did you do it?"

"I—" Black fog shrouded her thoughts, and she released another frustrated wail as she clawed at her head. "Get it out," she sobbed. "Get it out!"

When her nails did nothing but cut her skin, she reached through the bars blindingly fast and snatched the dagger Willow wore on her belt and unsheathed it. But before she managed to stab herself in an attempt to purge the darkness, Sam caught her wrist and yanked the weapon away.

She crumpled onto the floor as pure agony ripped through her head. She fought against the black magic, but the harder she fought, the more it hurt. She writhed on the ground and sobbed, both from frustration and from the heartache of losing her mate.

What had she done? What had she done?

"Jesper," she whimpered. "Jesper."

"Call for Zachariah," Willow ordered, but Sam shook his head.

"I think we need Ingrid."

They both paused, and although she felt their gazes on her, she only managed to weep. If only she could open her mouth and explain. If only she could remember what she wanted to say. But each time she reached for a word, it floated just out of reach.

Another wail climbed her throat as she clawed at her head until ribbons of blood trailed down her face and neck. But no matter how hard she tried, the darkness remained.

She picked up the wooden cot in the corner and snapped one of the legs off. But before she managed the attempt to knock the fog out of herself, the metal door of her cell screeched open. Sam grabbed her arm and stabbed her with a needle.

Immediately, her head became woozy in a physical sense rather than within her mind. She stumbled on her feet as her vision darkened, and she was barely aware of a pair of arms catching her before she hit the ground.

Jesper slowly opened his eyes, blinking back the bright light entering the windows. He recognized his own room enough to know he wasn't dead, but he sure felt like it. His chest hurt. Every breath he took pained him. His head throbbed with a fierce ache. He still tasted blood in his mouth.

He blinked against the ache in the back of his skull and turned his head to find Kiara cuddled next to him on the bed while Sam stood at the window, staring out with his hands behind his back.

"Sam," he croaked, wincing at the pain of speaking.

His brother spun around and reached the bed in a few strides while Kiara's grip tightened on his arm where she lay next to him. "Thank the stars," Sam muttered. "We were worried you wouldn't ever wake."

Despite the gentle hand Sam placed over his heart, Jesper grunted at the pain, and it was all he could do to hold back the sting in his eyes. His brother kept his hand there for half a minute as if testing to see how strong his heart beat.

Mild relief followed when he took his hand off his chest, but it still burned. He glanced down to find himself without a shirt, a white bandage wrapped around his torso. Alavara had stabbed him with the intent to kill.

"Where is my mate?"

"In the dungeon still."

"And what of my people? Do they know what happened?"

Sam shook his head. "We concocted a story about you consuming bad blood from the kitchens. It's enough of an excuse for you to stay bedridden, but we had to punish the butcher to make the story more believable."

Jesper didn't want to ask what they did to the poor man as punishment. At the moment, he was too exhausted to care.

His mother slipped into the room, and as if overjoyed to find him conscious, she rushed to his side and kissed his forehead and both cheeks. He normally would have rolled his eyes and pushed her away, but his body felt so weak that he could hardly even lift his hand.

He needed to know.

"Did you speak to Alavara?"

Her eyes hardened. "Sam and I tried. There is something not right about her. She thinks you are dead, and I convinced her you are to give her the benefit of the doubt, to see her reaction. She was devastated."

He sighed in relief but winced when the action pained him. "Then she's innocent."

"I don't know." His mother bit her lip. "We summoned Ingrid to the palace. She might be able to figure out what's happening to Alavara."

"Ingrid the witch?"

She nodded. "But you must be prepared to face the fact that she might have tried to kill you on purpose."

His chin trembled. This time not from pain, but from intense heartache. He willed himself to keep from falling apart in front of Sam who watched quietly at the foot of the bed, but the raw emotion refused to let him have his way.

"But mates can't kill one another." If he hadn't moved a fraction before she'd stabbed him, he would be dead right now.

His mother's eyebrows furrowed as she produced an empty glass vial from the pocket of her skirts. "She consumed an elixir that would strip her of all emotions. Your father makes them all the time for our customers when they can no longer handle the grief of losing a loved one. But those elixirs usually last days. This one was infused with magic to only last a minute."

Understanding dawned on him. Sixty seconds was long enough to kill him, and when the elixir wore off, her inevitable grief over his death would have saved her from accusation.

"No." His voice sounded wet to his ears. "No. She wouldn't have killed me. She loves me. I know she does."

Even his words were hollow as uncertainty leaked through his voice. How could he be so certain of her love? She had never told him of her feelings. Besides, one didn't stab the person they loved.

"I'm so sorry, Jesper," she whispered. "This doesn't look good. But we are holding onto hope until Ingrid arrives."

Fire erupted through his chest as he reached to move aside the blankets covering him, but before his feet touched the ground, his mother tried to push him back into the pillows.

"I need to speak to her. I need to hear it from her own mouth."

"Jesper, no. You are weak. If you lose any more blood, you can still die."

"I need to see her. I need to." He fought against her again despite his protesting wound. "I need to see her!" he shouted.

She ended up winning, and the moment she pushed him onto his back, his aching heart burst with anguish. A sob bubbled up his throat, then another, and soon enough, the flow of tears refused to yield. He buried his face in his right arm, the only one he could lift, and wept.

Despite the uncertainty surrounding the incident, if he survived the stabbing, if the wound healed, he feared his heart would forever be broken.

Sam refused to leave Jesper's side for a single moment since the stabbing. What was he afraid of? He wasn't sure. Maybe that Alavara or her wicked father would return to finish the job. Another part of him didn't want his brother to face this by himself. He couldn't imagine anything more heart-wrenching than being betrayed by his mate.

He watched as Jesper lay unmoving in his bed while staring out the window with bleak, hopeless eyes. Jesper was broken. Completely, utterly broken.

"What?" Jesper asked without breaking his gaze from the window. "Nothing to say? It's so unlike you."

When Sam spoke, his voice was raspy. "What can I possibly say? This...this is unforgivable. You almost *died*, Jesper."

"Death would be a better alternative than this." His brother took in a slow breath and released a melancholy exhale as if his fragile spirit cracked a little more. How many more cracks would it take for it to break completely?

His own heart ached fiercely for his brother. The pain he must be in...

He noticed Jesper's bandages were soaked through again, and he moved toward the door with the intent to send for Zachariah for more. However, Jesper's voice stopped him in his tracks.

"What would you have done if Natalia had done it to you?"

He swallowed. Just the thought of Natalia using him, deceiving him, playing with his emotions, and then trying to kill him created an overwhelming ache in his body. They still didn't know if that's what happened with Alavara, but... It seemed very likely considering the evidence. "I don't know. I can't even begin to imagine."

Jesper said nothing more as he returned his defeated gaze to the window.

265

CHAPTER 25

THE DUNGEON DOORS shrieked open, followed by slow, labored footsteps. Alavara tucked herself tighter into a ball and stared with empty eyes at the wall. All her tears had dried a long time ago, and nothing else remained. Her heart ached so fiercely that death would have been a much more compassionate alternative. Her dear Jesper... Dead at her hands.

How could she have done such a thing?

The wicked, black smoke within her curled around her heart. Choking. Suffocating.

Dark elf.

Her mother had once told her that dark magic didn't just have to be used with malicious intent. It could be used to protect, to heal, to love. All she had used it for was to lie, to hurt, to kill, albeit against her will. But if she had been stronger, perhaps this wouldn't have happened.

The footsteps stopped just outside her cell. Labored breathing filled the silence of the dungeon. Her body ached too much to turn her head, so she simply continued to stare at the slick, rocky walls, at the moisture collecting on the surface and dripping slowly to the ground.

Whoever stood outside the cell said nothing, but they didn't leave. A grunt, then the sound of someone sliding back against the wall and sitting. The guards never stayed to watch her. Unless the guard was Cornell.

A familiar scent wafted past her nose, the fresh scent of forest leaves the same color as beautiful green eyes like the summer trees in Varesia.

Alavara gasped, her head snapping in the direction of the new arrival. He sat with his back against the wall, his head between his knees. But the deep red color of the hair was unmistakable. The broad shoulders. The lean build. And the scent. She would never forget his scent.

"Jesper," she breathed, launching herself to her feet and grasping onto the bars of the cell. Her heart thrummed back to life as she took a breath of him, her gaze roaming across every speck of him. "You're alive," she choked. "You're alive."

He breathed in and out, in and out, and he still didn't lift his head to look at her. If only she could break through these bars and hold him in her arms. But she lost the right to do such a thing the moment she'd plunged a dagger into his chest.

Besides, she feared her father's magic might take control of her again and finish the deed.

Finally, he said, "Mates are supposed to trust each other. I trusted you, Alavara. And then you stabbed me."

Her chin trembled. Her hands shook. "You don't understand." But her words halted in her mouth, and she fought for the explanation slipping through her fingers like sand.

He lifted his head, not to look at her, but to lean back and stare at the ceiling. Red-tinted tears escaped his eyes, and he didn't bother hiding them. She had never seen him cry before. Never.

"Please don't cry, Jesper. I cannot bear it."

Her heart stopped beating for a moment as she took in his unbuttoned shirt, which revealed the white bandage wrapped around his chest and shoulder. Patches of red leaked through, as if the trek to the dungeons had cost him.

"Jesper," she rasped. "You're bleeding."

"Of course, I'm bleeding," he snapped. Then in an exhausted, watery tone, he said, "You stabbed me with an iron blade."

The silence that followed filled her soul with agony. "What are you going to do to me? Am I to expect an execution?"

"An execution?" Finally, his gaze found hers in the dim light of the dungeon. "Never. But we need to have a serious conversation. My mother has spoken with a witch through a magic mirror. Ingrid thinks you might be controlled by dark magic."

Alavara sagged against the bars in relief, and her eyes fluttered closed.

"I'll take that as a yes," he continued before he grunted as he changed positions. "I keep going over every conversation we'd had. You were trying to warn me about the iron blade inside the glass sheath near the window. And you were so scared that night... Is this why? Because you knew what was going to happen to me?"

Her eyebrows pinched together as she sifted through her thoughts, but when they scattered, she sighed. "I don't remember."

Another grunt as he moved closer. "You weren't the same after you came back from seeing your father. What did he do to you?"

She vaguely recalled white tents, a shimmering ward, and a swift horseback ride. And then...

"My brother." Pain flashed in her mind, and she dug her nails into her head. "Make it stop," she whimpered. "I beg you."

"We'll try, love," he murmured as he reached through the bars and intertwined his fingers with hers. "We'll try."

Emotion shook her to the core as she stared at their hands. She'd held those hands many times. She'd kissed them. She'd memorized each indent and groove. "Why are you being so kind? I tried to kill you."

He squeezed her fingers and lowered his voice until his words intimately caressed her. "Because you are my mate. Whatever is going on, we will figure it out together."

Despite the heartache resting between them, she cracked a smile. "I thought you hated names of endearment."

He chuckled but winced. Perspiration dotted his entire face, and her concern for his welfare burned hotter. "I'm still unsure about it. But it's growing on me." He reached through the bars with his other hand and threaded his fingers through her hair, and she sighed at his gentle touch. She'd thought she'd never get to hold him again. "You've had a difficult time answering my questions. Let's try 'yes' and 'no' instead. Look to the right for yes, and the left for no."

"I can't…"

"Just try." He squeezed her hand again. "Is your mother truly dead?"

She managed to answer out loud. "Yes."

"Did your father kill her?"

Her eyelids shuttered closed as the dark fog clamped her mouth shut. But before it took her thoughts, too, she smiled sadly. "My mother was a beautiful woman. I miss her so much. He—" The fog threatened to scatter her thoughts, so she attempted to take it in another direction. "Many of my memories of her are gone."

And then she glanced to the right, grateful when it worked.

"Gone?" he asked. "Where did they go?"

An ache pounded in her head like an unforgiving drum, and she placed her hand against her temple.

"Did your father take them?" he prodded.

"Why do you assume he has done anything?"

"Because he was the last person you saw. I am putting the puzzle pieces together. But I need your help."

With a nod, she leaned her aching head against the bars, and he rested his temple against hers. She shuddered with relief at having him near. "Yes or no questions," she reminded.

They leaned away from each other so he could watch her respond to his inquiries.

"Do you want to kill me?" he asked.

She glanced to the left.

"Does your father?"

She swallowed and glanced to the right.

"Why?" he murmured, almost to himself. "I have upheld the treaty. I have done everything he asked of me." His fingers glanced over the skin on her hand as if to tell her he didn't regret it. "What is he trying to gain?"

But then a shuddering breath escaped his lips, and he swayed where he sat. Shame crowned her head like a wreath of broken glass as he sucked in a sharp breath, his eyes squeezing shut as if overcome by a sudden pain. Her heart dropped to her feet. She could only watch helplessly while he fought through pain she had caused.

A whimper escaped her lips, her head bowed. She would make this right. She swore it to herself. No matter what she had to do to accomplish her goal. Even at her own expense.

He blew out a long breath as he grimaced. "Mother, I know you're listening. Can you help me to my chambers?"

The dungeon door squeaked open immediately, and Willow rushed inside. She wrapped her arm around Jesper's waist, and he groaned as she hoisted him to his feet. Hostility in the woman's gaze stared back at her. Caution. Distrust.

"She didn't answer all of your questions," Willow said.

Jesper breathed heavily as he swayed where he stood, eyes closed. "I'm going to pass out. Is Ingrid here yet?"

"No, not yet."

Perspiration matted his hair and dripped down his face as he gazed regretfully at Alavara. "Forgive me. You need to remain here. I'm not strong enough to fight you off if you..." He trailed off, and she lowered her gaze in shame.

"I understand." She gripped the bars as she blinked back tears. "I'm so sorry for my hand in this. I wish I could tell you everything. I just can't remember."

The faint twitch of his mouth indicated he'd heard her, but then he slumped more heavily against his mother as she took the brunt of his weight. Cornell rushed down the steps and took Jesper's other side.

Alavara's hand clamped over her mouth as she held back a sob. Jesper was not all right. He was alive, yes, but she feared he might still die.

Their footsteps faded and disappeared completely when the large metal door squeaked closed behind them. She stared at the spot Jesper had occupied a minute before. She was relieved he had survived her attempt to kill him. But she also despised herself more than she despised anything. Gaining his trust was the ultimate gift. She had thrown his gift on the ground and stomped on it until it bled.

"Forgive me, Jesper," she whispered to the wall.

But only silence answered back.

CHAPTER 26

HEAT BURNED JESPER'S forehead, his body, his mind. A daze overtook him, and he placed a hand to his dizzy head from where he sat in a soft, red-velvet chair in the drawing room with his family surrounding him. He made sure to stay out of sight, away from servants' and nobles' eyes and ears, and especially keeping King Ruvyn in the dark about his state of health. Of course, the elf had retreated to the safety of his soldiers, which only reinforced his suspicion that he'd had a hand in the stabbing.

What do you want from me? he asked himself.

"What if we tried—" his mother started, but he interrupted.

"I'm a hopeless case." He threw up his hands but hissed when the action tugged on his wound. "Instead of focusing on what we can't change, let's focus on what we can. Where is Alavara?"

As if listening through the door, Captain Cornell entered with his head bowed, Sam at his heels.

"Sire," the captain of the guard greeted. "We bear grave news."

Dread pulled drapes of darkness across his vision. "What happened to my mate?"

Sam shook his head. "Alavara is…fine. But Ruvyn has slowly moved to surround the city with his army. We're under siege."

He swore and stood quickly, regretting it when his surroundings spun. His father grasped his forearms to keep him standing. "How? When? But the treaty." He peered outside the window and blinked through his unfocused vision to find pinpricks of light in the distance. It wasn't the light of friendly allies but a hostile enemy. "What do they expect? That they'll starve us out? We'll simply feast on their blood."

"But how many vampires will turn feral in the process?"

Jesper frowned. Feral vampires would do anything for a taste of blood, even attack other vampires. What of the children who fed every few hours to every few days? What of the females with child that might lose their pregnancies if they didn't receive sustenance?

His mother murmured, "Ingrid is still out there. She will never be able to sneak past Ruvyn's men now."

He wanted to swear up a storm and pull his hair out. He'd signed a treaty so this very thing would never happen! "I need to speak with my mate."

Both Sam and Cornell grimaced. The captain spoke. "She's…indisposed."

His heart stopped for mere moments as he stared back at the other two. "What do you mean? I spoke to her only yesterday."

"I warn you," Sam said. "Something's not right with her. Her demeanor is strange, and she keeps trying to escape."

Exhausted at the mere thought of traversing the hallways and descending the stairs to the dungeon, he ordered, "Bring her here."

"I don't know if it's wise to do so. She's not herself." His brother winced. "Or, perhaps she is."

Rage tempted him to tackle Sam at merely suggesting his mate was capable of lies and betrayal, though he quickly reminded himself that the situation was complicated. "Detain her with vodryx."

"We both know she is deadly with her hands alone. Vodryx may take away her vampire abilities, but it won't stop her."

"There is an army on our doorstep. We don't have a choice."

Cornell bowed and ducked out of the room. Jesper opened his mouth to give the next order when his entire body froze in shock. A familiar scent wafted past his nose, barely discernible but recognizable all the same.

Slowly, he turned toward the second door of the drawing room seconds before someone rapped quietly on the other side. His family exchanged looks but he only stared intensely at the closed door.

His father drew a dagger from his belt as he approached the door, and in a quick movement, he threw it open to reveal a witch with blonde hair carrying a wooden scepter with a blue glass orb on top. But Jesper didn't care about the witch as much as he cared about...

"Cybil," he croaked.

Another figure stepped into his line of sight. Small. Fierce. But uncertainty revealed itself in the hunch of her shoulders, in the hair covering her face as she stared at the floor, in the way she bit her lip. Ingrid entered the room first, but Cybil lagged behind.

Despite his unsteady feet, he stumbled across the room and pulled her into as much of an embrace as his wound would allow. "You are the worst!" he growled at her. "A letter? You wrote me a letter and tried to disappear forever? What is wrong with you?"

She chuckled against him as she returned the embrace. "What's going on? You don't do embraces."

"I do sometimes," he defended as they broke apart, but she laughed.

"No, you have never once embraced me. And I've never witnessed you do it for your family, either. Your mate has made you soft."

"I've just missed you. You're my best friend."

Instead of seeming upset over the title, she smiled warmly and gently punched his right shoulder, but not hard enough to jar his injury as if she sensed he wasn't quite all right. "I'm happy to see you happy." She bit her lip again. "At least, I think you are happy?"

He was confused about so many things, but he refused to give up on Alavara. He loved her. "Ingrid," he said, turning to the witch, "how did you cross the border?"

The witch gestured to Cybil with her scepter. "We crossed paths. She snuck me into the city. Though, I'm not sure this is the position I want to be in right now. Why have you summoned me?"

His mother guided him to a chair and started unbuttoning his shirt but paused when she glanced toward Cybil. He barely managed to wave away her concern with his hand when his arms barely allowed him to lift them. His entire torso ached, made worse by the sheen of perspiration on his skin. Besides, Cybil had seen him shirtless often enough when they'd sparred in the past.

Jesper hissed as his mother peeled away his bloodied bandage, and the room collectively winced.

His father spoke this time. "He's received a...grave wound. Can you heal it?"

Ingrid approached with eyebrows drawn. Her fingers hovered over the injury without touching it. "Who did this to you?"

Not wanting to divulge Alavara's involvement, he avoided looking at Cybil and said, "An assassin finally got me."

But Cybil inhaled sharply as if she managed to place the pieces of the puzzle immediately, and when their gazes locked, only fury stared back at him. "I am going to kill that elf."

"That *elf* is my *mate*," he growled back. "And she's innocent. We summoned Ingrid to prove it."

Thankfully, his father roughly explained the situation and allowed Jesper to sit back against the chair. Ingrid's hands lit up with a silver light as she hovered them over his chest. The witch's eyebrows furrowed more by the minute.

"Why isn't it working?" Jesper's father asked as he stood off to the side, arms folded. Each of his family members stared intensely as Ingrid's silver magic emitted from her hands and bathed Jesper's chest in a cool light. But instead of healing, the magic glanced off his skin like sunlight off a mirror.

"The wound is too serious," Ingrid murmured as her magic flickered out, leaving a foreboding silence behind in the room.

"But all the iron is out of his body," Zachariah protested as he rebound the wound with new bandages. "He should be healing."

The witch nodded. "Yes, but the blade barely missed his heart. I fear the repercussions of iron so close to an immortal organ."

Jesper's lips thinned as his unfocused gaze moved toward the window, looking anywhere but at the mournful expressions of his family members. If he hadn't moved at the last second when Alavara had stabbed him, he would be dead. But what if it had only delayed the inevitable?

The rattling of chains perked his ears up, and he glanced toward the door. Moments later, Cornell entered with Alavara in tow, wearing a cloak that shrouded her face and figure. Manacles clamped around her wrists, jangling with each step she took into the room. But when Cornell closed the door behind them and pulled his mate's hood back...

His lips slowly parted when he stared back at black, soulless eyes. They were dead. Lifeless. Empty.

Heart trembling, he approached her and brushed his fingers along her cheek. She didn't respond to his touch but simply remained standing. "Where are you?" he murmured.

Alavara's fangs sprouted from her mouth, making him jump at the sudden, unexpected movement. A low growl emitted from his throat. And despite everything, he couldn't help but chuckle as he glanced over his shoulder, relieved that he could reach his mate, even this way.

"I'm thinking she doesn't like Cybil's scent on my shirt."

"Really?" Kiara laughed. "Then she clearly doesn't understand how insanely in love you are with her."

His face flushed, but before he could hide it by turning back to Alavara, she struck out at him with a finger jab to his shoulder. His entire arm became limp. He raised his hand to block her next attack, but lifting his arm proved too excruciating, and she jabbed him in the throat.

He stumbled backward, gasping for air as he clutched his neck. The momentary distraction gave her enough time to produce a dagger hidden within her cloak. She jumped on him and pinned him to the ground. Jesper's eyes widened in horror as the blade glinted beneath candlelight. She stabbed downward.

Before the tip of the blade managed to pierce his flesh, Cybil tackled Alavara off him, and the two fought weapon against weapon. Growls and snapping fangs filled the room as the two rolled over each other, each trying to gain the advantage over the other. The scent of blood filled his nostrils as they bit, scratched, and even stabbed one another.

Kiara helped him stand on shaky feet, and his body barely managed to heal enough for him to gasp in a deep, pained breath into his lungs. He watched the spectacle with wide eyes. Alavara's dagger wasn't made of iron, but even a stab wound to the heart would have killed him with his current injury.

Cybil had saved his life.

Sam and their father wrenched Alavara off Cybil and pinned her to the ground. As Alavara tried to wriggle free and fight back, Ingrid pressed the orb of her staff to Alavara's forehead.

His mate screamed.

"What are you doing to her!" he shouted. He rushed toward them and was about to push Ingrid away from Alavara when his mother grabbed him from behind and restrained him. "You're hurting her!"

Ingrid gritted her teeth, eyes flashing silver. "Her mind is filled with dark magic. I must pull it out and destroy it."

Unable to bear the sound of her agony, he fell to his knees and gripped Alavara's hand. She bucked and thrashed but he refused to release her. Somewhere in there, Alavara knew his name, knew his scent, and he desperately believed she didn't truly want to end his life.

The scepter pulled black wisps of magic out of Alavara, and the more she extracted, the more his mate howled and screamed. The black wisps caught on fire and burned into nothing but slithering smoke.

At last, the scepter's orb flickered out. Alavara lay still with her eyes closed, her head falling limp to the side.

After a few moments of silence, he ventured, "Alavara?"

When she didn't respond, he leaned over her, but his brother pushed him back.

"Don't get too close," Sam cautioned. "I'm quite sure she's out for your blood."

The scratch marks, bite marks, and stab wounds slowly healed across her and Cybil's skin as the long moments ticked by. Jesper held his breath, watching, waiting. But she didn't open her eyes.

Just when he began to pose a question to Ingrid, Alavara's chest shook with heaving breaths, followed by laughter escaping her mouth. Tears trailed down her cheeks and disappeared into her dark hair, but then a smile stretched across her face even though her eyes remained closed.

"He's gone," she murmured. "I'm free."

Sam helped her into a sitting position while pushing Jesper away once again as if to maintain distance between the two of them. He desperately wanted to touch her, to scent her, to pull her into an embrace. But he also didn't want to die.

Alavara's eyelids fluttered open, her dark lashes framing even darker eyes. But the presence within them was unmistakable. They were no longer empty and void of life. But they were teeming with intelligence.

And regret…

Her gaze dipped to his bandaged torso, now bloody again when the wound had ripped open once more after she'd attacked him. "Forgive me," she said in a raspy whisper. "I despise myself for what I've done to you."

He shook his head and dared to reach out to her. She met him halfway, and instead of attacking again, she threaded her fingers through his. "I'm guessing your father was controlling you."

A shuddering breath escaped her as she nodded.

He caressed the back of her hand with his thumb. "How much do you remember?" He swallowed. "How much was real for you?"

"Us," she answered resolutely. "That's what was real. I remember everything now. And I will tell you all of it." She ran her fingers lightly over his chest, over his bandages, and his lips pressed together with discomfort when he realized his family watched every little movement. Thankfully, she dropped her fingers and sighed. "I'm so sorry…"

"It's not your fault."

She squeezed her eyes shut. "I am partly to blame. It takes a good deal of strength to fight my father's magic. When I was turned, my strength faded away almost entirely with the absence of my magic. I wish I could have fought harder."

"How long have you been fighting him?"

Her dark eyes skimmed their audience before landing on him again. "My entire life. But I've done so many despicable things under his influence." Her eyes fluttered closed again. "My brother, Thalanil, took the brunt of my father's attention, and now I fear he is lost forever. I received what was left over. I had control over my thoughts and actions most of the time. Until I didn't."

His mother spoke next. "King Ruvyn has surrounded Ichor Knell."

Alavara frowned. "Then my father knows his plan has failed. This is his contingency plan should he not get what he wants through peaceful means."

Jesper snorted. "Peaceful? What does that even mean?"

But his mate simply glanced away from him and bit her lip as she turned her silver bracelet around on her wrist.

"Alavara?" he prompted when she didn't answer for the longest time.

She shrugged and grunted as she lifted herself up and sat heavily in a chair. But the motion seemed to sicken her, as she pressed a hand to her mouth and breathed deeply. "I don't know what to say. I'm afraid you will be furious at me."

"I already told you it's not your fault. You were not the perpetrator."

"But it feels like I was!" She threw her hands up. "*I* picked up the dagger. *I* stabbed you. *I've* been wearing this blasted bracelet. I have been deceiving you and it feels awful."

More than anything, Jesper wished to hold this conversation in private. But the moment Alavara had stabbed him was the moment this mess involved his entire family, even the entire population of Ichor Knell.

"Then you're telling me you have been deceiving me on purpose."

She sighed and shook her head. "Never." She spun the bracelet around on her wrist, bringing his attention back to the piece of jewelry. She'd mentioned the night she'd stabbed him that the important thing she'd needed to tell him had to do with her bracelet.

"What—"

Something struck the castle in a deafening crash, seeming to shake the entire structure. Or was it vertigo? He wasn't sure.

But one thing he was sure of...

His subjects were bound to be scared. They needed to take action. Now.

"Our people need us to lead." He gripped her by the elbows and stared intensely into her eyes. "That's your father out there. Can you lead by my side, Alavara?"

She returned his grip and nodded. "Always." And then she swallowed. "My father has hurt countless people. My loyalty is with you."

For better or for worse, they were in this together. And they would see it through to the end.

CHAPTER 27

WITH THE DARKNESS dispersed from her mind, Alavara's thoughts became clearer, her actions more focused. No longer did her father sway her motivations with his dark magic. She relished the complete feeling of freedom, a feeling she hadn't experienced in many years. In fact, she didn't remember the last time she'd lived an unfettered life.

She followed her mate, staying by his side as he barked out orders to the captain of the guard and to determined soldiers ready to protect their homes and their families. Like herself, he wore black, vampiric armor made of nearly impenetrable smelted gemstones. Jesper looked ruthless wearing it, like a king born from darkness eternal.

"Where do you want me?" Cybil asked, also wearing her own armor but one made of steel to fit her small body.

"On the battlefield with the rest of the soldiers," Jesper answered.

Slowly, Cybil's mouth dropped open, her eyes wide. "Are you sure? I'm not a soldier."

"You are now."

She smiled from ear to ear and pumped her fist. "I swear you won't regret this."

"Yes, well, you owe me a drink once this is over and done."

The castle shook again as the elves launched a sphere of magic past their borders. Screams lifted into the air. Vampires raced into the castle for refuge while others ran toward the danger to fight.

Cybil laughed and followed the others with sword in hand. "If we survive today, that drink is yours."

Jesper grabbed Alavara's hand, and despite the perspiration running down his face, despite his sluggish movements, he remained strong as they exited the castle to meet her people in battle.

He bit his lip, glancing sideways at her. "Do you mind if I spent time with Cybil? I should have asked you first."

Alavara ran a hand over his armored shoulder and shook her head. "She's your best friend. You are allowed to have a life outside our union, Jesper." But then a wicked smile pulled up on her lips. "Though, if you return with her scent all over you like earlier today, I make no promises about allowing her to keep both her eyes."

He snorted as they ascended several stairs onto a parapet to give them a vantage point of the battle. "After witnessing the two of you fight, I'm not sure who would come out on top."

Roars filled the skies as vampires charged against their elven foes. Alavara watched with quiet intensity. She didn't want these good people to die. Vampires *and* elves. Despite the vampire blood running through her veins, she was still an elf.

"Archers, ready!" Jesper held up his hand, and a chorus of bow strings being pulled taut filled her ears. After several long moments, he closed his fist, and the arrows whizzed through the air, striking the enemy.

She closed her eyes at the lives lost, at the sting of her people dying by vampires' hands. She had to stop this, and she knew of only one way to do it.

"My people are loyal to the crown," she said over the ruckus of shouting and clanging blades. "Not my father. And likely because he has some degree of control over them. But even my father has limits on his power." She swallowed as she watched a vampire cut down an elf. "If we defeat the source, the rest are bound to lay down their weapons."

Her mate turned to her, serious eyes boring into her. Any other person might have flinched away from the intensity of *him*, but she wouldn't shy away. Ever.

"Do you think it can be accomplished?"

She nodded, though she knew she was foolish for feeling so much hope. "Yes. I will do it myself."

"Not without me. We go together or not at all."

The words held immense meaning. Despite everything she'd done, despite everything she'd been a part of, he would die for her.

And she would die for him.

Clasping his forearm, she said, "Don't let my father close enough to touch you. If he threads his magic into your mind, it's not likely you will escape." Her gaze briefly flickered to the armor covering his chest, concealing the deadly wound beneath. Once this was over, she swore she would find a way to heal it. No matter what it cost her.

Blades of grass reached out of the compacted earth with long, outstretched fingers as Jesper and Alavara slithered past with Cornell flying from tree to tree above them. His scales blended in with the green and brown earth tones far better than her stark white physique. He worried someone might spot her. This plan rode heavily on sneaking into enemy territory undetected, even as the chaos of fighting ensued around them.

Enemy...

Did Alavara view her people the same way he did? Not likely. Whenever she spoke of them, only love shone in her eyes. Her father, on the other hand... He doubted she would miss him if he were to meet an unfortunate accident.

Jesper hissed quietly at the thought. Ruvyn had played him a fool. The only thing he didn't regret from this entire incident was taking Alavara as his mate. But the elven king had broken the treaty by attacking. Now, they had no choice but to protect their people, their kingdom, and their resources by defeating him.

His heart beat faster, followed by terrible pain, not from his confusing thoughts but from the exertion he expended moving smoothly through the grass. Dizziness clutched onto either side of his head, and his surroundings blurred momentarily. He squeezed his eyes shut and opened them slowly—at least as much as a serpent was able to. Although his vision righted once more, his body ached. Every inch of it, but the pain flared most at his chest.

Are you all right? Alavara slowed her progress and stared at him with her beady black eyes. Vampires didn't need to speak with just their tongues. They could speak with the back of their throats in a way only other vampires could understand.

I'm fine. Keep moving.

But Jesper—

We cannot afford to stop. Our window is small. If we wait any longer, we might be too late.

If they weren't too late already.

Her tongue flicked out of her mouth as she saw through his lie. She crossed his path and slithered over his body. Even in her serpent form, her touch caused shivers to run from his snout to his tail. For a moment, rational thought fled his mind.

But he forced himself to focus as they snuck closer to the back of Ruvyn's army where the elven king sat on his horse, barking orders and spreading his dark magic to the nearby soldiers.

A shiver ran down Jesper's spine as he stared at the black, soulless eyes of the man on the horse next to him. He looked similar to Alavara with the same dark hair and creamy complexion. He sat stiff in his saddle, hardly moving aside from his occasional breath.

Thalanil, Alavara explained with a rueful tone to her voice. *It won't be easy to get past my father with him nearby. My brother moves fast, even faster than me.* She flicked out her tongue and gave him a regretful look. *In your current state, you don't stand a chance. I'll engage Thalanil. You try to take down my father.*

He simply nodded, not wanting to expend any further energy by speaking. He motioned with his head toward a nearby tree. Only he slithered up, and he huffed with the effort it took to drape himself across an overhanging branch. Cornell landed beside him in his aviary form, ruffling his feathers while keeping both eyes trained on the enemy. The element of using their vampiric transformations would only last so long before someone noticed them. They needed to be quick.

Jesper blinked back another wave of dizziness and gazed out over the soldiers below. A part of him wanted to succumb to his body's protests, but another part thought of his family, of Alavara, of Kiara. They gave him the strength he needed to continue forward.

Instead of dizziness, his thoughts swam with confusion. Most of Ruvyn's army had journeyed back home after the treaty was struck. If Alavara had managed to kill Jesper, the elven king had kept just enough soldiers to move into the city in a moment of chaos, such as Jesper's death. But still, he couldn't wrap his mind around *how*. Alavara, being a female, wouldn't inherit the throne in his stead. Ruvyn had already made it clear he didn't plan on invading Ichor Knell through forceful means, at least until now. How did this connect?

Ruvyn's plan, as detailed by Alavara, didn't add up. What was Jesper missing?

He glanced down at her hidden in a tall patch of grass at the base of the tree. Her white, coiled scales stood out in the shadows of late afternoon. He wondered if she was hiding information from him, or if she was as in the dark about the elven king's plans as he was.

A familiar voice drew his attention away from his mate. Fury spread across Ruvyn's face after one of his guards whispered in his ear.

"What do you mean you haven't seen her? I don't care how many men you send to do the task. Bring her back. Alive!" he roared to the man, who flinched as spittle hit his face.

I think they are talking about you, he warned Alavara. *You shouldn't be here. You should go—*

His head spun, and a wave of dizziness shook him to the core, stronger than the one before. Every muscle in his serpent body loosened as his vision blacked out momentarily. But by the time his vision returned, he couldn't grasp onto the branch quickly enough to stop his fall. He lost control of his transformation and dropped to the green earth in his vampire form with a *thump* like a bird falling from a slingshot. The air whooshed from his lungs, his head aching as if lightning crackled through his veins.

Dozens of swords slid from their sheaths, and Jesper stumbled to his feet and drew his own sword. He turned in a full circle, watching warily as elven guards advanced slowly while exuding caution. The circle of blades closed in on him further, and his gaze darted for an opening to escape through. To his dismay, he found none. The soldiers were clearly well-trained.

A guard cried out.

Jesper snapped his attention in the direction of the cry to find Alavara taking down guards with only her hands. She jabbed one. Elbowed another. Limbs fell useless. She moved fluidly, slipping through grab attempts and dodging attacks.

She made an opening large enough for him to slip through, and Cornell fought behind him to keep him from getting surrounded again. He used his sword to defend himself from oncoming attacks, but when within close enough range, he fought only with his hands and feet, following her example. If he didn't have to kill the people she loved, then he wouldn't.

Daggers, he said in the back of his throat. *I messed up.*

Don't die, was her only response. *The plan stays the same.*

Alavara fought with him side by side against her own people. She fought to protect *him*, and with such ferocity as if she were afraid to lose him for a second time.

A surge of emotion overcame him. Right then, they were a team with a similar goal. He trusted her to have his back, which surprised him after everything that had transpired between them. And as much as he was able, he would have her back, too.

War cries rang out behind them as his people tried to break through the enemy lines. The strength of his subjects gave him the courage to continue fighting all while keeping his sights on Ruvyn. The man watched from atop his horse as if he were watching a game rather than a war. If he could only reach him, they could end this war for good.

Agonizing pain tore at his wound, a dizziness taking a hold of his head and threatening to drag him into dark, watery depths. He continued fighting with everything he had. For himself. For Alavara. For his kingdom. But when he took down one elf, another one cropped up in his place.

From across the fighting ground, Alavara met his eye and nodded. Together, they advanced toward Ruvyn and Thalanil. She moved smoothly as she jumped and dodged and weaved through her opponents. He moved more sloppily but managed all the same.

In a terrifying blink of an eye, Thalanil shifted from his horse and suddenly stood in front of Alavara. But she seemed to expect it, and with determination in her brows, she met him in combat with a series of kicks, jabs, and slices. Thalanil moved faster. But Alavara managed to keep up.

Focusing on the task at hand, Jesper transformed into a snake and weaved through legs as he tried to hide himself from the enemy. Feet attempted to trample him. Weapons tried to injure him. But he moved quietly and swiftly. With Ruvyn's focus on attempting to find him within the grass, he struck out at the horse's legs. The creature whinnied in fright and reared violently enough to throw its rider.

Ruvyn crashed to the ground in a heap of leather armor and weapons. Jesper darted forward in his vampire form once more and barely managed to scratch the man across the face with his sharp fingernails before a guard swung a sword at him.

He ducked and engaged the soldiers who surrounded him, all while cursing that he hadn't been able to deliver a killing blow to the elven king. He'd had his chance. And he'd missed it.

"Fight me man to man!" Jesper shouted as he blocked blow after blow with his sword. "King to king!"

Through gaps in leather armor, he spotted Ruvyn grinning as he dusted himself off. The man held out his hands to gesture to the battlefield. "Have you not noticed? You have been fighting me this entire time."

Knowing he hadn't much strength left, Jesper roared as he fought off his attackers, and when he found an opening, he charged through, straight at Ruvyn. They met in a clash of swords. The force reverberated up his arm, through his shoulder, and over his chest, nearly causing him to drop his weapon. But he breathed heavily through the pain and continued to fight.

The scent of perspiration and smoke filled his nostrils, reminding him of the battle his grandfather had died in. Just the thought fueled his actions and gave him enough energy to fight.

Block. Jab. Swing. Block.

The two of them fought without interference from the soldiers. Although Ruvyn was around four times his own age, the unpracticed footwork told him the man relied on his magic more than the sword.

Because Alavara was currently fighting his sword.

Jesper desperately wanted to glance her way, to make sure she was succeeding against Thalanil, but one killing blow would end this. One killing blow would protect her from harm.

Desperation churned within him as metal scraped against metal, as blow struck against blow. As if realizing Jesper's weakness, Ruvyn began attacking his left side, forcing him to block, block, block until his entire body screamed out in protest.

He changed from offense to defense as he struggled to keep up with the man's ruthless attacks. Slowly, they edged backward toward several trees. He gritted his teeth together when he realized the elven king was trying to trap him.

Don't let my father close enough to touch you. Alavara's earlier warning surfaced in his head. *If he threads his magic into your mind, it's not likely you will escape.*

Jesper attempted to switch back to the offensive to give him berth from the blockade of trees, but his body refused to obey him. His strength fled from him. His regeneration refused to work.

He was not going to come out as the victor.

I'm sorry, he wept in his own mind. *You should have taken someone else in my stead. I am not capable enough.*

In a swift blow, Ruvyn disarmed him. His sword clattered against a boulder, out of reach. Soldiers surrounded him and Cornell, grabbing hold of either side of him to prevent him from attacking further. He wasn't sure he could find the energy even if he tried.

At the same moment, Alavara cried out suddenly. Jesper's attention snapped toward her, only for fear to grip his heart and squeeze. Thalanil held a knife to his own sister's throat, and even though it wasn't made of iron, Jesper froze. He eyed the steel metal as the edge of the blade pressed against her skin.

He gave the soldiers holding him little heed, but rather watched the defiant fear blossom in Alavara's eyes as they gazed at each other across the short distance. Despite giving their all, they had failed.

"What a clever trick," Ruvyn chuckled. "I didn't even see the two of you coming."

"Don't hurt him," Alavara begged. "Please." When she squirmed against her brother's grip, the knife at her throat cut her skin, and a trickle of blood dripped down her neck. The sight of her blood enraged him.

"Put your knife down," Jesper growled, flexing his fingers as he readied for an attack. "Or you will learn just how fast I can pull your spine out of your body."

The soldiers on either side of him took an uncomfortable step away from him while still restraining his arms.

"Are you trying to protect her?" Ruvyn laughed as he approached Alavara and angled a knife toward her wrist. "Do you know how many lies she's told you?"

"*Your* lies, don't you mean? I know what you've done to her. I know what you've made her do."

Shame stared back at him in Alavara's dark eyes, and she lowered her gaze.

"She has already told me everything."

"Everything?" The elf slid the tip of the knife beneath the silver bracelet she wore and paused. Jesper held his breath as he stared at the weapon. If he so much as drew one more drop of her blood, he would make him regret ever laying a hand on her.

"Forgive me, Jesper," Alavara said, choking on her words. "I tried to tell you. Several times. I'm so sorry."

"Release her," he demanded despite knowing he wasn't in a position to bargain. "Now."

Still, Ruvyn's grin lingered on his face. "But I thought you'd want to know Alavara's last, mountainous secret."

He cut the bracelet off her wrist, and the metal beads scattered across the grass. Jesper struggled against his captors' grip as he prepared to leap forward and attack the elf, but the faintest of sounds made him pause in his tracks.

Thump thump. Thump thump. Thump thump.

The small heartbeat stood out against the slower, steadier heartbeats that were a chorus of background noise he'd learned to ignore over the years. The rhythm emanated from near Ruvyn, and Jesper cocked his head to the side as he listened. What was that noise? Where had he heard it before?

His face paled as he recalled pressing his ear to his mother's pregnant belly when Kiara had been within her womb. Her heartbeat had sounded so small and fragile, similar to...

His gaze darted to Alavara's stomach as he realized the source of the heartbeat. "What?" he gasped. "What..." He shook his head. It wasn't possible. It wasn't! Vampires weren't very fertile. She wouldn't be with child yet. She *couldn't*!

By the way she wouldn't meet his gaze told him she had already known about the pregnancy. But then he recalled the time during their chess game when she'd tried to tell him something about the bracelet but forgot. And then again in their bedroom when she'd wept in his arms, unable to remember the important event shrouded around the piece of jewelry.

King Ruvyn had done this. He'd wanted a grandchild to put on the throne after disposing of Jesper. To control the vampire kingdom free of his influence.

"Surprised?" Ruvyn smiled maliciously. "It was difficult to get our hands on a dwarven potion to increase vampire fertility. Alavara slipped it into your drink on your union day. And it was even more difficult to procure a dwarven bracelet to hide the sounds of the child's heartbeat."

Jesper shook his head in denial, his eyes glazing over with rest mist. It couldn't be true. "Kiara gave me that drink."

"Your sister is naive and far too trusting for her own good. Who do you think gave Kiara the drink to give to you?"

"No..." His heart squeezed painfully as the last piece of the puzzle finally fell into place. Ruvyn had something to gain from his death. He had named his nonexistent son as his heir, but little had he known that his child had been under his nose all this time. With Jesper out of the way, should the child be born a male, Ruvyn would have won.

"Please," he whispered to his mate, and he knew she heard when her long ears twitched. "Please tell me you didn't deliberately hide this from me for *hours* today. That your father planned to kill me to place our child on the throne."

Her hand flew to her mouth as if she'd suddenly crumpled inside, her expression distraught. "When was the best time to tell you this? My mouth and mind were sealed for weeks. I didn't want to tell you until the fighting was over."

Jesper swallowed the emotion clogging his throat. "You didn't want me to keep you away from the battle."

She shook her head. "This is my fight."

"And that's my child. And you're my mate." Vampire children were stronger than human children within the womb, but if the mother died, so did the baby. Now all three of them were doomed to die. Ichor Knell was going to fall. Because he was foolish and didn't name a second heir should Jesper *and* his heir die.

"I had a *right* to know."

"Yes, you did. Forgive me, Jesper."

But this wasn't Alavara's fault. A far more sinister man held all the cards, and he'd been blinded from the very first move.

His fangs sprouted in a burst of rage at his predicament, startling the guards on either side of him. But despite his weak struggling, he couldn't break free.

Another wave of dizziness washed over him, and he struggled to remain upright. If it hadn't been for his captors' grip, he feared he might have fallen flat on his face. Several beads of perspiration gathered on his forehead as his body temperature rose another fraction.

Holding this conversation in front of an audience while they were both captives was far too characteristic of their relationship than he would have liked. Should they both be more concerned about their situation? Most definitely. But Jesper only saw red. He had a child on the way, and no one had bothered to tell him. How long had it been since their union? Too long to not know about the baby, even if Ruvyn had deliberately hidden the child's existence from him.

Ruvyn gestured to the guards holding him, and in response, their grip tightened on his arms. "Hold the vampire steady. I will deal with him in a moment. As for you, my daughter..." Black smoke slithered up his hand and weaved through his fingers. Jesper blinked once, thinking his eyes were deceiving him. But the smoke still lingered. "It seems I can no longer wait the full nine months for this child to arrive. I need the child *now*."

"No!" Alavara screeched. She writhed out of Thalanil's hold, but not before Ruvyn placed a hand on her belly. Black wisps escaped between his fingers in smoky tendrils. A great and terrible scream permeated the air, and she doubled over while clutching her midsection.

His frustration, his anger evaporated at the sound of her pained screeches. Something snapped in him. His eyes flashed red. Strength flooded into his weakened body, and he ripped his arms out of the elves' grasp. Before they had a chance to react, he smashed his elbow into the face of one and shattered the other's kneecap with a well-aimed foot. The other elves were quick to act as they attacked with their weapons. A game of weaving and dodging began.

Alavara's screams grew louder, and she fell onto her hands and knees, still clutching her midsection.

Renewed determination filled him, and he fought harder and faster in an attempt to reach her side. He managed to break through the enemy lines, but then in a startling moment, he found himself face to face with Ruvyn.

The elf lifted his hand, and before Jesper could dodge, he touched his forehead.

The world around him seemed to swing upside down in a lurching movement, disorienting him as he crashed onto his back.

Something latched onto his feet, and then his wrists. He struggled against the invisible chains, but no matter how hard he fought, he couldn't break free.

Shadows slithered around his ankles like smoke curling from an unrestrained wildfire. It climbed up his legs, clinging to him, and no matter how hard he tried to kick them off, they remained. When they continued their trek up his body, he unsheathed the dagger hidden beneath his shirt and sliced into the wispy tendrils of darkness. The shadows parted for the weapon but didn't cease their journey.

He gasped and stumbled backward, but instantly regretted opening his mouth. The shadows raced inside and choked the air from his lungs. It spread through him until even his veins flowed with darkness. When he tried to cry out, the shadows pressed farther into him until it snuffed out every last sliver of light.

Darkness fell over him like a tent trapping him with no way out. It surrounded him on all sides from the sky to his surroundings to the ground his hands touched. Alavara was gone. The trees and bushes and soldiers were gone. Only silent, ebony ribbons of ink remained. The tendrils of darkness buzzed around him, burning, suffocating, disorienting.

"Alavara!" he cried, but his own voice echoed back.

He reached for his dagger, only for dread to fill him when his fingers clasped around air.

"You think you can strut into my army and take what is mine?" a voice hissed like a snake.

He spun every which way to locate the source, but it resonated around him, as if it were in his mind alone.

"Show yourself!" Jesper shouted. He bared his fangs and held his hands outstretched on either side of him, his sharp fingernails ready for a brawl. "Fight me! Or are you too much of a coward?"

"Coward?" The voice chuckled, a shiver running down his spine as wisps of shadows licked at his face. "If it is a fight you want, vampire king, then it is a fight you will get."

A wall of darkness slammed into him and threw him backward, smashing him into something equally solid. He fell onto his hands and knees and gasped air into aching lungs. He rolled out of the way when a flurry of small black shards raced in his direction. One of the shards sliced into his arm. Blood dripped from the cut and healed far too slowly.

The black shards spun in their flight through the air, transforming into something much larger and terrifying. A dozen black monsters turned abruptly on their wings and flew toward him with sharp beaks and outstretched talons.

Having nowhere to run, he faced the monsters head on with his fingers outstretched. He sliced through one of them with his fingernails, but it vanished in a poof of smoke.

Violent tremors shivered up his arm upon touching the darkness, a chill racing through him. The chill climbed up his body and spread through his skull. He stumbled backward, clawing at his head in an attempt to pull the black magic out of himself.

Flashes of fear entered his mind in the form of vivid images. Kiara's lifeless and bloodied form staring up at the sky. His mother ambushed and slaughtered by the enemy. Dracula's final words before succumbing to death.

Fear gripped him, and he collapsed to the ground when his useless body couldn't handle the strain. Dark, dark, dark. Everything was dark, and he was nothing—just a speck of dust in a sea of black.

Pure agony ripped through him, starting from his mind and traveling through the rest of his body. There was no greater pain, no greater torment, no greater—

A grunt.

The darkness and pain snapped into Ruvyn's hand as if he had called it back, and Jesper once again found himself surrounded by soldiers while he lay in a fetal position on the ground. But it wasn't Ruvyn's hand that drew his attention. It was the dagger protruding from his chest.

His lips parted when he recognized the very weapon his grandfather had received as a gift from the dwarves, one he hadn't realized had gone missing from the Ichor Knell vault.

Thalanil's hand shook as he twisted the dagger within his father's chest, as if he barely managed to maintain control of his own mind. A snarl lay on the man's lips, and his eyes flickered back and forth from empty to lucid, but not once did his grip slip on the weapon.

"Th-Thalanil," Ruvyn gasped. He fell to his knees. Blood gurgled from his throat and dripped from the corner of his mouth. His words were garbled when he tried to speak again. "What have you done?"

A tendril of shadow slithered out of Ruvyn's hand, but Thalanil moved far quicker as if taking advantage of his momentary control. His hand glowed blue before he placed it over his father's head. It was as if his hand sucked the elven king's soul out of his body when blue wisps wove around his fingertips.

Finally, he released the dagger and lifted his other hand into the sky. The blue wisps circled his wrist, jumped to his palm, and traveled to his fingertips, and then they vanished into the air like fading smoke.

Ruvyn's eyes rolled back into his head, and his body pitched forward onto the grass and lay still. He didn't move again. He was dead.

Jesper's eyes widened as he stared at Thalanil, the elf's eyes now completely lucid. The power he wielded... With magic like his, how hadn't he escaped Ruvyn's hold all this time?

Fighting suddenly stopped around him with a dizzying halt as the elves retreated from the Ichor Knell grounds. The dagger slowly disintegrated into a pile of ash after its single use disappeared, no longer resembling the destructive weapon it had once been.

There was only one person he knew who could have stolen it out of the treasury beneath his nose.

"Alavara," he grunted as he pushed himself to his feet. Panic raced through him when her cries no longer lifted into the skies. What had Ruvyn done to her? Where was she? Was she dead?

Please, no.

The confused soldiers didn't stop him as he barreled past while following Alavara's scent, not knowing how long, exactly, Ruvyn had held him captive in his own mind. He darted toward the elven camp, past rows of tents, leaped over ropes that held the tents aloft, and ducked beneath the flap of the tent where her scent lingered the strongest.

He breathed heavily, his eyes wide as he surveyed his surroundings. Blood was smeared across the ground. Once-white cloths were now stained red. A frail-looking elven woman stood with a pile of fabric in her arms, holding completely still as if afraid he might attack.

His gaze followed the trail of red, and he wasn't sure whether to sigh in relief or cry out in horror when he found Alavara lying on cushions, her body propped up by pillows.

Dry, red-tinted tears stained Alavara's exhausted face, a heavy weariness pinning her body to the cushions on the ground. His gaze traveled from the fear shining bright in her eyes to the blood soaking the bottom half of her dress, staining the grass red. Horror gripped him, and he almost rushed to her side when he caught an unfamiliar scent mingled with hers.

Jesper's body became rigid as he finally noticed the bundle of blankets in her arms. She held the blankets close to her chest, her eyes wide as she stared back at him.

A muffled gurgle caused his heart to stop for a moment. Shock rendered him speechless.

A baby. She was holding a baby.

Once again, his gaze traveled to her blood-soaked clothing, and he realized what had happened. Whatever Ruvyn's magic had done to her... It had sped up her pregnancy. She had given birth to their child.

And he had missed it.

He blinked once. Twice. Emotion tugged at him, buffeted by a strong wind. He took a step toward his mate. And then another.

"Where is my father?" she asked in a trembling tone.

"Dead." He nodded toward the exit of the tent. "Thalanil killed him with that dagger you stole from me." His mouth twitched with humor even though he felt like falling apart.

Alavara released a long breath of relief, her eyes closing momentarily. "We're all free." She clasped a hand over her mouth as if hardly able to take in the truth of the situation.

"What…" He swallowed and angled his head to catch a glimpse of a head of thick dark hair. Breath struggled to enter his lungs. "What is it?"

Alavara's eyes opened, and she cradled the baby closer, effectively hiding it from him. She was afraid. Afraid he would take the baby away or hurt it or something.

"We have a son," she whispered.

With a nod, he took another cautious step forward, afraid to startle a violent reaction out of her. Of course, the baby was a male. Only a male would have been able to inherit the throne should he die. But he wasn't angry. Not at all. He was surprisingly moved.

"Will you allow me to hold him?"

She paused, searching his eyes as if looking for malintent. That's when he realized she was searching for traces of her father's magic within him.

As if not finding it, she finally nodded and handed the child to the elven female, who bounced the baby a few times as if it were a natural female instinct. She carefully handed the child to him.

"I'm not sure if I'm holding him correctly," he said, the bundle awkward in his arms.

"You are doing fine, Your Majesty," the woman answered.

Taking a deep, steadying breath, he looked down at the face of his son.

His beautiful son.

The baby's eyes were halfway closed, his eyes dark, dark, dark. Just like Alavara's. His cheeks were plump, his lips gentle and curved. His ears came to a point, though not quite as long as Alavara's.

He was so *small*.

And he appeared far too peaceful for his abrupt emergence into the world.

Emotion caught in his throat as he gazed down at the life he and Alavara had created together. Suddenly, nothing mattered anymore—her unwilling betrayal, her unintended lies, her forced attempt to kill him. For a moment, everything was right in the world.

The child cooed before opening his mouth in an enormous yawn.

He glanced toward Alavara to find her mouth upturned in the slightest of smiles, though a trace of fear still lived in her eyes. Even with the tear-stained cheeks, the exhausted expression, and her own blood covering her, she had never looked more beautiful. He loved her. So much.

With enough caution to feel silly, he lowered himself next to her on the cushions, arm to arm, shoulder to shoulder, and together they gazed down at their handsome baby boy.

"Have you named him?" Jesper asked, turning his head to find her only close.

She shook her head. "No. In my culture, it is customary for the father to name their children."

He returned his tender gaze to his sleeping boy and slowly sprouted his fangs as to not startle her. He pricked his finger on the point of one fang, blood oozing out of the puncture wound. Because of his iron-poisoned state, it didn't heal quickly like it should.

Lightly touching the blood-covered finger to his son's forehead, he started drawing an image that was more or less supposed to resemble a phoenix. Unfortunately, he didn't have his sister's artistic abilities.

"Zoran Degore," he said as he finished the image on his son, who didn't stir. "I give you a name and the title of heir to the Ichor Knell throne. I also give you the symbol of a phoenix. Though you were born from darkness, from ashes, it has only made you stronger, and those around you will see the bright, shining light you carry in your heart."

"Jesper," Alavara whispered, and he turned to find a deep sadness in her eyes. "Please don't take him away from me. Don't send me away without him."

"Send you away?" He gawked when he realized she was serious. "Why do you think I would do such a thing?" Now he understood her previous fear.

"How can you possibly want to keep me here after everything I've done?"

Careful not to jostle Zoran, he reached for his mate and threaded his fingers through hers. The movement stretched his wound, but he tried his best to hide his agony. "All right, so our start wasn't quite ideal. But I want you here. I want Zoran here. We'll start anew." He caressed the side of their son's face, admiring the deep hair color on his infant head. "The name Zoran means dawn. A phoenix symbolizes rebirth. It's not just for him, but for us."

She nodded, the relief evident in her eyes. "Yes, yes. Thank you, Jesper. Thank you."

As if not able to keep away from their son for too long, she took him back and kissed both plump cheeks and then his nose. The other matronly elf worked to clean up the mess from the birth and helped change her into different clothing while she held the baby. The woman soon left, leaving the three of them alone in the tent.

"Sam won't be happy with me." His mouth lifted in a wry smile. "He's tried for a child for fifty years. I get one within the first few months."

She ducked her head sheepishly. "I suspect he already knows. I caught him staring at my bracelet the day after I put it on. He didn't look upset."

"And he didn't tell me?"

"I'm sure he didn't want to ruin the surprise."

"Shock is more like it. I am utterly shocked." And disappointed that his brother may have found out first. He'd felt like a fool enough to last him a lifetime.

Something touched his hand, and he jumped in surprise to find Alavara's fingers resting on top of his. "I know you said you never wanted children. Are you angry?"

Honestly, Jesper wasn't sure how to piece together the mixed emotions in his heart. Children terrified him. There, he admitted it, if only to himself. What was he supposed to do with Zoran? How was he supposed to be a good father, especially when he was still learning how to be a good mate?

But as he gazed at Alavara, he realized they were in this together. They would love and support one another, even when he felt unqualified for the beautiful gift in her arms.

Not knowing how to speak his mind, he instead kissed each on the forehead, and then he stood and approached the entrance of the tent to look out.

Cornell guarded the tent with his sword drawn, though no one paid him any heed. Soldiers bowed to Thalanil, and despite the grogginess in his expression, he gave orders like a king as he hastily withdrew his soldiers from Ichor Knell.

Sudden exhaustion overcame him, and he was more aware than ever of the throbbing in his chest. His wound pulsed with pain, each heartbeat striking him like a whip. His own blood soaked the front of his shirt beneath his armor. He needed a physician. He needed Zachariah.

"We will return to Ichor Knell at dusk," he replied quietly. "I am assuming your brother's soldiers will allow us to pass."

She nodded. "My brother will be a good king. I know it."

When he turned fully to face his mate, only relief filled her expression, and she sank farther into the cushion as if fully resting for the first time in many years. "We are waiting for dusk then? Why?"

"First, you need to rest. And second... There are a few things I need to do before I publicly claim Zoran as my heir."

CHAPTER 28

IT TOOK HOURS to clean up the mess between the elves and vampires and agree to a new treaty with Thalanil as the new king, one where the elves gave money and resources to make up for the breach of treaty, although involuntary on many of their parts. A hesitant peace formed between them, and the elves promised to pull their troops out of vampire lands immediately. Cybil, acting underneath Cornell's orders, seemed to make it her mission to make sure they left for good.

By the end of the day, a deadly exhaustion consumed Jesper, but he did his best as they returned to the castle and he helped his mate up the too-long staircase and bore most of her weight as he guided her down the hallway, Cornell helping at her other side. He couldn't decide if he was foolish when he opened his chambers to her and placed her on top of the bed while the captain fetched a maidservant.

Alavara breathed heavily, winded after the long journey. "I thought vampires healed quickly."

"They usually do," he replied, tucking the sheets around her while doing his best to ignore the pulsing ache of his wound. "I know it takes humans a month or two at least to fully heal from giving birth. Vampires need time as well. At least a couple weeks. You will likely be in bed for a while."

He was surprised when he reached for Zoran, and she allowed him to take him from her. But the moment he started toward the door, a note of panic hit her voice.

"Where are you going with him?"

"Relax, he is safe with me. I will return shortly."

"Jesper." She released a strangled, anxious whine, and he attempted to give her a reassuring smile.

"No harm will come to him. You have my word."

Despite his reassurance, her worried gaze followed him as he left the room. Zoran continued to sleep bundled in his arms, the blood wiped from his forehead, and he couldn't deny his own worry. Why was he still asleep? Was something wrong with him? How could Jesper move so much, and the baby not jostle awake?

Following the fresh scent of his mother, he soon found himself standing in front of the drawing room, recovering from the battle earlier that day. He took a deep breath and opened the door slowly. When he peeked his head inside, his heart jumped to the roof when he found his entire family within. His mother and father sat in armchairs on one side of the hearth, and Kiara and Sam sat on the other side. His father was nodding off but startled awake, his hand flying to his sword strapped to his belt.

And then he realized what was happening. They were afraid to leave each other alone after what transpired today.

"Jesper." His mother leaped to her feet, followed by the others. "You returned. We've been so worried about you. What happened?"

He took another deep breath and bit his lip when he stared back at Sam, who watched with an uncharacteristically serious expression. "Something happened. Well, a lot of things happened. The armies are gone. We're on the road toward peace again." He shook his head. "But that's beside the point." At least the immediate point. "Alavara…" He swallowed and stepped inside. Several gasps and stunned expressions greeted him upon seeing the baby in his arms. "Alavara gave birth. Ruvyn's dark magic progressed the pregnancy, and well…" Vulnerability showed in his expression, and he hated being unable to push it away. "I trust Alavara. I do. But I need to know for sure. How do I know he's mine?"

"Oh, Jesper," Kiara murmured before taking Zoran away from him and bouncing him in her arms. What was it with females and baby instinct? "He's beautiful. He *has* to be yours."

Shrugging, he wilted into a chair and buried his head in his arms on top of the table when his head swam with dizziness. His voice came out muffled. "He looks like Alavara. I'm not sure if he looks like me."

A light hand touched his shoulder, and he didn't need to lift his head to know it was his mother. "If the baby is yours, he will have been born with fangs. If he is not, and he was conceived before your union, then there will be no fangs. Have you checked?"

He shook his head. "I don't want to. I'm afraid of the answer."

"I'll check," Sam said, and Jesper's entire body tensed as he waited. "Fangs. He *is* yours, Jesper."

A sigh of relief escaped him, and he continued to breathe slowly into his arms, nodding off just like his father. At least until Zoran started whimpering, and those whimpers turned into piercing cries. He stood abruptly, wincing when the action tugged on his wound.

"What do I do?" He took Zoran back from his sister, surprising himself by falling over the edge of panic so quickly. "How do I make him stop crying?"

"He sounds hungry." His mother placed a goblet of blood on the table in front of him. "Try feeding him."

"No." He scrunched his nose with distaste. "I am not feeding a baby. You do it."

"He is *your* baby. You need to learn, Jesper."

"I can barely even hold a baby. You expect me to feed one?"

Zoran's wailing grew louder, deafening to their sensitive vampire ears. His father was the only one who didn't flinch. He finally relented and picked up the goblet, but when he brought the rim to the baby's lips, his mother shook her head and almost had to shout over the crying.

"You saw how I fed Kiara when she was a baby. Do it correctly."

Again, he grimaced. "I will spill everywhere."

"Perhaps, but you have to start somewhere."

He considered taking Zoran back to Alavara to make her do it, but that required transporting a ravenous, screaming baby vampire through the halls and gaining unwanted attention for himself. His wound hurt, he was exhausted, and the last thing he wanted to deal with was a screaming baby.

He picked up the goblet of blood and downed its contents. He attempted to hold Zoran's mouth open as he'd seen his mother do with Kiara and latched his mouth over his son's while regurgitating the blood he'd just consumed.

A trickle of blood dribbled from the corner of his mouth, but for the most part, the blood managed to get into the baby's mouth. Zoran choked on his cry but then hungrily swallowed what Jesper offered. The chokes became sniffs. The sniffs became contented sighs.

Little by little his eyes drifted closed, his swallows less frequent, and finally Jesper unlatched his mouth.

"Daggers," he grunted when blood dripped down Zoran's sleeping face, but Kiara caught it quickly with a handkerchief.

"What did you name him?" Sam asked quietly, and again, Jesper felt guilty that he had a son when Sam had wanted a child of his own all this time. It seemed as though things never changed.

"Zoran." He looked to each of his family members with pleading eyes. "He will be my heir. I want all of you to support my decision."

"I mean no disrespect," his mother started with uncertainty written across her expression. "But are you sure you want to take that risk should the elves make a second attempt to take the throne?"

Although she made a good point, he nodded. "I'm sure."

Alavara stopped short in the doorway, one hand against the wall to support herself. All eyes turned in her direction. Silence ensued as if the wind had stopped blowing on a particularly stormy day.

After hearing Zoran's piercing wails all the way from hers and Jesper's bedchambers, her anxious heart wouldn't allow her to stay in bed. She had followed the sound, only to find her baby sleeping soundly in Jesper's arms, unharmed.

"I'm sorry," she said to the entire family. "For my hand in this."

Kiara stood first, and when Alavara expected anger, hatred, or someone to lash out at her, the other woman pulled her into an embrace.

"I wish we could have helped you sooner."

Next, Sam and Willow joined the embrace, though Jesper and his father remained sitting. She almost laughed when she realized where Jesper's aversion to public affection came from.

"He will hate it," Willow said quietly, gesturing with a nod toward Jesper, "but force him to stay in bed for the next week. He won't heal at this rate."

She nodded and vowed to herself to fix what she had done.

Bidding the others a goodnight, she allowed her mate to support her around the waist and guide her down the hallway and toward their chambers. Her entire body ached from giving birth. No one was meant to grow a baby inside them within the span of a few minutes and expect to give birth immediately after.

"I mean it when I say to stay in bed," Jesper chided. "If you are up and about, it will take much longer for you to heal."

She nearly snorted. *You are one to talk.*

"I heard Zoran crying. I was worried. I haven't fed him yet. Is he hungry?"

He shook his head. "I fed him. He will be fine for a little while." When she gave him a confused stare, he explained, "Vampire babies drink blood, not milk. I will show you how to do it when he's hungry again."

"How do you know he's a vampire?" Zoran was conceived on their union night, and a part of her thought it was entirely possible for him to be an elf instead of a vampire.

"He has fangs."

"Oh." There was so much about being a vampire she didn't know.

They reached their chambers, and she couldn't have been more grateful to fall back onto the bed. Her entire body ached from her back to her lower regions to her legs. And the exhaustion… It didn't have anything to do with a baby keeping her up at night. Not yet, at least.

But still, she couldn't help but feel showered with relief. Her dear boys were alive. And after her father had been killed, the memories of her mother he'd trapped in his glowing orb had returned to her. She remembered everything. And she treasured every single memory.

Jesper sat in a chair beside the bed and reached for her hand, though he said nothing as he hunched over and stared into his lap.

Not liking the serious note to his expression, she squeezed his fingers and dared to say the words she'd kept from him all this time. "I love you. Words cannot express how grateful I am to you for staying by me, for helping me, for believing in me."

He blinked several times as he lifted his head and stared at her as if trying to gauge if he'd heard her correctly. When his disbelieving stare lasted several moments too long, she laughed and shook her head.

"Are my feelings unwelcome?" she teased and nudged him with her foot. "Should I have kept them to myself?"

"No!" he said in a rush. "I just…" He ran a hand over his mouth. "I've never heard those words directed at me before from a woman. Romantically."

"Do I need to give you another year to digest them?" She slowly ran her fingernails up his arm, loving the way his breath hitched at her touch. "Or are you going to tell me you return my affection with irrefutable, undeniable—"

"I love you," he gasped before he smiled wide. "By the nine, I love you, Alavara."

He cradled her face and pulled her into a kiss sweet enough to stop her heart, entrapped in a moment of time in his beautiful caress. If this was the last kiss she ever received from him, she could move on to the next life happily and without reservation.

Someone knocked on the door, and they startled at the sound.

Jesper tenderly brushed his thumb along her bottom lip before he said, "Come."

The door opened to reveal Zachariah carrying a bowl of water and a medical bag. He placed his bag on the table and began to unpack. "Who first? You, Alavara, or the baby?"

"Baby," Jesper and Alavara answered at the same time.

Anxiety rose to her throat when Zachariah took Zoran, a pit of worry forming in her stomach. But the pit shrank slowly as he handled their son carefully. The baby grunted in protest at being unwrapped from his blanket and being exposed to the cold. He otherwise didn't stir much other than to stretch.

She watched as Zachariah placed Zoran on the bed and pushed on his legs, forced open his eyelids, checked his ears, felt his head, and he stilled for a minute as if listening to his heart. Her anxiety grew by the moment when he continued his assessment by snapping his fingers beside each ear and looking into his mouth, pulling on his upper lip to reveal a set of small fangs.

Was something wrong with their son? There had to be. Despite being a fully grown newborn, he hadn't spent the full nine months inside her womb.

At last, he spoke while swaddling him with practiced hands. "Zoran appears to be perfectly healthy. I won't even pretend to know anything about dark magic and how it works. You should count yourself lucky. This scenario could have ended far differently."

Thankfully, he handed her sweet baby boy back to her and not Jesper. She needed the reassurance of holding him in her arms, thanking the forces of nature for Zoran's good health.

"Alavara, would you like to be seen by me or a midwife?"

She brushed her thumb against Zoran's dark, silky hair and traced his pointed ears. "I already had the baby. I don't need to be seen by anyone."

"On the contrary. Until you stop bleeding, and we make certain you don't have any blood clots, you will need medical care."

"A midwife then."

He nodded and moved onto Jesper next. Although she tried to appear preoccupied by Zoran, she watched carefully as Zachariah peeled Jesper's bloody shirt away from his wound. Worry knotted her stomach when Zachariah lost his professional composure and grimaced. Her gaze darted to Jesper's chest, and her heart dropped like an apple plucked off a tree by the wind only to hit the ground with a *thud*. A slit as large as the dagger she'd wielded rested over his heart, but the wound oozed with a mixture of fluids ranging from clear to yellow to red.

"You tore open your stitches. Jesper, your wound is infected."

"And?" Jesper sounded more than just a bit grouchy. He must have been as exhausted as she was.

Zachariah looked hesitantly at her, and she was sure he saw the immense guilt in her expression.

"Just say it," Jesper sighed. "I don't care that she's here."

"You can still die. It's not looking good."

You can still die.

His words spiraled her into a pit of unending darkness, and no matter how hard she tried to reach for footing, she only met air. She couldn't breathe as if a shadowy current pulled her beneath a sinister surface. Her father may have been gone, but Jesper was not safe from his grasp, from *her* grasp. She had to fix this, and there was only one way she knew how.

Feeling Jesper's forehead, he continued, "Fever, chills, rapid heart rate. Any confusion or disorientation?"

"I'm fine," Jesper muttered. Beads of sweat clung to his forehead, his face flushed. "I can get through this. What will you tell the court? I don't think the excuse of drinking bad blood will work a second time."

"You may have to tell them the truth."

Alavara paled. What would the court do to her if they found out she'd tried to take his life under her father's dark, magical influence? No one in Ichor Knell would bow under her rule. No one would respect her. Her life here would be miserable.

"The *truth*," Jesper grunted through Zachariah's administration, "is that while Alavara and I fought against the elves, Ruvyn stabbed me with an iron weapon. The elf king progressed Alavara's pregnancy, and we now have a child. Alavara's brother escaped Ruvyn's hold, and he killed him. We came back to Ichor Knell escorted by Captain Cornell, who saw the entire thing and can vouch for our story."

"Jesper." She wasn't sure whether to object or thank him.

"That's what happened. Do you remember it any differently?"

She shrugged. "It's hard to say. Half the time I was busy growing a baby and giving birth."

"Exactly."

Zachariah finished wrapping the wound in a clean bandage. "I will send for a midwife when I get back to the infirmary. Jesper, you need to rest. I can ask a maid to make up a separate room for you."

He shook his head. "I'm sleeping in here with my family." Silence.

Zachariah looked between them, and his obvious distress showed on his face. Well-deserved, she thought. It hurt each time someone looked at her as if she were born from the pit of darkness itself, but she knew she deserved it after what happened.

"Jesper, can we talk outside?"

"No. We all know Alavara almost killed me. We all worry she might do it again should some of the darkness remain in her mind. I will take care of it. Everyone else doesn't need to." Yes, Jesper certainly was grouchy. "Now I want to sleep."

Zachariah hesitated, but with one more commanding look from Jesper, he started packing his things. "Send for me if the pain worsens or if the infection spreads. I will check back on you tomorrow."

The moment he disappeared, they sighed at the same time. She set Zoran in the cradle beside the bed, one a maidservant had brought in earlier. Her entire body still ached, especially her back. Females weren't meant to grow babies so quickly. It was excruciating. Almost more so than the actual birthing part.

Jesper blew out the candle and climbed into the bed with her. Thankfully, he didn't shy away from her touch when she reached out for him. She dragged her fingertips along his cheek and jaw, staring into his eyes. Words weren't enough to convey her gratitude for how much he'd done for her, so she allowed her eyes to speak for her.

Finally, she said, "I know of an ancient healing spell. It will cure you."

"If you say so." By the tone of his voice, he didn't seem to believe her as if he thought himself a hopeless case. And then in a more jesting tone, he said, "If you try to kill me tonight, I think I might be too tired to stop you."

"Good. That means if you wake up tomorrow, you can be sure I won't try to kill you again."

Silence fell between them. For a moment, she listened to both Jesper's and Zoran's breathing, praying to Goddess Nature with thanks that she still had them in her life.

He grunted and wrapped an arm around her waist to pull her closer. Almost the moment he laid his head on her shoulder, his breathing deepened but his heart didn't slow. It raced quickly while his body fought the infection spreading through him like a poison.

Tomorrow, the infection would be gone.

Tomorrow, he would be healed.

CHAPTER 29

THE INFECTION WAS getting worse.

Jesper's head spun as he sat in a chair beside the window, looking out over the kingdom below. He lost all sense of time and place. His eyes glazed over and sweat clung to his skin. Last night had been awful to endure. Night sweats. Heaviness on his chest as if someone had sat on him. Tossing and turning with both hot and cold flashes. One moment, he had kicked the blankets off, and the next, all the blankets in the palace couldn't have kept him warm.

When Zachariah had arrived earlier that morning, his expression had been grave. His family members had visited as well. Mostly to see the baby, though they were concerned about him as well. Sam had left earlier that morning, saying he'd been away from Natalia long enough and needed to return home. Although they hadn't fought, their parting had been full of uncharacteristic melancholy. He knew Sam was happy for him for having Zoran. But he also knew it hurt his brother.

"Jesper."

He continued to stare out the window, his head still spinning. His body floated on a cloud of darkness. No, a cloud of fire. Lots of fire. Hot. Hot. Hot.

"Jesper."

He jumped when a hand touched his shoulder, and his gaze darted to the attacker. No, not attacker. Alavara. She looked lovely today. Dark eyes bored into his. Dark hair flowed loose over her shoulders. A lavender and light blue dress hugged her curves, the sleeves dripping off her shoulders.

"Mmm," he murmured as he reached for her hair and brought it to his nose, inhaling her scent. His hand drifted on a breeze of embers, disconnected from him as if some other source other than himself lifted it. "I think I might want to marry you."

Despite the worry in her eyes, she smiled. "We are already mates, Jesper. Though, elves have a custom to renew their vows for each new year of marriage."

The breath he inhaled sank deep into his lungs, and he let it out as a slow sigh. "Why don't we live in a giant tree for the next year instead of...instead of..." He squinted his eyes shut, trying to recall the words he wanted.

"Ichor Knell?"

"Right." How had he forgotten those words? He had lived here most of his life. "Of course, we must bring Kiara with us. She can find a handsome elf for her mate."

Alavara touched the back of her fingers to his cheek. The chill of her skin was a relief to his flushed face. "You are starting to sound like Sam. I thought you didn't care for romance."

"Romance?" He grimaced. "No, no, no. A mate wouldn't do. We will hide her in a tree instead. Then she can't find a mate." What was wrong with him? The words escaped as if on their own accord. "Wait. Do elves live in trees? Or do they have cities like...like..."

"Like vampires? It depends on the settlement. My home was made of beautiful, shimmering glass. If the sunlight caught it just right, it would sparkle and shimmer. Other elves live deep within the forest, making their homes out of large sequoias."

"You make sunlight seem like something wonderful."

Another wave of dizziness clutched his head, and he leaned back in the chair, waiting for it to pass. Was he drunk? No, he couldn't be. Had someone drugged him then? He felt like a half-wit.

Instead of continuing the conversation about sunlight, she crossed the room to peer over Zoran's cradle and smiled down at his sleeping face. She touched his cheek and kissed his forehead. Sadness lingered in her eyes, though when he squeezed his eyes shut and opened them again, the emotion was gone.

"Do you remember what I said last night about the healing spell?" she asked. "Are you ready?"

He nodded, his head heavy with the movement. "Where should we do this?"

"Let's go somewhere private. Private and beautiful. As close to the sunlight as you can take me."

He knew of such a place. Sam had taken a few females there in his courting years to impress them. Not that he wanted to impress Alavara...

The moment he pushed himself to his feet, his head spun sickeningly, and he pitched to the side. His fingers latched onto the curtains, but it was almost as if his spirit only had one foot inside his body, as he wasn't sure if he managed to grab them or not.

A steadying hand appeared at his elbow. After squeezing his eyes shut for a few moments, he opened them again to find that the world had steadied, and Alavara grasped him firmly. Worry knotted her forehead, and he smoothed it away with his thumb and a half-smile.

"Do you think you will make it?" she asked, concern lacing her voice. But he simply waved it away.

"A lapse of dizziness. Nothing too awful. I stood up too quickly."

She fastened a cloak around his shoulders, and he almost stopped her from making a fuss over him when her fingers brushed against his skin. The same spark like when they'd first touched raced across him, and this time he didn't shy away from it. He embraced it. He cherished it. His life had taken on a new meaning with her in his life.

After leaving Zoran with a maidservant, they made it outside without any further incidents, and he was all too aware of the dozens of eyes that followed them as they made the short trip to the carriage. Zachariah must have told the court what had happened. But all was fine. After the healing spell, he would be back to normal.

"Death," someone said under their breath.

Jesper's head snapped in the direction of the voice only to find the Diviner standing on the side of the street wearing long gold and white robes. The holy man stared at them as they passed, long enough for uneasiness to crawl through him like a wounded animal in its dark burrow. He likely looked awful. Even without the ability to see his own reflection, he knew as much.

But death?

No. He wouldn't die from this. He *couldn't* die from this. Alavara needed him. Zoran needed him. This kingdom needed him. Death was an expense he couldn't afford.

But this infection…

His chest burned with a fierce ache, throbbing with every pulse of his heart as they climbed into the carriage and with every jostle on the road. Surviving the stabbing, despite the blade not entering his heart, had been slim. Flakes of iron could have already entered his bloodstream.

His face paled, and not just from the exertion of keeping himself upright in his seat. No wound could have made his chest ache so fiercely. The iron had already reached his heart, despite Zachariah's administration. If not for Alavara's healing spell, he might be dead in a few days. Or less.

After several long minutes, they climbed out of the carriage. A foreboding green, grassy hill greeted them just outside the city boundaries. An emerald jewel tree stood elegantly at the top, shading a bench from sunlight.

Between the two of them, they pathetically climbed the hill, each panting for air at the very top. It was not a good time for a hike, no matter how small, what with him being injured and her recovering from birth. Why couldn't they have done this in their bedchambers or the drawing room or in the infirmary? Why here?

He searched for someone else with pointed ears, perhaps carrying a magical staff, but found they were the only two on the hill. "I thought you weren't capable of magic anymore."

"I'm not." When her panting slowed, she reached into her pocket and produced two necklaces. One with a red crystal dangling from the end and the other with a clear crystal. "I completed this particular spell back when I did have magic. I've been waiting to use it for a long time. Though, I never imagined I would willingly choose to be the one on this end of the spell."

"What do you mean?"

She only smiled. "You will see."

Emerald jewel leaves clattered gently together in a breeze drifting past. She pulled him onto the bench, and together, they admired the view down below. Jewel trees of all colors stretched from left to right, ranging from red rubies to green emeralds to yellow topaz to blue sapphires. Autumn. The scenery reminded him of autumn.

Beautiful. Breathtaking. And romantic?

He glanced at Alavara out of the corner of his eye to gauge her reaction. A smile graced her lips, water pooling in her eyes. After a moment, her head settled on his shoulder. His chest ached too much to lift his arm over her shoulders, so he wrapped it around her waist instead.

A sliver of sunlight broke through the clouds and encompassed the trees in an angelic glow. Hundreds of jewels hungrily drank in the light and sparkled with dazzling brilliance. Beside him, Alavara gasped before she reached for him and squeezed his fingers.

"Oh, it's beautiful," she said moments before the clouds blocked the sunlight again, returning the jewel grove to its original splendor.

He turned his head to find her gazing at him with dark, sparkling eyes. He gave in to the urge to kiss her and brushed his lips lightly against hers. Warmth flooded his entire body, raising his temperature at least a couple more degrees. His head burst with dizziness, forcing him to break away and take several steadying breaths. The fever climbed higher, burning his shoulders, his neck, his forehead. Perspiration clung to him and soaked his shirt through his back and chest. Yes, the view was beautiful, but he preferred to climb beneath his covers and hide away in the darkness.

"It's time," she said, wiping his forehead with the hem of her cloak. "I won't make you suffer any longer."

He nodded. "What do I need to do?"

"Nothing." She draped the clear crystal necklace over his neck while pulling the red over hers. "Dark magic doesn't just have to be used with malicious intent," she whispered as if reciting a prayer. "It can be used to protect, to heal, to love." A tear trailed down her cheek. "I think I understand now, Mother. I only wish it hadn't taken me so long."

The finalness in her voice concerned him, the crease in her eyebrows worrying him more. But when her expression relaxed, his anxiety fled. This was only a healing spell, nothing more.

Slowly, the pain in his chest ebbed, the raging wildfire turning into a bonfire, which then turned into a candle flame. Heat fled his body. Perspiration dried in its tracks. And his wound...

A tickling sensation spread across his chest, and he pulled the neck of his shirt open to find the wound disappearing as if it hadn't been there in the first place. It didn't even leave a scar.

The once-clear crystal around his neck transitioned into a murky red, which darkened more and more by the second to look like Alavara's.

He lifted his head to compare the two crystals, only for his face to pale. While his crystal grew darker, hers grew lighter. Her chin trembled. Her breaths escaped her in short, labored puffs. Blood seeped into her bodice over her heart, right where his own wound used to be.

"No!" he shouted. He grabbed a hold of both necklaces and yanked them off, but even with broken chains, the crystals continued to transfer colors. Alavara's eyes glazed over, perspiration clinging to her skin. When she began to pitch forward, he caught her and laid her on his lap. Her entire body trembled, and he watched helplessly as the colors from the crystals completed their transition.

"You lied!" he shouted, his voice watery. "The spell traded my injury for your health. I'm stronger than you. I can endure it."

"You can't."

"Reverse it. *Now.*"

"It cannot be reversed. It's a permanent spell." Her hands trembled violently as she slid her fingers into his. "I regret what I did to you, Jesper. This is the only way I know how to redeem my actions. I will gladly take your wound if it means I can right my wrongs."

"But...but you will die." No, no, no. This could not be happening. No!

"A worthy trade." She grunted, and her body became limper in his lap. "This feels awful. How could I have done this to you?"

He laughed humorlessly, but it did nothing to erase the ache of her suffering. "If you think this is bad, you should have experienced the first few days."

"Now I *really* feel awful for what I did to you." Her fingers tightened on his, her eyes searching his face. "At least you won't bear a scar anymore. Then you won't have a permanent reminder of my betrayal. Forgive me."

"I already have." He kissed her palm. "It was never your betrayal to begin with."

Panic raced through him when her arm hung limp. Dropping her fingers, he placed his hands on either side of her face. "There must be something we can do. Another spell. Tell me, Alavara. *Tell me what to do.*"

Her gaze drifted from his face to the boughs of emeralds hanging above them. Another burst of sunlight brushed the jewels, the sparkling effect rippling in the reflection of her eyes. Her gaze flickered back to him, and a peaceful smile lifted her lips. Slowly, her eyelids closed, her long, dark eyelashes casting a shadow over her cheekbones. Her head rolled to the side, now completely limp. Her chest didn't rise again.

Let's go somewhere private. Private and beautiful. As close to the sunlight as you can take me.

Alavara's words echoed in his mind, words he would never forget for as long as he lived. If only he had noticed the finality in her voice. If only he had taken more care to watch the sadness in her eyes when she'd said goodbye to their son. If only he had loved her better when he'd had her.

"One last deception," he whispered. He trailed his fingers through her hair and brought a strand to his nose to burn her scent into his memory, and then to his lips to kiss the sweet berry aroma of her. He then kissed each of her still fingers as unceasing tears trailed down his cheeks. "I lied, too. I said nothing could break me. But this has broken me. I cannot…" A tear plopped onto her lilac-colored sleeve. "I cannot live without you." He choked on his words. "Even until the very end, you kept your secrets. You promised me, Alavara. You promised to be honest with me. You lied." Another tear plopped onto her hand as he held it to his forehead. "How do you expect me to take care of Zoran without you? I don't know anything about children. I have a kingdom to rule. How do I rule a kingdom when all I want is to lie with you in the grave?"

"What a waste of the life she has given you," a voice said behind him, and his heart leaped to his throat as he spun around on the bench. His pounding heart stopped mid-beat as he beheld a familiar face with long, pointed ears, dark hair pulled into a bun, and piercing dark eyes.

His throat closed around his words, around his grief. He did not wish to share it with this stranger, even if he was his brother-in-law. He'd thought the man had returned to his own kingdom. Why was he still here?

Thalanil held a large pink crystal in his hand, a soft light pulsing through the gem like a dance of somber flames. He stared out over the jewel trees below as Alavara had done only minutes ago.

"I know my sister, though it has been ages since we've spent time together other than yesterday." Thalanil slowly turned to look at Alavara's lifeless form. A sadness entered his eyes, though he expressed no grief. "She will do anything for those she loves. And I mean *anything*. Tell me, Jesper. What would you do for her to return to you?"

Immediately, his heart picked up as he stared back at his brother-in-law. Did he wield such power?

"Anything," he breathed.

"That is a very heavy word. Would you give your right arm? Would you give your firstborn son? Would you give your own life? She gave her life for you. What would you do to reciprocate your love for her?"

Never mind that she had been the one to take it from him in the first place. He would do anything to have her back, alive and healthy. "Like I said, *anything*."

"Would you give your kingdom?"

His face paled as he remembered who Thalanil was and what he represented. The man before him was *Ruvyn's* son, now King of Varesia. He may have killed Ruvyn, and they may have struck a treaty with vampires. But Jesper had been deceived before.

"If you agree to spare my people, Ichor Knell is yours."

Thalanil leaned his weight against the nearby tree and tore his gaze away from his sister to stare back at him. Such deep pain and torture lingered in his eyes. He couldn't imagine what he must have gone through in the years beneath Ruvyn's total control. Jesper had only gotten a small taste of Ruvyn's dark magic, and he had wanted to cease existing.

"But you fought so hard to keep the kingdom out of my father's grasp. Why agree now?"

"Because I love Alavara, and I would do anything for her."

Anything.

He trailed the back of his fingers over his mate's cheek, which grew colder by the minute. An ache deeper than an iron wound scalded him through his heart. He regretted every awful thing he'd ever said to her. He only wished he had been kinder and more loving toward his beautiful, incredible mate. He only wished he'd had more time.

The elf king walked out from the cover of the jewel tree as a ray of sunshine broke through the clouds above. As he stepped into the sunlight, he lifted his face toward the sky as if basking in its warmth after so long of being trapped in the dark.

"What I require of you, Your Highness, is not your kingdom nor your right arm nor your son. What I need from you is half your lifespan. Should you be destined to live a thousand years more, you will now live five hundred. Should you be destined to live twenty years more, you will live only ten."

The entire world froze around him as he stared wide-eyed at the elf. He dared not hope. "And what of Alavara?"

Turning toward him, Thalanil placed the pink crystal against Jesper's chest, over his heart. "Alavara will live again as she once had. Healthy and whole and unaffected by the iron festering in her blood. However, she will only live as long as you do, as she will share the other half of your lifespan. If you die by an iron wound, or perhaps getting scorched by sunlight, the magic thread that binds the two of you will sever, and she will die alongside you."

He had absolutely no reservations in his mind. "I will do it. Bring her back. Please."

The elf's expression turned grave in warning. "As I said, I know my sister well. She would not have been able to live with the guilt of killing you." He nodded toward the pink crystal in his hand. "I caught her soul before it transitioned to the afterlife. If I bring her back, I expect you to treat her well, and I hope she will do the same for you."

"I swear I will." He clutched tight onto Alavara's limp hand. "I swear with every fiber of my being."

"Then you must protect her, and she must protect you. Remember, if you die, she will as well. If she dies, so will you."

The crystal began to glow brighter, and it sucked sinewy pink shadows from his body before he placed the crystal against Alavara's chest. Her body absorbed the essence, and when she sucked in a sharp breath, he laughed joyously. Her chest rose and fell with each breath. Her heart began beating once more.

"Jesper?" she croaked, squinting her eyes open.

"Alavara!" He cradled her face in his hands and kissed her cheeks, her nose, her forehead, and a gush of happiness rushed through him when he kissed her lips. His previously broken heart stitched itself back together thread by thread until it resembled something similar to what he'd started with.

In a moment of gratitude, he turned to thank Thalanil, but he was gone.

Not able to tear himself away for long, he gazed down at his beautiful mate still lying in his lap. Her eyes appeared unfocused as if she were trying to reorient herself in her newly healed body.

"I thought...I thought..." She placed her hand over her heart, her eyebrows furrowing with obvious confusion. "What happened?" Her face paled, and her attention turned to his chest. "The crystal didn't work."

"No, it worked, to which I owe you a thorough scolding." He trailed his fingers through her hair. He ran a thumb across each dark eyebrow. He traced the gentle outline of her jaw. He placed a hand just below her collarbone to feel the steady beat of her heart. "I traded half my lifespan to bring you back."

Her eyes widened. "Jesper, no. You shouldn't have—"

"I know exactly what I was giving up. It's a worthy trade, even just to have you in my life for a few more minutes."

Her chin quivered, and although she said nothing, the grateful look in her eyes said it all. Her gentle, *warm*, fingers touched the side of his face, tracing the stubble on his jaw.

"Besides," he continued with a straight face. "Who else is going to change Zoran's nappies?"

Alavara snorted and smacked him in the shoulder. "Oh, I will make sure you are well-practiced in the art well before the fortnight ends."

His gaze softened. "I had a hard time believing it at first, but I feel your love in here now," he whispered, resting her hand against his heart. "Just don't ever try to prove it to me in such a drastic way again."

"How else was I going to get you to believe it?"

He choked on his laughter and leaned close to nuzzle his nose against hers. "What a strange couple we are."

"Our relationship would be boring otherwise, don't you agree?" She bit her lip and struggled to sit. Emerald leaves tinkled in the breeze above them as she leaned in to brush her lips against his. "I love you, Jesper."

He returned her kiss with one of his own. "I know, Alavara. I truly know."

They kissed again. Both of them smiled into it, their hearts beating as one.

CHAPTER 30

ONE YEAR LATER

"Hold still!" Kiara giggled as she flipped Jesper's arm over to continue painting blue whorls across his skin. The elven design circled each finger, climbed across his hands and arms, and stood out stark and plain on his bare torso until he resembled something far more elven than vampiric.

Jesper huffed and moved his weight from one foot to the other while simultaneously shifting within the shade to keep himself and Kiara out of the waning dusk's sunlight. "I swear I've been standing still for an entire hour."

"It's only been twenty minutes, love!" Alavara called out from behind another tree where she stood with two of her elven sisters, receiving similar paint, he presumed.

Beside him, his entire family laughed at his expense, even little Zoran, who attempted to grab Sam's nose as his brother held him. When he failed, he reached over and tried again with Natalia. But the boy's attention quickly shifted to the baby in Natalia's arms, a female vampire they'd adopted from a young woman whose unfortunate circumstances made her unable to care for the child.

Zoran rested his head on baby Emilie's stomach with a brief snuggle before he tried to grab her cheeks. She simply gurgled, and Natalia and Sam released a synchronized "awww" of adoration.

Jesper turned slightly to hide his smile. He wasn't about to let Sam know he didn't *completely* hate his guts and was happy for him. No, not at all.

At last, Kiara finished the final swirl, and he held both of his arms out to admire her handiwork. The fluid paint strokes came together to form a beautiful pattern, symbolic of life, marriage, fertility, love, and long-lasting happiness.

Today, he and Alavara were getting married.

Again.

But this time, renewing their marriage vows was their choice and no one was forcing them into it. Loving each other, choosing each other... This ceremony was symbolic of free will and the rebirth of their union. However, they were doing it with her customs, the way they should have done it the first time to involve her culture.

The moment the sun slipped behind the mountains, a hush of reverence blanketed the group, aside from baby gurgles, infant squeals, and the water rushing through the languid brook.

And then Alavara stepped out from behind the tree, joined by her two sisters and brother. Words fled his tongue, and his lips parted in dumbstruck awe. His mate wore a white, silk gown, the style plain but immensely flattering to her figure, revealing enough to show off the blue whorls adorning every inch of her exposed skin. A sheer cape lay against her back like a silken waterfall, rippling across the forest floor as she walked. A tiara lay across her head, weaved elegantly into her dark hair with silver beads dripping down her back.

A mischievous grin pulled up on her face as she shifted in just the right way to reveal the slit in her dress traveling all the way to her thigh. Flames climbed his neck at the brief show of skin.

"You like?" she asked.

"Yes." He cleared his throat in embarrassment at his eager reply. But when he glanced toward his family to gauge their reactions, Alavara approached, and her fingers brushed his chin and turned his head back to face her.

"Thank you for allowing me this tradition."

"Any tradition you want, it's yours. You've already sacrificed so much. I don't want you to part with any more than you have to."

Her mischievous grin returned as she ran a flirtatious hand down his arm. "I recall you saying on our wedding day a year ago that you hated me, and our union meant nothing."

"He says he hates me all the time!" Sam laughed. "I think what he means is his threats mean nothing and *hate* actually means *love*."

He glared at his brother. Was he trying to goad him today of all days? He was not above pummeling him into a ball and stuffing him inside a tree.

But his anger dissipated like smoke in the wind the moment Alavara wrapped her long fingers around his and pulled him toward the water. With bare feet, he stepped into the cool river, the water climbing up to his calves. She lifted the bottom of her flowing white dress as he helped her stand beside him. The moment she dropped the fabric, the river snagged the train until it splayed out behind her in a beautiful shimmer of silver, making her one with nature. And with the sky a molten copper mixed with pink and orange, there was no better backdrop to such an important day.

Thalanil and Alavara's two sisters moved to stand on one side of the river while his family stood on the other. He and his mate clasped hands, and he lifted his gaze to stare into her dark eyes. Beautiful. Mysterious. Deadly. But playful at the same time.

His mate.

Thalanil handed them two crown wreaths weaved with branches and flowers. Jesper placed the smaller of the two over Alavara's brow, and she placed the other over his.

The elven king nodded. "You may present your gifts and recite your vows."

Taking a deep breath, Jesper accepted a box from his mother and opened it to reveal the shimmer of a silver petal flower resting on a silver comb. Alavara inhaled sharply as he gently took it out, handed the box back to his mother, and held it up. The silver petals caught the light of dusk, revealing a breathtaking shimmer.

"I scoured Varesia for this," he started, running a thumb over each petal hardened with magic so it would never deteriorate or die. "I don't believe you mentioned it would be so difficult to find."

She chuckled and swiped a tear from her eye as he tucked the comb into her hair, the dark strands contrasting against the flower. "You told me you would never put in the effort to find one for me, that it was more like Sam to do such a thing."

Jesper shrugged sheepishly as everyone's laughter surrounded him. He wasn't comfortable with public affection, so he tucked the letter he'd written her detailing his entire heart and feelings into her pocket and kept his words short and to the point. "I lied. On our union day a year ago, I lied. I did not plan to love you or cherish you in this life and into the afterlife. I'm grateful plans can change. I promise to love you, to cherish you, and to stay by your side for the rest of our days together."

"So you admit I'm a boon to your existence."

He chuckled and shrugged again. "Well, life is never boring with you, to be sure."

Tenderly, she lifted his hand and placed a kiss on his palm. He tried to ignore the fluster climbing his neck and forced himself to keep his gaze on her and not on his family.

With a smile, she reached into her pocket and concealed something small within her palm. "Thankfully, I didn't need to scour the earth for this when I already knew where to find one." She opened her hand to reveal a ring with a black and red sheen and a smooth finish.

He had no idea what metal it consisted of, even as she slid it onto his middle finger. It hugged his finger like a cool, comfortable caress.

"My family owns several dragon scales. My brother parted with this one, and I found someone who possessed the skills to make it into a ring."

Jesper inhaled sharply and inspected the piece of jewelry closer. As he tipped it every which way, the design shimmered like lava racing across black sand.

"I never thought I could love being a vampire," she said, pulling his attention back to her, "but after a year with you, you have made me love life more than I ever have before. I'm happy. I'm free. I'm yours. And I only hope to give you a measure of the happiness you give me."

"I assure you," he said in a raspy tone, "you do."

And then Sam handed Zoran to Jesper. He held his son close, in between his mate and himself, a family of three, forever connected through time and eternity.

Thalanil stepped forward, and silver magic sparked in his upturned hand. The elven king took a moment to look from him, to Alavara, to baby Zoran before he smiled. "I bless this union. May it prosper with love, friendship, and happiness as you journey into the world together as husband and wife, parents, and mates. As a family. Goddess Nature bestows upon your crowns the blessings of peace and prosperity and binds your love forever."

He tossed the silver magic into the air like a ball, but instead of arching back down, it exploded above their heads in a burst of shimmering light. Jesper inhaled sharply as silver sparkles rained over their heads, reflecting off the surface of the river, which magnified the hidden rainbow of colors tenfold.

Through the haze of color, Jesper met Alavara's gaze, holding tight onto her hand with their child between them. He loved his mate. And all the pain and heartache had been worth it just to stand here with her in this moment.

They laughed joyously as Zoran reached for the sparkles and tried to close his small fists around the fragments of light. With both arms around his mate and his son, a smile of gratitude spread across his face. Fate had been kind to him, indeed. No longer was his heart filled with cobwebs and echoes. It was filled with warmth, a flame too resilient to extinguish. It was filled with love.

353

ABOUT THE AUTHOR

Sydney Winward is an award-winning fantasy and paranormal romance author who dabbles in the occasional historical fiction. She loves building complex worlds filled with magic, strong characters, and emotional stories that can make you laugh and cry.

Sydney is the author of the Sunlight and Shadows Series and the best-selling Bloodborn Series, and when she's not writing, she's reading, thinking about stories, or going on adventures with her children. She lives in Utah with her husband and three amazing kids.

www.sydneywinward.com